TROLL BLOOD

ALSO BY KATHERINE LANGRISH

TROLL FELL

TROLL MILL

KATHERINE LANGRISH

TROLL BLOOD

AN IMPRINT OF HARPERCOLLINSPUBLISHERS

Eos is an imprint of HarperCollins Publishers.

Troll Blood

Library of Congress Cataloging-in-Publication Data
Langrish, Katherine.
    Troll blood / Katherine Langrish. — 1st U. S. ed.
        p.   cm.
    "First published in hardcover in Great Britain by HarperCollins
Children's Books in 2007."
    Sequel to: Troll Mill.
    Summary: When the cunning seafaring trader Gunnar, and his
short-tempered, sword-wielding son, Harald Silkenhair, land in
Trollsvik looking for a crew for a journey to Vinland, fifteen-year-
old Peer, suspicious of their motives, reluctantly agrees to join them,
mostly to watch over his friend Hilde who is eager to sail to the New
World as companion to Gunnar's wife Astrid.
    ISBN 978-0-06-111674-2 (trade bdg.)
    ISBN 978-0-06-111675-9 (lib. bdg.)
    1. Vikings—Juvenile fiction. [1. Vikings—Fiction. 2. Voyages and
travel—Fiction. 3. Supernatural—Fiction. 4. Micmac Indians—
Fiction. 5. Indians of North America—Maritime Provinces—
Fiction. 6. Adventure and adventurers—Fiction.] I. Title.
PZ7.L2697Tro 2008   2007021237
[Fic]—dc22   CIP
                                                              AC

Typography by Christopher Stengel
1 2 3 4 5 6 7 8 9 10
❖
First published in hardcover in Great Britain by
HarperCollins Children's Books in 2007.
First U. S. Edition, 2008

For all my family

Many thanks to

Phil Scott, for telling me about the Viking Ship Museum

the staff of the Viking Ship Museum, Roskilde, Denmark,

who showed me how to sail a reconstructed Viking-age ship

Diane Chisholm of the Mi'kmaq Resource Centre,

Cape Breton University, Nova Scotia

who patiently answered my many inquiries

Dr. Ruth Holmes Whitehead, who kindly read the manuscript

and made many invaluable suggestions concerning Mi'kmaq lore.

As always, any remaining mistakes are my own responsibility.

approx track of "Water Snake"

GREENLAND

HELLULAND

MARKLAND

Serpent's Bay

VINLAND

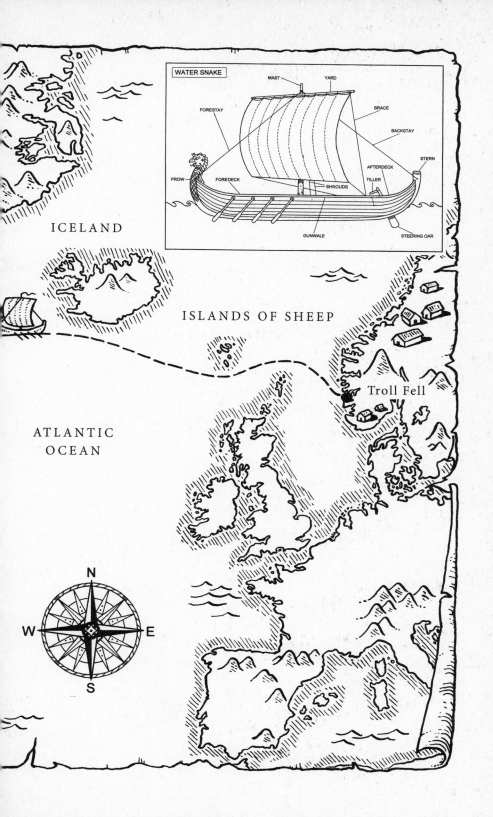

ICELAND

ISLANDS OF SHEEP

ATLANTIC
OCEAN

Troll Fell

WATER SNAKE

MAST   YARD

FORESTAY   BRACE

BACKSTAY

STERN

AFTERDECK

PROW   TILLER

FOREDECK   SHROUDS

GUNWALE   STEERING OAR

N

W   E

S

Contents

CHAPTER 1

Murder in Vinland

The Mist Persons are busy, crouching on wave-splashed rocks out in the gulf, blowing chilly whiteness over the sea. Their breath rolls like a tide over the beach and the boggy meadowlands near the river mouth, and flows far up the valley, spreading into the dark woods on either side.

A birchbark canoe comes whirling downriver through the wet fog. Kneeling in the prow, Kwimu braces himself against the crosspiece. He lifts a long pole like a lance, ready to fend off rocks. Each bend, each stretch of rapids comes as a surprise. Even the banks are hard to see.

The canoe bucks. Kwimu feels the river hump its back like an animal. The canoe shoots over the hump and goes arrowing into a narrow gorge, where tall cliffs squeeze the water into a mad downhill dash. Spray splashes in, and Fox, curled against his knees, shakes an irritated head. Fox hates getting wet.

A rock! Kwimu jabs the pole, swaying to keep his balance as the canoe swerves lightly away. It hurtles down a sleek slope and goes shivering and bouncing into roaring white water at the bottom. Again and again Kwimu flicks out the pole, striking here and there, turning the canoe between the rocks. Sometimes a whirlpool catches them, trying to hold them back and pull them down, but Kwimu's father, Sinumkw, kneeling behind him, gives a mighty thrust with his paddle and sends them shooting on.

A bend in the river. More rocks. Kwimu throws back his wet hair, every muscle tense. They dart down, twining into the curve, hugging the base of the cliff, where the water is deeper and smoother. It's cold here; the wet, grainy stone drips, and the mist writhes in eerie shapes. There's a splash and an echo, and it's not just the paddle. The canoe tilts, veers. Fox springs up snarling, showing his white teeth and black gums, and for a heartbeat Kwimu sees a thin muddy hand clutch at the prow. A head plastered with wet hair rises from the water. It winks at him with an expression of sullen glee, and ducks under.

Cold with shock, Kwimu flings a wild glance back at his father. But Sinumkw simply shouts, "Look what you're doing!" And they're snatched into the next stretch of rapids.

They hurtle into the crosscurrents, Sinumkw paddling grimly. Kwimu thrusts and fends with dripping hair and aching arms until the gorge widens, the cliffs drop back, and the canoe spills out into calm water flowing between high banks covered with trees. On either side, the gray-robed forest rises, fading into mist.

Kwimu twists around, panting. "Did you see?" he bursts out. "Did you see the Water Person—the Grabber-from-Beneath?"

Sinumkw frowns, but says calmly, "I saw nothing but the rocks and the rapids."

"He was there," Kwimu insists. "And Fox saw him too."

His father nods. "Maybe. But if you'd taken your eyes off the water for a moment longer, we'd have capsized. So his trick didn't work. Anyway, well done! That's the worst stretch over. No more rapids between here and the sea. And we'll land here, I think."

He drives his paddle into the water. The canoe pivots toward the shore.

"But I thought we were going all the way down to the sea. Can't we go on in the canoe? It's so much quicker than walking," Kwimu pleads as they lift the canoe out of the water.

"Quicker, yes," says Sinumkw drily. "Speed isn't everything. Just look around. Somebody's been cutting trees." Kwimu looks up in surprise, and his father is right—the bank is littered with chips of yellow wood, and studded with stumps like broken teeth. Piles of lopped branches lie in the trampled undergrowth.

Sinumkw picks up some scattered chips. "These aren't fresh. This was done moons ago, before the winter."

"Who would need so many trees?" Kwimu asks quietly. His

scalp prickles. There are Other Persons in the woods. One of them cuts down trees. Sometimes, in lonely parts of the forest, hunters hear the sound of an ax chopping—and a tree comes crashing down, though no one is visible.

But his father is thinking along more practical lines. "See here. They rolled the trunks into the river and floated them downstream. Who did it? It could be enemies: the Kwetejk, perhaps. What if they've built a stockade at the river mouth, in just the spot we want to use?"

"Oh!" Kwimu thinks with a shiver of their fierce rivals from the northwest woods. "What shall we do?"

His father shrugs. "This is why we came, *n'kwis*, ahead of everyone else, to find the best place for the summer camp, and to look out for danger. Imagine if the whole clan was with us now—grandmothers, babies, cooking gear, and all! No. We'll leave the canoe and come back for it later. We'll circle into the woods and climb the bluffs above the river. We can look down on the bay from there." He turns, setting off on a long uphill slant into the forest.

Kwimu follows. The encircling fog fills the woods with secrets. It's a shape-changer, turning the trees into looming giants that drip and tiptoe and creak and murmur. Anything might lurk there, or stealthily follow them at the edges of sight. But if there was danger, Fox would sense it; Fox would warn them. Reassured by the thought, Kwimu strokes Fox's cold fur, and hurries after his father.

Snow still lingers under the hemlocks and firs, and the

buds on the birches aren't open yet. The forest is colorless, black, white, and gray. A dozen paces ahead, Sinumkw climbs silently through the swirls and pockets of vapor, like a ghost passing through world after world.

The woods are full of mysteries. . . .

Grandmother said that yesterday evening, her bright bird-like eyes blinking in her soft wrinkled face. Kwimu thinks of her now, as he trudges uphill under the dripping trees. He can see her in his head, like a little partridge with bright plumage, wrapped in her big beaver-fur cloak with the colored quill-work glinting in the firelight. She's so tiny, but so strong. And she has the Sight. Everyone listens when she speaks.

Long ago, in the time of the Old Ones . . .

All the stories begin like this.

. . . in the old days, two brothers go hunting. And they find a deep ditch, too wide to jump. A strange, smooth ditch, scoured out of sticky red mud, twisting along between the trees. The track of a Horned Serpent: a jipijka'm track.

Now this track is full of power.

One of the brothers climbs into the ditch to see what sort of thing made it.

Aha!

At once, his body changes. It bloats and swells and pulls out like an earthworm, growing longer and longer. His eyes widen and blaze, and two horns sprout from his head, one yellow, one red. He fills the ditch from top to bottom; he raises his head and hisses at his brother; he slithers away like a snake.

The track leads into the lake. He plunges deep into the water, and no one ever sees him again.

The woods are full of mysteries. . . .

In spite of his thick moose-hide robes, Kwimu is cold. Why did Grandmother tell that story? What does it mean? Everywhere he looks he sees omens. Layers of fungus, like thick lips that might open and speak. A rotten log like a corpse rolled up in birch bark.

Can anything good happen on such a day?

The slope steepens, broken by small ravines where icy creeks hurry down to join the river. There are voices in the creeks, Kwimu is sure, quarrelsome voices that squabble and bicker. Perhaps it's the Spreaders, the nasty little people who peg you to the ground if you fall asleep by the streamside.

They cross one creek near a waterfall. Spray has coated the boulders with ice, and the pool boils and froths like a black kettle. Just the place for Grandmother's story to come to life! What if a huge head crowned with twiggy horns emerged from the water, snaking toward them on a long slimy neck? In this haunted fog, anything seems possible.

It grows lighter. The woods thin. Kwimu follows his father along a knobbly headland that juts out from the forest into the white nothingness of the mist. He feels giddy, as if walking out into the Sky World. He knows that down there, where the ground plunges steeply away, there's a fine gravel beach and grasslands beside the river. The bay, their summer home, where the women will gather shellfish, and the men and boys will take the canoes out past the sandbars and right over deep water to the islands, to fish and to gather birds' eggs. Right now none of that is visible. A mother-of-pearl sun peers through the haze.

All is quiet except for the hushing of the sea. But the mist tastes of smoke, sweet dry smoke floating up from below.

Fox growls quietly. His fur bristles, full of prickling, warning life. Kwimu and his father exchange anxious looks.

They hunker down in the wet bushes, ill at ease. Smoke means people, but a friendly village would be noisy with dogs, children, women chattering—so why the silence? If only the mist would clear. Straining his ears, Kwimu begins to think he can pick up the muffled sound of voices. Men talking—or arguing, for the sound becomes louder and sharper.

And then an appalling scream tears through the fog. Kwimu grabs his father. The scream soars into bubbling hysteria, and breaks into a series of sharp, yipping howls like a mad wolf. The morning erupts in shouts of anger and alarm, and a ring-ding, hard-edged clashing. Flocks of screeching birds clatter up from the forest.

As if their wings are fanning it away, the mist thins and vanishes. At last Kwimu and Sinumkw see what is going on below them, down by the river mouth.

The earth has been flayed. Instead of grassland, pits and scars of bare red soil show where the turf has been lifted. Two strange lumpish sod houses have been thrown up on a rising crescent of ground between the edge of the forest and the sea.

They look like burrows, for the withered grass grows right over them, but smoke rises from holes in the tops. Between these houses—these burrows—men are swarming.

Men? Their faces are white as paint, and they seem shaggy around the head, like a lynx or bobcat. These are not the Kwetejk, nor like any men Kwimu has ever seen. Are they the dead then, returned from the Ghost World? But some are pursuing others, hacking them with long axes, stabbing with lances. Some lie motionless on the ground.

Sinumkw taps Kwimu's shoulder. "Look!" His voice is awed, shocked. "In the river. *Jipijka'maq!*"

Kwimu drags his eyes from the scene below, and the hairs rise on his neck. Floating in the wide shallows where the river meets the sea are two things—bigger than the biggest canoe—and surely they are alive. For each has a head, staring shoreward from the top of a long neck. Each head is that of a Horned Serpent.

The smaller of the two is painted red, and the horned head snarls open-jawed from the top of a slender curving neck. The larger one is painted in red and black stripes, and it lifts a goggle-eyed head, beaked like a screaming eagle.

"Grandmother's story," whispers Kwimu. "This is what it meant."

These people are *jipijka'maq*—Horned Serpent people, shape-changers. They come from out of the water and under the ground. Their whiteness is not paint, but the bleached pallor of things you find under stones. But why are they fighting, and why are they here? Kwimu moistens his lips, staring at the sprawled figures on the ground. Perhaps they're not dead. Perhaps any moment now their feet and hands will vanish, their bodies will swell and lengthen, and they will slither off on their bellies into their dark earth houses?

But they never move.

"Hah!" With a cough of disdainful laughter, Sinumkw points suddenly. "See the coward there!"

A man in a green cloak is escaping, running away from the fight. He's dragging a child along with him, a young boy. Just past the end of the nearest house he stops, and pushes the child, pointing to the woods. The message is clear. "Run!" he's saying. "Run and hide yourself. Go!" The child hesitates, and is sent staggering with a hard shove between the shoulder blades. The man whirls and goes racing back.

So he's not a coward after all; he was trying to save the child. And he's unarmed, except for a knife. His enemies are coming to meet him. In the lead is a burly, bearlike man, obviously a chief. By his side is a boy no older than Kwimu, with long, loose golden hair that floats behind him as he runs, yelling. The burly chief shouts an order to his warriors. They spread out to catch the man in green, who dodges two of them and dashes on like a hunted animal, heading for the river. And then he trips and falls.

The chieftain shouts again and points. His men scatter sideways. The chieftain's right arm comes up, balancing his spear. He pauses a second, and throws.

There's a ragged chorus of whoops and howls from the men. They run forward, closing in on the crumpled green bundle. The spear stands straight up, a marker pointing at the sky. It twitches suddenly, it wags to and fro. The green bundle is still moving, trying to crawl away. Kwimu's breath hisses through his teeth.

The boy with the golden hair strolls up behind the men. He is about Kwimu's age, maybe fifteen winters old. His weapon is shaped like the long-bladed leaves that grow in the marshes— but red with blood. The others part to let him through; the burly chieftain puts an arm around his shoulders. Together they gaze at the man on the ground. Then the chieftain tugs his spear out. The golden youth hooks a foot under the body, rolling it onto its back. The man's pale face comes into view. Still alive. His fingers open and close like claws.

Warriors taunt each other when they fight. If the man on the ground can still speak, this is the moment for his final defiance. And perhaps he does gasp something out. But the golden-haired youth laughs. The high, shrill sound echoes upward. He puts the point of his long red blade to the man's throat, and shoves it in. Kwimu shuts his eyes. Only a blink, but when he opens them again, it's over.

He turns his face away, and freezes. That child—the child the man in green was trying to save! He hasn't run off; he's peering around the corner of the nearest house, clutching the sod walls with both hands, craning his neck to see what's happening. He sees the dead man, and shrinks like a snail when you tap its shell.

The burly chieftain gives orders, pointing this way and that. His men fan out and start searching between the houses. Kwimu sucks in his bottom lip. *They're hunting for the child. And they'll find him; there's nowhere to run.*

The child presses against the wall. Any moment now the men will simply come around the building, and there he'll be.

Then Kwimu almost shouts. The child turns and flings himself at the soft sod wall, digging fingers and toes into the cracks and crannies. He scurries up like a mouse, pulling himself onto the roof just as the nearest man rounds the corner. He lies flat. His light hair and clothes blend with the pale grasses growing on the turf roof, but he's still completely visible to anyone who glances up. In fact, Kwimu can see one of his feet sticking over the edge.

But the man doesn't look up. He strides along with his head down, staring at the ground. Kwimu bites his lip, hardly able to breathe. *Don't move. He's gone, but there's another one coming. Don't move!*

Neither man looks up. It seems crazy, but they don't. Kwimu sighs silently, surprised by the strength of his feelings for this strange foreign child. Beside him, Sinumkw shakes with admiring laughter. "That little weasel! To fool all those warriors with one simple trick! Look, they can't think where he's gone."

And it is funny, in a way, seeing the men poking and prodding around the houses, and gazing into the woods, when all the time he's a few feet above their heads, as still as a sitting bird. All the same, Kwimu's nails are cutting into his palms by the time the men give up. Maybe their hearts are not really in this search for a small boy. They return to the chief and his golden son empty-handed.

The chief shrugs. It's clear he thinks it doesn't matter much. He gestures to the bodies lying on the ground, and goes on talking to his son. Obediently the men drag the bodies down to the water's edge. They wade yelling into the cold river, carrying the dead out to the smaller, slenderer of the Serpents, which jerks and snubs at its tether as if outraged at being given such a cargo. One by one, the bodies are tumbled in.

Where's the child?

Sidling up the roof like a crab.

At least he's pulled his foot in—no, don't go near the ridge!

As if he hears, the child sinks down just below the ridge, but he keeps popping up his head and peering over. Kwimu bites his nails in agony. *Stop doing that, they'll see you!*

The chief gives another order. Whatever it is, the child on the roof understands: He flattens himself again, and the men troop back to the houses and begin emptying them. Everything is carried out. They stagger down to the river under bundles of furs, and heave them into the belly of the second Horned Serpent, the big one with the eagle's beak. They bring out gear, pots, sacks, weapons. Shouting, they load up with timber: logs and planks from a pile on the other side of the houses. The creature—vessel, it must be some kind of vessel—sways this way and that as they adjust the cargo till it's riding level, a lot lower in the water.

"They're leaving!" Kwimu says with a gasp of relief. "They're going away!"

Sinumkw makes a brushing movement with his hand: *Quiet*. He watches the scene below with a hunter's intensity.

At last, all is ready. A small, fat canoe collects the burly chieftain and his golden son—*they* don't have to wade through the freezing water. The chieftain hoists himself aboard the big Serpent, but his son is ferried to the smaller vessel, and nimbly leaps aboard. Kwimu shades his eyes. The boy strides up and down, pouring something out of a big pot. He upends the pot, shakes out the last drops, and tosses it overboard. With an arm twined around the Horned Serpent's painted neck, he leans out and catches a rope that uncoils through the air from the bigger vessel. He knots it at the base of the neck, and jumps down into the waiting canoe. In moments, he's back with his father.

The men lift out long, thin paddles: It's as if the Serpent is putting out legs like a beetle. Slowly it turns away from the shore, swinging with the current till it's pointing out to sea.

Kwimu has never seen paddling like this before, with all the men facing the wrong way. How can they see where to go? But it seems to work. The red and black *jipijka'm* is crawling away out of the river, loaded with furs and timber, and towing its companion behind it—the red Serpent of the Dead.

So they're going, and they haven't found the child. Does he know he's safe? Kwimu glances down at the roof.

The child is sitting up, staring.

Get down, get down—they might still see you. . . .

But the child gets slowly to his feet. He stands in full view of the river, conspicuous on the rooftop. He lifts his arm, both arms, and starts to wave and scream. He's dancing on the roof, yelling in a shrill voice.

"He mocks his enemies!" says Sinumkw in deep appreciation.

But Kwimu isn't so sure. He's got a cold feeling that if he could understand, the child might be screaming, "Come back, come back! Don't leave me!"

For a second, the crawling motion falters as some of the men lift their arms to point. Then it picks up again. They're not stopping; they're not turning. They're leaving the river now, heading into the bay. There's still a lot of haze on the water: You can't see the horizon.

They're doing something else now: casting off the rope. A feather of fire flies through the air, curving into the red Serpent. A moment later, flames splutter fiercely up.

"Oil." Sinumkw nods. "They poured in oil to make it burn."

Kwimu can actually hear it, crackling like a hundred spits. Black smoke pours up in a tall column. The neck and proud horned head show clearly, but the long serpent body seems writhing in flames.

Down below, the child is scrambling off the roof. He drops the last few feet and goes racing down over the ravaged grasslands toward the beach.

"Let's get him!" Kwimu turns to Sinumkw. "Please, *nujj* . . ."

His father shakes his head. "No."

"Oh, please, *nujj*. He's only little, and he's brave. . . ."

"A bear cub is little and brave," says Sinumkw grimly, "and if you take one for a pet, it will grow up into a big bear and claw your arm off."

Kwimu swallows. "I know, but . . . can we leave him to die?"

"*They* have." Sinumkw nods toward the bay. "He's not one of the People, Kwimu. Not one of us."

"You like him, though," says Kwimu desperately. "You laughed at the way he tricked the warriors. See—Fox approves!" Fox twists his head and licks Kwimu's hand suddenly, as though to encourage him. Kwimu hardly dares to go on, but the words come anyway, forcing their way up from deep inside him, like a spring of water that has to bubble out. "He might become your son, *nujj*. My brother."

Sinumkw looks at him. His chest rises and falls in a sigh. "Well, we can try. Perhaps the cub is young enough to tame. Don't be surprised if he bites you."

They turn, for the slope ahead is too steep to descend, and it will be necessary to go back into the woods and find another way down. Kwimu casts a backward glance at the burning vessel, and is in time to see it tip up and slide neatly backward under the water. The snarling serpent head vanishes last, and then it's as though it has never existed, except for the smoke drifting higher and higher, a fading stain against the sky.

The other *jipijka'm* is already out of the bay and turning up the gulf toward the open sea; and from this distance it looks more like a serpent than ever—a living serpent, swimming quietly away through the haze.

Down on the shore, nine-year-old Ottar, young son of Thorolf the Seafarer, stands knee-deep in the cold waves. Tears pour down his cheeks. He's alone, orphaned, desperate, stranded in this horrible place on the wrong side of the world. He hears a shout from the beach behind him. He turns, his heart leaping in wild, unbelieving hope. Somehow it's going to be all right— it's been a bad dream or an even worse joke—and he won't even be angry. He's going to run to whomever it is, and cling to them, and sob until the sobbing turns into laughter.

And then he sees. His mouth goes dry. Coming toward him on the rising ground between him and the houses are two terrible figures. Their long hair is as black as pitch, and tied with colored strings. Their clothes are daubed with magic signs. Furs dangle from their belts. They are both carrying bows. But the frightening thing—the really frightening thing about them—is that you can't see their expressions at all. Half of their faces are covered in black paint, the other half in red. Their eyes glitter white and black.

"Skraelings!" Ottar whispers. "Dirty Skraelings!"

He prepares to die.

CHAPTER 2

Water Snake

The green sea wrapped itself around Peer Ulfsson's waist, and rose to his chest with a slopping sound. "Yow!" he yelled. As the wave plunged past he sucked in his breath, and bent quickly to look through the water.

There! In the heaving brown-green glimmer he saw it: the hammer he'd dropped, lying on the stones. He groped with his arm, his fingers closed on the handle, and the next wave swept past his ears and knocked him over. There was a dizzy moment of being rolled backward in a freezing froth of bubbles and sand. He struggled up, spluttering but brandishing the hammer in triumph.

"Got it!"

"So I see." Bjorn's face was one wide grin. "If you'd tied it to your wrist like I told you, you wouldn't have had to do that.

Get dressed: You look like a plucked chicken."

Peer laughed through chattering teeth. He bounded back to shore and dragged his discarded jerkin over his head, fighting wet arms through the sleeves. It fell in warm folds almost to his knees, and he hugged his arms across his chest. "Aaah, that's better. I'll leave my breeches till I've dried off a bit. . . . What's that? Who's shouting?"

Torn by the wind, an alarmed cry had reached his ears. He couldn't make out the words. Up on the jetty Bjorn stiffened, shading his eyes to look down the fjord. "It's Harald. He's seen a ship. Yes—there's a strange ship coming."

Peer jumped up beside Bjorn, noticing with pride how firm and solid the jetty was. The two of them had been building it for almost a month now, in between their other work, and in Peer's opinion it made the tiny beach at Trollsvik look like a proper harbor. It was a stout plank walkway between a double row of posts. Bjorn's new faering, or fishing boat, bobbed beside it.

He joined Bjorn at the unfinished end, where the last few planks waited to be nailed down. It was late afternoon, the tide flowing in. Out where the shining fjord met the pale spring sky he saw a large reddish sail, square-on, and the thin line of an upthrust prow like the neck of a snail. A big ship running into Trollsvik before the wind.

"Who is it?" he blurted.

Bjorn didn't take his eyes off the ship. "I don't know. Don't know the sail. Could be raiders. Best not take chances. Run for help, Peer. Tell everyone you can."

A lonely little village like Trollsvik could expect no mercy from a shipful of Viking raiders if they took the place by surprise. The best thing was to meet them with a show of force. Peer turned without argument. Then he saw a scatter of people hurrying over the dunes. "Look, Harald's raised the alarm already. Here he comes, with Snorri and Einar...."

"Hey, Harald!" Bjorn bawled at the top of his voice. "Whose ship is that?"

A bandy-legged man with straggling gray hair raised an arm in reply as he puffed across the shingle and climbed painfully onto the jetty. "No idea," he wheezed, bending double to catch his breath. "I was cleaning my nets—looked up and saw it. Shouted at you and ran for the others. You don't know it either?"

"Not me," said Bjorn. Peer looked at the ship—already much closer—then back at the little crowd. Most of the men had snatched up some kind of weapon. Snorri One-Eye carried a pitchfork, and old Thorkell came hobbling along with a hoe, using the handle as a walking stick. Einar had a harpoon. Snorri's fierce, gray-haired wife, Gerd, came limping after him over the stones, clutching a wicked-looking knife. Even Einar's two little boys had begun piling up big round stones to throw at the visitors. Peer wondered if he should join them. Then he realized he was holding a weapon already. His hammer.

He hefted it. It was long-handled and heavy. The dull iron

head had one flat end for banging big nails in. The other end tapered to a sharp wedge. When he swung it, it seemed to pull his hand after it. As if it wanted to strike.

Could I really hit anyone with this? He imagined it smashing into someone's head, and sucked a wincing breath.

The neighbors were arguing. "No need to fear!" yelled Gerd, lowering her knife. "See the dragonhead? That's Thorolf's ship—that is, the old *Long Serpent* that Ralf Eiriksson sailed on."

"It is not!" Snorri turned on his wife. "Thorolf's been gone two years now, went off to Vinland."

"So what?" Gerd was undaunted. "He can come back, can't he?"

"Fool of a woman," Snorri shouted. "That's not his ship, I say!"

"How d'you know?" Gerd shrilled.

"Because this one's as broad in the beam as you are, that's why—the *Long Serpent* was narrower. . ."

"That isn't the *Long Serpent*," said Peer. "I should know. My father helped to build her."

"This ship looks like a trader," Einar said. "Built for cargo, not war."

"That's all very well, Einar. Plenty of traders turn into raiders when it suits them—doesn't mean her crew won't fight."

"What do you think, Bjorn?" asked Peer in a low voice.

Bjorn gave him an odd glance, half humorous, half sympathetic. "I don't know, Peer. Let's just put on a good show and hope they're friendly."

Peer stood unhappily clutching his hammer. The ship was so close now that he could see the sea stains on the ocher red sail. The hull was painted in faded red and black stripes. A man stood in the bow, just behind the upward swoop of its tall dragon-neck.

We could be fighting in a few minutes. A gull shrieked, swooping low overhead, and its keen cry made him jump. Odd to think that the gull might soon be swinging and circling over a battle, and that its shrieks might be joined by the screams of wounded or dying men and women. *I might die. . . .* And with a jump of his heart he thought of his best friend, Hilde, safe for the moment at her father's farm on Troll Fell. What if he never saw her again? And what would happen to her if these men were dangerous?

There was a flurry of activity on board. The yard swung and tipped, spilling wind. Down came the sail in vast folds. Oars came out to guide the ship in. Behind Peer and Bjorn, the villagers bunched like sheep.

The man in the bow leaned out, cupped a hand around his mouth, and yelled, "Bjorn!"

Bjorn threw his head up. "Arnë!" he shouted back. "Is that you?"

Arnë, Bjorn's brother! The villagers broke into relieved, lively chatter. Peer unclenched stiff fingers from the haft of his hammer. He wouldn't have to use it as a weapon after all. *And a good thing, too*, said a secret little voice at the back of his head, *because you know you couldn't have hit anyone.*

The thought bothered him. Was it true? Would he be no good in a fight? The word *coward* brushed across his mind. Then, with a shrug that was half a shudder, he dismissed the idea. It didn't matter now.

"The ship's called *Water Snake*," Arnë shouted across the narrowing gap of water. "Gunnar Ingolfsson's the skipper. I've brought him here to meet Ralf Eiriksson."

"Who's this Gunnar? Why does he want Ralf?" Peer wondered aloud, as the ship closed on the jetty.

"Gunnar Ingolfsson. Gunnar . . ." Bjorn snapped his fingers. "He's the man Thorolf took on as partner a couple of years ago. Got a name as a sea rover, a bit of a Viking. Thorolf and he sailed off to Vinland together in two ships. So what's he doing here, and why's Arnë with him?"

Peer shrugged. He wasn't curious about Arnë.

"Vinland? Vinland?" muttered Einar. "Where's that?"

"Don't you remember?" Snorri said helpfully. "A few years back, Ralf and Thorolf got blown off course and found a new land all covered in forests. . . ."

"The land beyond the sunset," Peer said eagerly.

"I knew that," Einar huffed, "but I thought they called it Woodland."

"They did!" Snorri waved a triumphant finger. "But other ships went there and found vines. Vines—Vinland, see? It's all the same coast. This Gunnar must be making a second trip.

I've heard you can bring back a fortune in timber and furs and grapes. I've got half a mind to go myself."

"Ho, yes," scoffed Einar. "And how would you know what a grape looks like? Have you ever seen one?"

"Arnë's a wild one," Bjorn said to Peer. "What's he done with his fishing boat? Sold it, I suppose, to join this trip. Well, he's crazy, that's all."

"He always wanted to go a-Viking," Peer pointed out.

"I know." Bjorn grinned suddenly. "That's why I say he's crazy!"

Peer nodded. *And that's why Hilde likes him,* he thought, as a black-edged cloud slipped over the sun. The hills and the shore and the flashing water lost their colors. The jetty he had taken such pride in suddenly seemed a rough-and-ready thing of no interest. He wished he could do something exciting or brave.

How was it that Arnë always managed to do things that would impress Hilde? Of course, it helped that he was tall, strong, and good-looking. And seven years older than Peer: Girls took older men more seriously. *If he's sailing off to Vinland, I won't get a word in this evening, then. She'll be talking to Arnë all night.*

The big ship came nudging up to the jetty. Seven or eight men were busy on board, stowing the yard fore and aft, lifting the oars in, collecting their gear. Arnë threw a rope up to Bjorn. "Nice new jetty," he called, laughing. "Did you build it specially for us? It's good, this'll be easier for Astrid."

23

"Astrid?"

"The skipper's wife."

Everyone stared. Peer got a glimpse of a girl in a blue cloak, huddled under an awning that had been rigged up behind the mast. Arnë climbed onto the jetty and wrung Bjorn's hand. He clapped Peer on the shoulder and said, "Fancy a voyage to Vinland?" before turning to offer a helping hand to the girl. She was finding it difficult, clutching some kind of pouch or bag. A giant of a fellow with a shock of almost white fair hair tried to boost her up from the ship.

Peer watched scornfully. *Hilde wouldn't need helping out of a boat. She'd just kilt up her dress and jump out, laughing!*

Hilde, Hilde! She teased Peer, bossed him about, and drove him crazy. Last spring, he'd made the mistake of impulsively kissing her, and she'd laughed at him. He hadn't dared to do it since, except in dreams.

We belong together, he thought. She'd been his best friend and ally for years, ever since he'd come to Troll Fell as an orphan to work for his two brutal uncles at their dilapidated mill. Peer had helped to save Hilde's young brother and sister from the trolls, and her family had taken him in and treated him like a son. Hilde was fond of him, Peer knew that. But she kept him at arm's length.

One day, he swore to himself, *one day when the time is right, I'll go to Hilde and ask her . . . or perhaps I'll say . . .*

No, I'll tell her: "We just belong together."

But would she agree?

"Hey! You!"

Lost in thought, Peer didn't notice the voice hailing him from the ship.

"You there—Barelegs!"

"Peer!" Einar jogged him in the ribs. "The young lord's talking to you."

"What?" Peer woke up. Had he heard what he thought he'd heard?

"He means you," Einar chortled, pointing. "Anyone else around here with no breeches on?"

Barelegs? Peer turned around and met the light, cold gaze of a boy his own age—a youth of sixteen or so, wearing a dark checkered traveling cloak wrapped around his shoulders, pinned with a large silver brooch. Because the jetty was higher than the ship, his head was currently at about Peer's waist level, but this disadvantage didn't seem to bother him. He tilted up a tanned face as smooth as a girl's, but wider in the jaw, heavier across the brow. Loose golden hair fell about his shoulders and cascaded in a wind-whipped tangle halfway down his back. But his eyes . . . they reminded Peer of something. Einar once had a dog with eyes like that, odd milky blue eyes—*wolf eyes*, he'd called them. And the dog was treacherous; you couldn't get anywhere near it.

The boy snapped his fingers. "Are you deaf? I told you to help my father up onto the jetty. He's not well."

He took the elbow of a man standing beside him. This must be the skipper, the famous Gunnar Ingolfsson. He was a powerful figure, short-legged and barrel-chested, but he did look ill. His face was flushed and glistening. When he glanced up at Peer his eyes were the same pale blue as his son's, but the rims were slack, and the flesh under them was pouchy and stained. Impatiently he stretched up his hand. Gold arm rings slid back to his elbow.

Peer hesitated, but the boy's rudeness didn't seem enough reason to ignore his father. He reached down. Gunnar's grasp was cold, and slick with sweat. And then Peer saw with a shock that Gunnar's other hand was gone. The left arm swung short; the wrist was a clumsily cobbled-together stump of puckered flesh with a weeping red core. *One hand, look, only one hand. . . .* The whisper ran through the crowd as Gunnar dragged on Peer's arm, trod hard on the ship's gunwale, and pulled himself onto the jetty with a grunt of effort. He let go of Peer without a word, and turned immediately to join his wife.

The boy sprang up after him. "That's better, Barelegs," he said to Peer.

"My name's not Barelegs," said Peer, his temper rising.

"No?" The boy's eyebrows went up, and he glanced deliberately around at the villagers. "Does he actually own a pair of breeches?"

Einar snorted, Gerd giggled, and Einar's eldest boy made things worse by shouting out, "Yes, he does, and they're over there!"

There was a burst of laughter. Peer went red.

The boy smiled at Peer. "Now why did you have to take

those trousers off in such a hurry? Were you caught short? Did our big ship scare you that much, Barelegs?"

Peer struck out, completely forgetting the hammer in his hand. The boy twisted like a cat, there was a swirl of cloak and a rasping sound. Something flashed into the air. With a shout, Bjorn grabbed Peer's arm, forcing it down. He wrenched the hammer away and hurled it onto the beach.

Peer bent over, rubbing his numbed fingers. "I'm s-sorry," he stammered to Bjorn. "I lost my—I wouldn't have hurt him—"

"No," said Bjorn in a savage undertone, "you'd have been gutted." And he nodded at the boy, who stood watching Peer with dancing eyes, holding a long steel sword at a casual slant.

Peer gaped. He'd never actually seen a sword before. Nobody in the village was rich enough to have one. Subtle patterns seemed to play and move on the flat steel surface. The frighteningly sharp edges had been honed to fresh silver.

That could cut my arm off.

At the edges of vision he half saw the crowd: Gerd disapproving; Harald worried; Einar and Snorri, their grins wearing off like old paint; the sailors from the ship edging together, watchful, glancing at their leader, Gunnar; the tall girl, Gunnar's wife, looking on with cool disdainful eyes, as if nothing surprised her.

Then the boy pushed the sword into its sheath. He tossed his hair back and said in a light, amused way, "He started it."

"And just who are you?" demanded Bjorn before Peer could reply.

The boy waited for a second as if he expected Bjorn to add, "young master," and Gunnar interrupted. "He's my son, Harald Gunnarsson, my firstborn." His voice was gruff, thick with pride, and Peer saw, without surprise this time, that he too was wearing a sword. "My young lion, eh, Harald?" Affectionately he cuffed the boy's head with his sound right hand. "I'll get me other sons one day, perhaps, but none to equal this one. Look at him, pretty as a girl, no wonder they call him 'Harald Silkenhair.' But don't be fooled. See this?" He lifted his left arm to show the missing fist, and turned slowly around, grinning at the villagers. "Seen it? All had a good look?" His voice changed to a snarl. "But the man who did it lost his *head*, and it was my boy here who took it off him."

There was scattered applause. "A brave lad, to defend his father!"

"A fine young hero. And so handsome, too!" Gerd clasped her red hands.

"'*Bare is back without brother behind*,'" old Thorkell quoted in pompous approval.

"Well said, Granddad." Gunnar nodded. "And a good son will guard your back as well as any brother. Quick with his sword, and quick with his tongue, too; he can string you a verse together as fast as any of the king's skalds."

"A little too quick with his tongue, perhaps," said Bjorn drily.

Gunnar hesitated. Then he burst out laughing, his red face darkening as he fought for breath. "All right," he coughed, "all

28

right. We can't let the young dogs bark too loudly, can we? Harald—and you . . . What's your name—Peer? No more quarreling. Shake hands."

"Yes, Father," said Harald, to an appreciative mutter from the villagers. He stepped forward, holding out his hand. Peer eyed him without taking it. His heart beat in his throat, and his mouth was sour with tension as he met Harald's bright gaze.

Harald grinned unpleasantly. "Hey, come on, Barelegs. Can't you take a joke?"

Peer nearly burst. He turned his back and shouldered his way along the jetty, leaving Bjorn and the others to deal with the newcomers. Down on the shingle, he hastily pulled on his breeches while Einar's little boys peeped at him around the posts of the jetty, giggling and whispering, "Barelegs, Barelegs." He pretended not to hear, but it was the sort of name that stuck. He would never live it down.

Bjorn called to him, "Arnë's taking Gunnar up to Ralf's farm. Why don't you go with them? It'll be sunset soon anyway."

"No," said Peer gruffly. "I'll be along later. I've work to finish here."

He watched them pick their way across the beach, heading for the path to the village. Gunnar's young wife, Astrid, clung to his arm, mincing across the pebbles. Probably her shoes were too thin, Peer thought sourly. How would she ever make it up to the farm, a good two miles of rough track? But perhaps they'd borrow a pony.

He walked slowly back along the jetty, taking his time, unwilling to talk even to Bjorn. The tide was full. *Water Snake* had risen with it.

Against the sky the knob of the dragonhead stood black, like a club or a clenched fist. The angry wooden eyes bulged outward as if likely to explode. The gaping jaws curved together like pincers. An undulating tongue licked forward between them, the damp wood splitting along the grain.

The ship was empty—the crew had all disappeared to the village. Peer glanced about. No one was looking. He quietly jumped on board.

The ship smelled of pinewood and fresh tar. The rope he clutched left a sticky line on his palm. There was decking fore and aft. The waist of the ship was an orderly clutter of crates and barrels: luggage and supplies. A white hen stuck its head out of a wicker crate and clucked gently.

Fancy a trip to Vinland, Peer?

He clambered across the cargo and up the curve of the ship into the stern, where he stood for a moment holding the tiller and gazing out westward. The sun was low over the fjord, laying a bright track on the water: a road studded with glittering cobblestones. It stung his heart and dazzled his eyes.

And Harald Silkenhair, no older than Peer, had traveled that road. Harald had sailed across the world, proved himself in battles, been to places Peer would never see.

He thought of Thorolf's ship, his father's ship, the *Long*

Serpent, beached on the shores of Vinland far across the world, and felt a surge of longing. Life was a tangle that tied him to the shore. What would it be like to cut free, shake off the land, and go gliding away into the very heart of the sun? He closed his eyes and tried to imagine he was out at sea.

"What are you doing?" Bjorn looked down at him from the jetty. Peer snatched his hand off the tiller, feeling every kind of fool for being discovered playing at sailing like some little boy.

"Looking at the, oh, the workmanship." He made an effort. "I don't think the dragonhead's as fine as the one my father made. But it's still good work."

"Mm," said Bjorn. After a moment he said, "And what do you make of Harald Troublemaker?"

Their eyes met. Peer said, "He just picked a fight with me. For no reason at all."

"I know."

"What was I supposed to do? Stand there and take it? Did you hear what he said to me?"

Bjorn blew out a troubled breath. "Peer, better to take an insult than a sword in your guts. You don't have to play Harald's games."

"How can your brother sail with someone like that?"

Bjorn shook his head. "Arnë can be a bit of a fool sometimes."

"Let me get off this boat." Peer climbed over the side and onto the jetty, feeling *Water Snake* balance and adjust as his weight left her.

"Don't play Harald's games," Bjorn repeated.

"I won't." Half comforted, Peer straightened and stretched. "You're right," he added. What was the point of letting Harald get to him? Let him strut. Let Arnë have his evening with Hilde. Tomorrow they'd both sail away.

CHAPTER 3

"Be Careful What You Wish For . . ."

Hilde rubbed tired eyes. It was almost too dark to see the pattern she was weaving. Drafts snuffled and whined under the door. The wooden shutters were tightly fastened. The fire smoked. She longed for a breath of air.

Farther up the room, in the glow of the long hearth, nine-year-old Sigrid was telling little Eirik a bedtime story.

"So there was a terrible storm. And Halvor's ship was blown along and blown along until he landed in a beautiful country. And then he got out, and he came to a castle where there was an enormous troll with three heads."

"Isn't he rather young for that story?" Hilde interrupted. "He's only two."

"He likes it," said Sigrid. "Anyway, it's keeping him quiet. And the troll said, '*Hutututu!* I smell the blood of a mortal man!' So Halvor pulled out his sword, and chopped off the troll's heads."

"Chop, chop, chop!" chuckled Eirik. Hilde rolled her eyes.

"And he rescued a princess, a beautiful princess, and got married to her. And they lived in the castle together, ever so happily, till one day Halvor began to miss his poor mother and father, who would think he had drowned."

Hilde wove a few more rows, half listening while the princess gave Halvor a magical ring that would carry him back over the sea, with a warning never to forget her. "'Or I shall have to go away to Soria Moria Castle, to marry a troll with nine heads.'"

Now there was less bloodshed in the story, Eirik lost interest. He lay kicking his legs in the air, then turned on his stomach and began squirming eel-like over the edge of the bed. Sigrid dragged him back. "Lie still, Eirik, or I won't go on."

"Ma," grumbled Hilde, "I can hardly see."

"Then stop," said Gudrun. She was slicing onions, and paused with the knife in her hand to wipe her streaming eyes. "Thank goodness Elli's asleep at last. I'll be so glad when she's finished teething. All that wailing really wears you out. . . ."

"Shall I finish the onions for you?"

"No, go and help with Eirik, I've nearly done."

"Come on, Eirik," said Hilde, "sit on my knee and listen to Siggy's nice story. Better chop off a few more heads," she advised Sigrid from the side of her mouth.

"Halvor was so happy to get home that he quite forgot the

poor princess was waiting for him," said Sigrid rapidly. "And she waited and waited, and then she said, 'He's forgotten me, and now I must go to Soria Moria Castle and marry the troll with nine heads.'"

"Excellent!" exclaimed Hilde, trying to stop Eirik slithering off her lap. "Nine heads coming off soon, Eirik."

"So Halvor had to find Soria Moria Castle, which was east of the sun and west of the moon, but nobody knew the way. Oh, Eirik, I wish you'd *listen*!"

"Eirik," said Hilde ruthlessly, "listen to the end of the story! The prince chopped off the troll's heads. Chop, chop, chop!"

"Chop, chop, *chop*!" chanted Eirik.

"You've wrecked my story!" Sigrid cried.

"I told you, Sigrid: He's too little." She let Eirik slide to the floor. "And he isn't sleepy. He wants to play. I don't blame him, either. I know how he feels."

Gudrun looked at her. "What do you mean?"

"Nothing." Hilde prowled up the room. "Just—I'm sick of being cooped up indoors. Peer's having fun on the beach, building that jetty with Bjorn. Pa and Sigurd are on the fell with Loki and the new puppy. It isn't fair. I wish something interesting would happen to me."

"Be careful what you wish for," said Gudrun, "you might get it. It was *interesting* last summer when the house was attacked by trolls, but I wouldn't want to go through that again. Life isn't fair, and you may as well get used to it."

"You always say that!" Hilde wailed. "I'm so *tired* of being shut up in here, doing the same things, cooking and spinning and weaving, for ever and ever and ever."

"Hilde!" said Gudrun in surprise. She set down the knife and smoothed Hilde's hair with a damp hand. "We all feel low at the end of winter. But spring's here, and soon the weather will be warm again. Think of sitting outside in the long evenings."

"I suppose," Hilde muttered.

Sigrid said, "Now your hair will smell of onions."

"Well, thanks!" Hilde began, when there was a bang at the door. Alf, the old sheepdog, struggled up with a startled bark.

Gudrun's hand flew to her mouth. "Who's this knocking after dark?"

"Trolls?" said Sigrid apprehensively.

Hilde got to her feet. "*I'll* open it. And if there are any trolls out there, I'll make them wish they hadn't bothered."

"Chop, chop, chop!" shouted Eirik. With a nervous giggle, Sigrid hoisted him into her arms, and Hilde grabbed a broom and flung the door open. "Who is it, and what do you want?"

Then she threw down the broom with a cry of delight. "Arnë!"

Arnë Egilsson ducked in under the lintel, pulling off his cap, a broad smile on his face. "Hello, Hilde—don't hit me! Is Ralf here? Gudrun, I've brought visitors." He paused before announcing grandly, "Here's Gunnar Ingolfsson of Vinland, with his wife, Astrid, and his son, Harald Silkenhair. Gunnar wants to speak to Ralf. Guess what, Hilde? I've joined

36

Gunnar's ship. I'm sailing with him to Vinland!"

Hilde gasped. "Arnë, you lucky, lucky thing!"

"Yes, but I'll miss you. Will you miss me?" he whispered, leaning close. She stepped back with a bright smile. *If my hair really smells of onions, I'll kill Ma. . . .*

A moment later, people were crowding in. Gunnar Ingolfsson filled the doorframe, a thickset, sandy-bearded man in a heavy wolfskin cloak. After him came a tall, pale girl. A flustered Gudrun came forward to greet them, wiping her hands on her apron. And the last to come in . . .

Hilde blinked. In walked a boy who made Arnë look like an overgrown, ruddy-faced farmhand. He wore his fine cloak with a confident swagger. Long golden hair tumbled over his shoulders and down his back. Harald Silkenhair?

He's like a young hero from a saga.

"He's just like a prince from a fairy tale," Sigrid breathed. "Hilde, look, he's even got a sword!"

Eirik struggled, kicking Sigrid with his bare toes till she put him down. He ran forward, a sturdy little figure in a nightshirt, blocking Harald's way, and gazed up in wide-eyed admiration. "Show me your sword," he demanded.

Harald's lips quirked, and he went down on one knee. He slid his sword a few inches out of the sheath. "Meet Bonebiter. No!" he warned, as Eirik's chubby hand went out. "She's sharp. Touch the handle."

Rather uneasily Hilde watched Eirik stretch out a finger. The hilt of the sword was wrapped with silver wire. "Shiny," said Eirik, his voice soft with awe. He looked up at Harald. "Did you cut off the twoll's head?"

Harald frowned. Hilde cut in. "It's just a story he's been listening to. He thinks—"

"He thinks you're a prince who killed some trolls," blurted Sigrid, blushing.

Harald ran the sword back into its sheath. "Not trolls," he said, laughing, "not trolls." He leaned forward and ruffled Eirik's hair. "When you're a man, maybe you'll have a sword like this." And he got to his feet.

"Wasn't that nice of him?" Sigrid whispered to Hilde.

"I . . . suppose so," said Hilde slowly. Sigrid was right. It was very nice of this young warrior to take notice of a small boy. So why should she feel so uncomfortable about it? *Meet Bonebiter.* Little boys always worshipped heroes, didn't they? What could be wrong with that?

Harald turned to Gudrun. "Lady!" He bowed over her rough hand as though it were the white hand of a queen, and declaimed with a flourish:

"Far have we fared on the wide ocean,
where seabirds scream and the whales wander.
Glad of our landfall, thanks we give
to our fair hostess for this fine welcome."

"Goodness!" Gudrun fluttered as Harald let go of her hand. "Poetry!"

"His own." Gunnar watched his son with a kind of rough delight.

"I'm honored," Gudrun exclaimed. "You're most welcome. What a shame my father-in-law isn't still alive. He was such a fine poet himself. He would so much have enjoyed this meeting."

Would he? thought Hilde, watching her mother's pleased pink flush. *Or would he have thought Master Harald Silkenhair was a young whippersnapper?*

She looked at Harald, wondering how many times he'd used that verse. Could he possibly be poking fun? But before she could consider the matter any further, Arnë tapped her shoulder. "Hilde, this is Gunnar's wife, Astrid."

Hilde turned, nearly bumping against a tall girl standing close behind her, muffled in an expensive-looking dark blue cloak with the hood up. A brown and white goatskin bag was slung over her shoulder on a long strap, which she clutched with long thin-wristed hands. She had ice-maiden skin, so white and thin that the blue veins glistened through, wide gray eyes, a neat straight nose like a cat's with little curling nostrils, and pale closely shut lips.

Their eyes met. For a second Hilde felt she was looking into the eyes of a deer or a hare, a wild animal that glares at you before bolting.

Then Astrid pushed her hood down. Out sprang a bright cloud of amber hair, frizzing and fizzling, catching the light in a million fiery glints. The hair transformed her cold, still face.

With her hood down, she was beautiful.

Hilde held out her hand, puzzled. *Gunnar's wife? She doesn't look much older than me. She can't possibly be that boy's mother!*

Astrid touched Hilde's hand with chilly fingers. There was a pause, and Hilde racked her brains for something to say. "Have you been to Vinland, too?"

"No!" said Astrid in a low, curt voice. After a moment she added with reluctance, "Gunnar and I were only married in the fall. He's an old friend of my father, Grimolf Sigurdsson of Westfold. He came to stay with us, and—I suppose he liked the look of me. I'm his second wife."

So that's it. Poor girl. Gunnar looks older than Pa. I'm glad I don't have to marry an old man just because he's rich. Aloud Hilde said, "How exciting! And now you can travel with him right across the world."

But perhaps Astrid could tell what Hilde was thinking. Instead of answering she merely raised a scornful eyebrow. Then she stared at the floor. Hilde pursed her lips in annoyance.

"Not everyone wants to travel across the world, Hilde," Arnë said with a smile. "Seafaring is hard for women."

"I'd love to go to Vinland," said Hilde immediately, determined to show Arnë that whatever most women were like, she was different.

Astrid looked up quickly, but before she or Arnë could reply, the door opened. A half-grown black puppy tumbled in and dashed around the room barking excitedly, followed by Peer's dog, Loki. A cheerful voice called, "Hey, hey, what's this? Visitors?"

"Ralf!" cried Gudrun. "Get down, Gryla, stop barking! Sigurd, tie your puppy up. Ralf, look who Arnë's brought to see us!"

The girls were left together. Hilde was about to make an excuse and slip away when Astrid touched her arm, and said stiffly, "Did you mean that? Would you really like to go to Vinland?"

Hilde opened her mouth to give some airy reply. Nothing came out. The warm, stifling world of the farmhouse wrapped around her throat like a tight scarf. She stared at Astrid, choking on the unfairness of it. Here was this awful boring girl, with her grand snooty manners, sailing off to Vinland while Hilde had to stay at home.

She doesn't know how lucky she is. Oh, if only I had her chance. I want to see something new. I want to go far away. I want to—I want to find Soria Moria Castle, east of the sun and west of the moon!

Astrid was watching her like a cat. "Come with me!" she said.

Hilde made a strangled noise between a laugh and a hiccup. "What?"

"Come with me. Ask your mother. I'll do my best to help you. I'll tell Gunnar I want another girl for company. It's true anyway. And then you'll be on my side, won't you?"

"On your s-side?" Hilde stammered, taken aback.

Something flashed at the back of Astrid's eyes. "Nobody asked *me* if I wanted to come to Vinland. Nobody asked me if I wanted to marry Gunnar. Well, my father *asked*, but he certainly wasn't listening for an answer. He'd already agreed. He wouldn't insult a man like Gunnar."

"Was—was there somebody else you liked?"

"There may have been," said Astrid warily.

"My father would never do that to me," said Hilde, appalled.

Astrid shrugged. "Lucky you. I thought of putting the cold curse on Gunnar, but someone's done it already. He's never warm. See?"

The cold curse? Hilde twisted around. Gunnar, still wrapped in his thick cloak, was hoisting Ralf's big chair closer to the fire.

Astrid tossed her head. "Anyway, you needn't feel sorry for me. I'm married, and I'm making the best of it. After all, Gunnar's a famous man. *You'll* never marry anyone half so well known. He treats me well, too. He's never once struck me. The men say he's as tough as Tyr, who put his hand in the wolf's mouth. But he needs me. He has fevers, and sometimes he tries to stay awake because of bad dreams. And he hates being alone in the dark." Her eyes narrowed. "I haven't found out why yet, but I will. I know herbs; I know how to mix drafts to give him peaceful sleep. I can wind him around my little finger," she boasted.

"What about Harald?" asked Hilde.

Astrid gave her a sharp glance. "Don't be fooled by his looks. His own mother died years ago, so he didn't mind me at first—he thought I was just a pretty little *thing* that his father might as well have. Now he knows better, and he's jealous. What do you think of him?"

"Um. Isn't he a little bit pleased with himself?"

Astrid laughed. "Oh, yes. There's no one quite like Harald Silkenhair. Well! You might do."

"Do?" Hilde decided all over again that she didn't like Astrid. "What for?"

Astrid raised her eyebrows. "Don't be like that. We could have fun together. You want to come to Vinland, don't you? Or was that just talk?" she added scornfully.

"No! I meant it." Hilde swallowed. "But . . ."

Astrid seemed to realize that she hadn't been making a great impression. She looked at Hilde for a moment, as if wondering what to offer her. "I want you to come. Do you like secrets? If we're going to be friends, I'll tell you one."

"Go on," said Hilde, intrigued in spite of herself.

Astrid hesitated. "Shall I? Remember, I'm taking a risk, I'm trusting you. Are you easily shocked? No? All right, listen." Her pale eyes opened wide. "*There's troll blood in me.* Oh, yes, there is—a long way back, perhaps, but it's there. And I can see things other people can't."

"Troll blood?" A fascinated shiver ran down Hilde's back. "What do you mean?"

Astrid gave her a conspiratorial smile. "What I say." She leaned close and whispered, "My mother's mother was the daughter of Thorodd Half-Troll, and *his* mother was a troll out of the Dovrefell. My mother's dead now. But she passed down all kinds of tricks to me." She patted her big goatskin bag. "Gunnar thinks this is just herbs and medicines. Well, some of it is, and some of it isn't."

Hilde drew back in sudden suspicion. "You're making it up."

"Oh, am I?" Astrid looked around, but their low-voiced conversation was easily drowned out by loud laughter from the men chatting and joking by the fire. "All right then." She unbuckled the flap and plunged her arm into the bag. "Hold this."

She handed Hilde a little square box, yellowish in the dim firelight. Hilde rubbed her fingers over it. It was made of smooth bone or ivory, but there were some scratchings on the lid, runes or patterns. She looked up at Astrid. "Well?"

"Listen to it," said Astrid. "Put it to your ear."

Hilde did. The box buzzed. She almost dropped it, and listened again. Yes, when her ear was pressed close, the box was buzzing or humming. Or was it even a sleepy, angry voice, singing or chanting a very, very long way off?

"What's inside?" Hilde burned with curiosity. She pried at the lid.

"Don't open it!" Astrid snatched it back. "My mother gave it to me. It tells me things. Now do you believe me?"

Looking at Astrid in the flickering firelight, Hilde found

she did. There was a slant to her eyes, a play of shadows on the cheekbones that reminded Hilde of the troll princess who lived underneath Troll Fell.

"Does Gunnar know you've—got troll blood?" she almost whispered. Astrid smiled, showing a line of sharp little white teeth. "Oh, no, he's much too shockable. I told you, it's a secret. He only knows I can do a little *seidr*—magic. Are you wondering if I've got a tail? Don't worry, I haven't. But the troll blood's there. It makes me different. And I can see this, Hilde Ralfsdaughter. Like it or not, you're coming with us to Vinland." She pinched Hilde's arm. "You wait and see. Let's talk again later." She walked away to the fire.

Hilde's fingers prickled from touching the little buzzing box. Her breath came short. A smile of pure excitement curled her lips. *The cold curse. Troll blood. Like it or not, you're coming with us to Vinland.* And to think that only a short while ago she had thought Astrid conventional and dull!

Oh, she thought, *I do want to go with her. I must!*

CHAPTER 4

The Nis Amuses Itself

As Peer came out of the woods there was a rustling and pattering in the bushes: trolls probably, out foraging now that night had fallen. Troll Fell loomed above the farm like a dreaming giant, asleep with his head on his knees. Just over the giant's shoulder, a scraped-out moon bobbed in a flood of clouds.

Peer hesitated by the farmhouse door. All the way up the track he'd hurried along, imagining Harald picking a quarrel with Ralf, insulting Hilde, frightening the twins. He'd pictured himself striding in to the rescue. But now his imagination failed. Harald had a sword and would use it. It would be no good trying to pull him outside for a fistfight.

He wished now he'd come home earlier. He could have found Hilde, and told her all about it. And yet . . . the story made him look such a fool. What if Harald called him Barelegs in front of Hilde? *How can I stop him? What shall I do?*

"You don't have to play his games," Bjorn had said. But Peer had a feeling that Harald was good at pushing people into games they had no wish to play.

Reluctantly he lifted the latch, and something scampered across the yard and mewed at the bottom of the door like a hopeful cat. The Nis—their touchy little house spirit! It must have been accidentally shut out. As the door creaked open he got a glimpse of its beady eyes, skinny outline, and little red hat before it shot past his ankles and whizzed up the wall into the rafters.

He closed the door. The room was hot, bright, and crowded, the atmosphere unnaturally hushed. Peer's taut nerves twanged. *What's going on? Trouble?*

A strong voice chanted:

"The hound of heaven, the ship-seizer,
hunted us over the wild waters.
Weary wanderers, we fled before
the wide jaws of the wind-wolf!"

It was Harald, the center of attention, standing at the long trestle table reciting his poetry to the family. He made a brave sight, gold gleaming at his neck. Everyone listened in apparent admiration. No one had eyes for Peer.

Peer waited by the door, hungry and cross. In full flow,

Harald chanted on. It was all about the voyage to Vinland, and he was making it sound pretty stormy and adventurous. Once, he caught Peer's eye, and a faint smirk fled across his face.

Would the poem never end? Was Harald deliberately spinning it out to keep him waiting? Something scuffled overhead. Dust dropped in a fairy cascade. Suppressing a sneeze, Peer rubbed his eyes and saw flickering movement along the roof beams. It would be the Nis poking about among the cobwebs, chasing spiders—one of its favorite games. Good. At least the Nis couldn't be bothered with Harald Silkenhair!

At last Harald's voice rose in triumphant climax:

"But our sleek ship, our proud sea-serpent
 bore us swiftly to a safe haven,
 an empty land, fleeced in forests,
 land for our labors, land for claiming!"

Everyone but Peer clapped and cheered. Harald flung himself back on the bench, lifted his cup, and tossed down a draft of ale. "Great stuff!" roared Ralf, pounding the table. "Grand! 'Our sleek ship, our proud sea-serpent!' I've always wished I could make poetry. My father could, but I can't. 'An empty land, fleeced in forests.' That's not right, though. Vinland isn't empty. There are people there."

Harald's laugh was a jeer. "People? You mean the Skraelings?"

Peer didn't know what a Skraeling was, but nothing would have induced him to ask. He squeezed down the room and reached over Arnё's shoulder to grab some food. Gudrun smiled at him, and Hilde flipped him a wave, but the benches were full, so he folded himself into a corner near the fire, sitting on the earth floor with his back against one of the big wooden posts that held up the roof. Loki came out from under the table to greet him. Peer pulled him close and fed him a piece of cheese.

Sigurd was asking loudly, "What's a Skraeling?"

"Skraelings, laddie?" Gunnar set down his horn cup with a crack. "A Skraeling is a wretch, a pitiful rascal. It's what we call those creatures who live in Vinland. No better than trolls. They live in tents made from bits of tree bark. They dress in skins. Your little sister knows more than the Skraelings do. Why," he guffawed, "at one place we stopped they were so ignorant that they bartered good furs for a few miserable pieces of red cloth. And when we ran short of cloth, we tore it into thinner and thinner strips, and still the Skraelings paid in furs."

"That's not what Pa told us," said Hilde. Peer nodded agreement. Ralf's stories had made these people sound like tall forest spirits, flitting between the trees with bright feathers in their black hair.

Ralf said mildly, "I thought they were fine people. And why shouldn't they barter furs for cloth, if cloth was a rarity? I don't call that proof of ignorance."

49

Gunnar stared as though he wasn't used to being disagreed with. Gudrun broke in, "But aren't they dangerous? Isn't that how you lost your hand, Gunnar—fighting Skraelings?"

"Skraelings? No!" Gunnar's face darkened. "No. It happened in Westfold before I left. An argument in an alehouse." Here his wife gave him a cold glance, Peer noticed—perhaps she didn't approve of alehouse fights. "The man jumped me before I was ready for him. Luckily I had my boy here with me."

"What did Harald do?" Sigurd asked eagerly.

"Oh, I just cut the fellow's hair for him. With this," said Harald with a lazy wink, patting his sword. Sigurd laughed out loud, and Ralf grinned. Astrid studied her nails, and Gudrun shook her head. Peer stared at Harald in deep dislike.

Harald twitched. He brushed at his shoulder, frowning. A moment later he shook his head, combing his fingers through his hair. Then Peer realized. The Nis, perching in the rafters, was amusing itself by dropping things onto Harald's head— dead spiders and bits of grit and cobwebs. Brilliant! He tousled Loki's ears, grinning.

"Anyway, tell us about your settlement," exclaimed Ralf. "What's it called? What's it like? And how's my old friend Thorolf?"

Peer looked up. It would be good to hear news of Thorolf; he remembered him as a tall, pleasant-faced man who had often spoken to his father in the boat sheds at Hammerhaven.

A glance passed between Harald and Gunnar. "We've had no news of Thorolf since we left him in Vinland last year," said

Harald, yawning. "Have we, Father?"

"How could we?" Gunnar shivered suddenly, and the cup shook and splashed in his hand. He set it down. "Harald's right. We left him there last year. Haven't been back since."

"Ah, then you don't know what he's up to now," Ralf pointed out. "He may have come after you."

Gunnar mumbled something. Peer, who was sitting near him, saw in surprise that his face was beaded with sweat. He noticed Astrid giving her husband a sharp, curious glance.

Harald shook his hair. "I think we'll find Thorolf and his men right where we left them," he said, smiling. "I don't think he had any plans to leave."

Ralf leaned forward, rubbing his hands. "Didn't he, now? Maybe you're right. It's a wonderful land. Those green forests, full of game—the rivers bursting with fish. No wonder Thorolf wants to make a home there. And you, you're on your way back?"

Harald nodded. "We have two good solid houses in a sheltered bay, with a river running out of the woods, and good anchorage in the river mouth. We named it Serpent's Bay—because of the two ships, *Long Serpent* and *Water Snake*."

And I suppose that was your clever idea, thought Peer, watching mesmerized as a dried bean bounced off Harald's shoulder and skittered across the table. Sigurd noticed it this time. He nudged Sigrid, and the pair of them glanced upward and giggled.

Arnë broke in eagerly. "Ralf, why don't you come with us?

That's why I brought Gunnar here. He's looking for another man, and I told him you've always talked about another voyage."

Gudrun, who'd been going around the table with the jug, knocked Arnë's cup over. Ale washed across the table. Sigrid jumped up for a cloth, but Gudrun stood stock-still, eyes fixed on Ralf.

"Arnë's right." Gunnar wiped his face and looked steadier. "It's like this, Ralf: My old crew split up over the winter. On the profits of the last trip, some of them got married or bought land, and didn't want to set out again this season. So I've been looking for new men. Picked up a couple in Hammerhaven— Arnë, for one—but there's room for another. Interested?" He didn't wait for Ralf to reply, but went on: "Here's the plan. Setting out this early, we ought to reach Vinland by midsummer. The Greenlanders will pay anything for good timber, and it's there for the taking, great tall oaks and pines. Spend the winter trapping—fox and beaver. The place belongs to no one. No kings, no laws. It's all free. You can carve yourself a piece of land and be absolute master. Think about it. You could come home and buy Gudrun a gold necklace. Or a couple of cows or more land, whatever you like. What do you say?"

"I knew you'd ask," said Ralf slowly. "I've been thinking about it all evening, deciding what to do . . ."

Gunnar sat back. "Good! Let's drink to it."

". . . but I'm needed on the farm," Ralf went on. "Sigurd's not old enough to manage, and the last time I went away Gudrun had all sorts of trouble with the trolls. I can't leave her to cope alone."

Gudrun's eyes shone, but Gunnar's whiskered cheeks creased uneasily. "Trolls? You have many trolls here?"

Ralf laughed, and waved his hand. "We live on Troll Fell, Gunnar."

"Trolls." Gunnar shuddered. "I hate 'em. Unnatural vermin."

Astrid seemed to stir. Her lips parted, but before she could speak another dried bean dropped from the rafters, splashing into Harald's cup as he lifted it to his lips. Harald threw down the cup.

"That's enough, you!" He pointed at Peer, who scrambled to his feet. "Do you think I'm going to put up with this?"

Everyone stared. Harald put his hands on the table and leaned forward menacingly. "You've been throwing beans at me, haven't you, Barelegs? And you think it's funny?"

"I didn't do anything," said Peer, seriously alarmed.

"It wasn't Peer!" Sigrid cried.

"No. There's something dodging about in the roof," said Astrid, to Peer's great surprise. Most people couldn't see the Nis.

Everyone looked up into the smoky dark roof space, cluttered with fishing nets, strings of onions, old hay rakes, and scythes.

The Nis flung down its fistful of beans. A stinging shower

rattled onto Harald's upturned face, and as he cursed and ducked, the Nis followed it up by bouncing some small wrinkled apples off his back. Then it could be heard drumming its heels against the beam, and sniggering: *"Tee-hee-hee!"*

Astrid's face sharpened into a triangular smile. "There it is!" she breathed, fixing her eyes on a spot above Harald's head. The sniggering broke off.

"Where?" Harald spun around, golden hair spraying out. He dragged out his sword and angled it up, craning his neck to see into the rafters.

Everyone leaped to their feet. The dogs began barking. "Put that sword away," called Ralf. "Someone'll get hurt!"

"No swords in this house!" cried Gudrun.

"My apologies," said Harald between his teeth. "There's something up there. Stand back, and let me deal with it." He put a foot on the bench, obviously preparing to spring up onto the table. Peer heard a frightened squeak from the Nis.

"There it goes!" Peer shot out his arm and pointed. "Look, a troll! Running along that rafter, can't you see?" His finger followed the imaginary troll from beam to beam. "It's over the fire—oh!" He let his arm drop.

"What? Where?" gasped Gudrun, half convinced.

"It went out through the smoke hole," said Peer with disappointment in his voice.

"Then it's on the roof." Harald sprang for the door, Arnë and Gunnar and the dogs close behind him. Ralf followed more slowly, giving Peer the flicker of a wink.

Peer thought he had better dash for the door, too. He caught Hilde's eye and said loudly, "Let's hope they catch it!" Hilde was laughing silently.

The twins were already crowding outside, while Gudrun tried to pull them back. "Harald's got a sword out there!"

Then the wind was fresh on Peer's face. The moon skimmed between the clouds like a stone skipping over water, filling the yard with scuttling shadows. Harald was making Arnë give him a leg up onto the farmhouse's thick turf roof. Gunnar stood squarely in the patch of light from the open door, squinting up under his good hand. "Go on, son," he shouted. "A roof's no place to hide. We'll not be fooled by that again. . . ."

"I never thought he could have climbed up," said Harald over his shoulder.

What were they talking about? Peer looked at Ralf, who shrugged and said in a low voice, "I guess they've had adventures before."

Harald walked along the roof ridge, sword in hand, a sinister silhouette against the sky. The moonlight silvered his blowing hair. Peer shivered suddenly, and Ralf too must have felt uncomfortable about this prowling figure on his own roof, for he called out, "It's gone; you've missed it. Come on down."

But the dogs, which had been running about eagerly with their noses down, began to bark and growl, and make little dashes at a blackly shadowed corner of the yard near the cowshed.

"Don't tell me they've found a real troll," Ralf muttered. He crossed the yard in a couple of quick strides, Peer beside him, Gunnar close behind.

In the angle of the wall was a crawling darkness the size of a small child. "Gods!" Gunnar's voice clotted with horror. "Look at that. Where's its *head*?"

Peer's skin prickled. Then he saw the troll had merely crouched down, wrapping skinny arms protectively over its head. Its bare flanks gleamed dimly like oiled leather. There was a sound of chewing, and a strong stink of old herrings. So it had been robbing the fish-drying racks!

Ralf clapped his hands. "Go on! Get out of here! Shoo!" he shouted.

A pair of luminous green eyes winked open. The troll gaped in threat, and produced a dry, frightening hiss, accompanied by an even stronger smell of fish. Ralf dragged the dogs away by their collars. "Stand back, Peer—give it a chance to run."

Behind them, Harald leaped into the yard. He staggered, touching a hand to the ground to steady himself; then he was up, his naked blade glinting. "Out of my way!" he shouted, running at the troll.

The round green eyes scrunched into terrified half-moons. The troll dived away, fat sides pumping, long bald tail curving and switching. It scrambled around the corner of the cowshed. But Harald was faster. He threw himself forward and stamped down heavily on its tail, jerking it to a halt. The troll tugged and writhed to get free, squealing dreadfully. "Let it go! Let it go!" Ralf shouted. But Harald struck.

As the blow flashed down, the troll gave a final desperate wrench, and leaped crazily up the hillside as if shot from a catapult, leaving its narrow, tapering tail thrashing horribly under Harald's boot. There was a sickening smell of stale armpits and rotten eggs.

Harald leaped back in disgust and slammed his sword into its sheath. Ralf and Arnë broke out coughing, and the dogs whined, wiping their noses on their paws. With a shiver of loathing, Gunnar turned away from the jerkily wriggling tail. Peer rubbed a hand over his eyes. What had he and the Nis begun?

"I need a drink after that," said Ralf drily. He held open the farmhouse door and nodded for everyone to go in.

Gudrun, the twins, and Hilde and Astrid clustered around the door.

"Was there really a troll?"

"What happened?"

"What was that noise?"

"Poof!" Sigurd clutched his nose. "What's that *awful* smell?"

"There was a troll, all right," Peer said to Hilde.

"Harald was so fast," said Arnë in admiration. "What a warrior! He nearly got it!"

"He got its *tail*," said Peer with bitter sarcasm.

Softhearted Sigrid gasped. "Oh, the poor thing! Oh, that

must have hurt so much! Will it be all right?"

"It will grow a new one," Hilde soothed her.

Harald overheard. "Yes, a pity," he said to Hilde lightly. "Your little brother wanted me to kill a troll, didn't he? How the tales do come to life!"

"Why didn't you let the dogs pull it down?" Gunnar growled at Ralf. "You could have nailed the head to your barn door to scare the others. Like hanging up a dead crow. The best way to deal with vermin."

Ralf poured himself a cup of ale, and pushed the jug toward Gunnar and Harald. He looked as if he was struggling for words. "I didn't want it killed," he said at last, politely enough. "The trolls may be a nuisance, but they're our neighbors, Gunnar. We've got to live here with them. We've all got to get along."

"Get along with trolls?" Gunnar showed a set of brownish teeth through his bristly beard. "Root 'em up, smoke 'em out. That's what I'd do."

Peer thought of the labyrinthine passages underneath Troll Fell. *Smoke 'em out? We'd have hundreds of trolls down on us like angry bees.*

Gunnar sat down suddenly. His chest heaved. "Anyway," he got out between harsh breaths, "what about my offer? Be a man. Come with us."

Ralf and Gudrun looked at each other. She dropped onto the bench beside him, and he reached across and squeezed her hand. "No, I can't," he said firmly. "But ask in the village.

58

Maybe there's someone there who wants to go."

Gunnar gave him a black look. "I see I've wasted my time. Arnë swore you'd come, that's all. Well, I warn you, if the wind's right, we'll be leaving tomorrow. I won't lose a good wind in the sailing season. After tomorrow it'll be too late to change your mind."

Ralf shrugged. Peer beat his fist on his knee in silent satisfaction. *Good for Ralf! We don't want anything to do with them, any of them!*

Hilde stood up. "Ma, Pa . . ."

Peer saw her resolute face and his heart stopped. He knew what was coming.

"Astrid wants me to come to Vinland with her. And I'd like to go!"

The shocked silence stretched . . . and stretched. With a rustle, a half-burned log shifted in the fire like a sleepy dragon. Its bright underbelly flaked, shedding golden scales that dimmed and died.

Gudrun found her voice. "Hilde, you can't go to Vinland. It's ridiculous."

"It's not," said Hilde. "Astrid is going, so why shouldn't I?"

"But Astrid is married," exclaimed Gudrun.

"And I'd be with her. What's wrong with that?"

Gudrun spun around. "Ralf—say something!"

"Hold on, hold on." Ralf tried to sound soothing. "Hilde, your Ma doesn't like this idea, and I can't say I blame her. . . ."

Peer stopped listening. He knew Hilde would get her own

way. She would go to Vinland, without him. There'd be no news. He'd miss her every day, but he'd never know if she got there safely, or when she was coming back. When Ralf had sailed away years ago, they hadn't known if he was alive or dead until the day he came home.

He felt someone's gaze, looked up and saw Harald watching him.

"Gudrun, I know you're worried." Astrid's cool voice cut across the hubbub. "But please, please let Hilde come." Her eyes opened, wide and pleading. "We've made friends already. I swear we'll be just like sisters." She laid one hand on Gunnar's shoulder. "Gunnar wouldn't take me if it wasn't safe."

Gunnar grasped her hand. "Of course it will be safe," he declared.

"See!" Hilde turned to Gudrun. "If it's safe for Astrid, it's safe for me."

"Hilde, be quiet!" Gudrun was red and flustered. "Your father and I will judge what's safe."

"Why should I be quiet?" Hilde flared up. "It's so unfair! You expect me to stay at home, don't you, and—and *drudge* all my life? Now I've got this chance—Vinland, *Vinland*—and you won't let me go. . . ."

Gudrun dropped back onto the bench and put her hands over her eyes. "You know," Ralf said to Gudrun, as quietly as if no one was listening, "Hilde's like me. She wants to see the world a bit. She's nearly grown up. This is the chance of a lifetime for her, Gudrun. I think we should let her go."

"But it's so dangerous!" Gudrun looked up in tears. "All that sea—and when they get to Vinland, those Skraeling creatures, creeping about in the woods . . ."

"It's dangerous here, too," said Hilde more calmly. "Trolls under the fell, and Granny Green-teeth down in the mill-pond, and lubbers in the woods. If I've survived all those, I daresay I'll survive a few Skraelings."

"That's true," Ralf said to Gudrun. "She'll be safe enough. Gunnar's a sound skipper and the sort of man who—well, who looks after his friends. And when they get to Vinland, there's Thorolf: I'd trust him anywhere. And now I come to think of it, Thorolf's little son must be in Vinland with him. Ottar, he's called. He's about the same age as Sigurd. Isn't that right, Gunnar? Is Ottar there?"

"Of course," said Harald, before Gunnar could answer. "Remember Ottar, Father, the day we left? Climbing onto the roof of the house and waving to us?"

Gunnar grinned and nodded.

"His little boy is there?" asked Gudrun doubtfully.

Hilde flung her arms around her mother and gave her a squeeze. "Oh, please, Ma, let me go. Please?"

Gudrun faltered. It was hard for her to resist this sudden embrace.

Peer took a breath. He ought to tell Gudrun and Ralf everything he knew about Harald. Surely they would never let Hilde sail away with someone who had forced a quarrel on him, and threatened him with a sword. And yet . . . Hilde wanted to go so very badly, and he loved her for it—for being herself, adventurous and brave. How could he wreck her chances?

"Oh, Hilde." Gudrun's voice trembled. "How can we let you go when we don't know these people? Of course, they seem splendid, and I can see that Astrid ought to have another woman with her, but . . ." She stopped and tried again. "If your father had been going, he could have looked after you, but as it is—"

"Ma, you do know Arnë," pleaded Hilde.

"Arnë isn't one of the family," said Gudrun desperately.

Peer's heart pounded. He looked across the table and met Harald's bright, amused, contemptuous stare. He saw himself through those eyes: *Someone who builds boats, but never sails in them. Someone who won't take chances. Someone who might dream about crossing the sea, but would never do it. Someone who'd stay behind while Hilde sails away.*

"I'll go with her," he said.

Hilde swung around with wide, incredulous eyes. "You, Peer?"

Ralf gave him a long, steady stare. "You really mean this, Peer?" he asked gravely. "You'll take care of Hilde? You'll look after her?"

"Yes." It was like swearing an oath: the most serious thing he'd ever done. He didn't know how he'd manage, but he'd do it, or die trying. "I will. Don't worry, Ralf. Gudrun, I promise

I'll bring her home again."

There was a moment's silence. Then Ralf gave Peer a tiny nod, and looked at Gudrun. With an enormous sniff, Gudrun nodded too.

"Thank you! Oh, *thank you!*" Hilde nearly danced on the spot. Then she threw herself at Peer and hugged him. "Oh, Peer, I never thought you might want to come too. But you do, and it's perfect—absolutely perfect!"

She let him go. He looked dizzily around the room. No one else seemed very happy. Arnë was scowling. Harald lifted an ironic eyebrow. Gunnar frowned. "Who *is* this?" He jabbed his thumb at Peer as though he'd quite forgotten meeting him on the jetty. "What use will he be to me? Why should I take him on my ship?"

And Hilde said cheerfully, pulling him forward with her arm around him, "Oh, this is Peer. He's terribly useful. He can do anything with wood. His father was a boatbuilder. He's helped Bjorn make a new faering. And he's my brother. He's my foster brother!"

CHAPTER 5

The Journey Begins

Peer opened his eyes and saw a dark roof space crisscrossed with sunbeams like golden scaffolding. Straw prickled under him. To one side of him was a plank partition. Behind the planks something large was champing and stirring.

Slowly he remembered. He and the twins were sleeping in the cowshed to leave more room for the guests. "Do you mind, Peer?" Gudrun had whispered last night. He'd minded very much, but of course he'd lied and said he didn't.

He remembered more, and a pit of dread opened in his stomach. What had he done? Had he really promised to go away for an unknown period of time, on a strange ship, to a strange land? Spring was on the way. He'd been looking forward to seeing the lambs being born, watching the barley come up, rowing out of the fjord with Bjorn and Sigurd to gather seagulls' eggs from the islands. Now all that would go on without him.

He sat up. On mounded straw between him and the door, the twins slept, cocooned in blankets. Behind the partition, Bonny, the cow, swung up her head, rolled a large brown eye at him, and returned to munching and breathing and switching her tail. From a warm nest in the straw beside him, Loki got up, stretching and yawning.

Peer stared at his dog in dismay. *How could I have forgotten him? But is it fair to take him on a ship, for weeks at sea?*

Loki lifted a paw and scraped at Peer's arm, probably hoping for breakfast. Peer took it, feeling the dog's pads rough on his fingers. "Loki, old fellow," he murmured. "What shall we do? Do you want to come with me?" Loki's tail hit the ground, once, twice.

"Good boy!" Peer hugged him. He was fooling himself, and he knew it: Loki always wagged his tail when Peer spoke to him. But he didn't care. He could never leave Loki behind.

At least that was decided. He lay back in the straw, stared upward, and wished he could carry on sleeping—that today need never start—that he didn't have to remember what Hilde had said last night. *Peer's my brother.*

He burrowed under the blanket, trying to dive back into sleep and escape the aching throb of the memory. A brother! A safe, dependable brother, to be relied on and ignored. Didn't Hilde know how he felt about her?

Perhaps not: He'd been so careful to keep things friendly all year. Perhaps she thought he'd got over it. He wished he'd kissed her again, even if she'd been angry. He wished he'd tried.

Oh, what was the use? *Peer's my brother!* It was hopeless.

"Psst," came a piercing whisper. "Peer! Are you awake?"

He raised his hot face from the crackling straw and saw Sigrid sitting up, arms wrapped neatly around her knees.

"Are you really going away to Vinland, Peer?"

"Looks like it," he said gloomily.

"You don't have to go if you don't want to."

"But Hilde wants to, and I've promised to go with her."

"Oh, Hilde," said Sigrid crossly. "Why do you always do what she wants?"

"I don't!" He thought about it. "Do I?"

"Yes, you do." Sigrid sat up straighter and wagged her finger at him. Peer almost smiled, but she was quite serious. "You've got to be tougher, Peer. Sometimes Hilde ought to do what *you* want."

Peer stared at her, speechless, until Sigrid wriggled and said, "What?"

"You're a very clever girl, Siggy," he said slowly. "And you are absolutely right!"

She beamed with surprised pleasure, and Peer threw back his blankets. "Time to get up!" And he pulled open the creaking cowshed door and stuck his head out.

The morning was sunny, but a wind with ice in its teeth blew down from the mountains. A seagull tilted overhead, dark against the blue and white sky, then bright against the hillside as it went sweeping off down the valley. Peer watched it. *A fair wind for sailing west. So we really are leaving. Today.*

But Sigrid's simple words had acted like magic. He set his jaw. *I've messed about long enough, trying to be whatever Hilde wants. From now on, I'll act the way I feel!*

He stepped out, alive and determined, and nearly trod on something shriveled and whiplike lying by the corner of the cowshed. Loki ran to sniff at it, and backed off, sneezing. It was the troll's tail. Peer poked it with his foot, and when it didn't move, he picked it up gingerly by the tip. It was heavier and bonier than he'd expected, and cold to the touch. He threw it on the dung heap with a shudder. A rusty smear stained the bare earth where the tail had lain. Blood. He scuffed dirt over it so that Sigrid would not see, and went on into the house.

Gudrun and Hilde were sorting out clothes. Peer put away his faint hope that Hilde might have changed her mind. Astrid sat like a queen in Ralf's big chair, watching them. She had little Elli on her knee, and was letting the baby play with a bunch of keys that dangled from her belt, jigging her up and down and humming some strange little song that rose and fell. Ralf, Gunnar, and Harald were nowhere to be seen.

"Peer! Eat something quickly. Gunnar wants to catch the morning tide." Gudrun's voice was brittle.

"The men have gone down to the ship. Gunnar wants to load up more food and fresh water. We're going to follow as soon as we can," Hilde added. She glanced at Gudrun guiltily, but Peer could tell she was bursting with excitement.

"I don't know." Gudrun bundled up a big armful of cloaks, shifts, and dresses. "You'd better just take everything. Peer, you can have some of Ralf's winter things. You've grown so much this year. I was going to make new clothes for you, but now—" She broke off, folding her lips tight.

"Where's Eirik?" asked Peer.

"Pa took him along to show him the ship," said Hilde. "It would have been tricky to manage him and Elli and the baggage too. And of course Ma wants to come down to the ship as well because—" She stopped. But for once Peer wasn't interested in sparing Hilde's feelings. He completed the sentence for her: "You mean, because she wants to say good-bye?"

Hilde flushed. There was a moment when no one spoke, and in the interval they heard Astrid singing to Elli, clapping the baby's hands together at the end of each line:

> *"Two little children on a summer's night,*
> *Went to the well in the pale moonlight.*
> *The lonely moon-man, spotted and old,*
> *Scooped them up in his arms so cold.*
> *They live in the moon now, high in the air.*
> *When you are old and gray, darling,*
> *They'll still be there."*

"I'll take her, shall I?" Peer almost snatched Elli away from Astrid.

"What a strange rhyme," said Gudrun nervously.

Astrid looked up. "It's one my mother used to sing. What a lovely baby Elli is. Why has she got webbed fingers?"

"She's Bjorn's daughter," Peer snapped, as though that explained it. His friend's tragic marriage with a seal-woman was none of Astrid's business.

Gudrun must have thought so too, for she said, clearing her throat, "Now, I wonder where the Nis is. I haven't seen it this morning."

Peer made a startled, warning gesture toward Astrid. But Hilde shook her head. "It's all right, Astrid knows."

"Knows about the Nis?" Peer looked at Astrid in suspicious astonishment.

"I saw it," Astrid said. "I knew it wasn't a troll. And don't worry, I haven't told Harald." She gave him a sweet smile. "You're a good liar, aren't you, Peer? You fooled Gunnar and Harald, anyway. But not me. I asked Hilde, and she told me it was a Nis. I even put its food down last night—Gudrun showed me how after everyone went to bed. It likes groute, doesn't it? Barley porridge with a dab of butter? And then it does the housework."

"Or not," said Gudrun, "as the case may be." She put her hands on her hips. "Well, if Gunnar wants you on that boat before noon, we'd better move."

There seemed mountains of stuff to load onto the pony. "We'll never need all this, surely!" Hilde laughed.

"I'm sure you will," said her mother grimly.

"What's this?" Peer picked up a tightly rolled sausage of woolen fabric.

"That's a sleeping sack," said Gudrun. "Big enough for two. It's for you, Peer—we've only the one, and Astrid says she'll share hers with Hilde. Ralf used it last, when he went a-Viking."

"Thank you, Gudrun," Peer said with gratitude. He hadn't thought about Loki. He hadn't thought about sleeping arrangements. What else had he missed?

"My tools—I'd better bring them." He dashed back into the empty house and looked around, caught by the strangeness of it all. Would he ever come back?

"Nis," he called quietly, and then, using the little creature's secret name, "Nithing? Are you there?" He listened. Nothing rustled or scampered. No inquisitive nose came poking out over the roof beams. "Nis?"

Perhaps it was curled up somewhere, fast asleep after the shocks and excitement of last night. "I'm going," he called, raising his voice. "Good-bye, Nis . . . I'm going away. Look after the family." Again he waited, but only silence followed. "Till we meet again," he ended forlornly.

He picked up his heavy wooden toolbox and went out, closing the door behind him. The pony lowered its head and snorted indignantly as this last load was strapped on.

"On guard!" said Gudrun to gray-muzzled old Alf, who set-tled down in front of the doorstep, ears pricked. Hilde carried Elli. Astrid was wrapped in her blue cloak again, shoulder braced against the weight of her bulging goatskin bag.

Peer held out his hand. "Give that to me, Astrid. I'll carry it for you."

"No!" Astrid clutched the strap. "I'll carry it myself. It's quite light."

It looked heavy to Peer, but he didn't care enough to insist. "Are we ready, then? Off we go."

Through the woods and downhill to the old wooden bridge—each twist of the path so familiar Peer could have walked it with his eyes shut. Past the ruined mill, where a whiff of burning still lingered in the damp air, and into the trees again. On down the long slope till they came to the handful of shaggy little houses that made up Trollsvik. They swished through the prickly grass of the sand dunes and dropped down onto the crunching shingle.

The fjord was blue-gray; beyond the shelter of the little harbor it was rough with whitecaps. Short, stiff waves followed one another in to land, turning over and collapsing abruptly onto the pebbles. And there was the ship, *Water Snake*, bare mast towering over the little jetty, forestay and backstay making a great inverted *V*. It was a shock to see her, somehow—so real, so—

"So big!" Gudrun gasped.

Astrid stopped, her cloak flapping in the wind. Her face was somber, and she braced her shoulders. "Here we go again!"

Most of the village was there on the shore, trying to sell

things to Gunnar. "Chickens—you'll want more chickens. Fresh eggs and meat for the voyage!" That was old Thorkell, gripping a couple of hens by their legs and brandishing them, flapping, in Gunnar's face. The jetty bristled with people, on-lookers jostling against cursing sailors, who were man-handling barrels of fresh water and provisions into the ship.

There was Harald, his long hair clubbed back in a ponytail, heaving barrels and crates around with the crew. Peer's eye-brows rose in grudging respect: He'd thought Harald too much the "young lord" to bother with real work. He noticed with relief that neither Harald nor Gunnar were wearing swords this morning. That would even things out a bit. Of course, those long steel swords would rust so easily; they'd be packed away in greased wool for the voyage. *I suppose they got them out yesterday to impress us all,* he thought sourly.

Ralf and Arnë came to unload the pony. Ralf seized Hilde. "Are you sure about this?" he asked. And before Peer could hear her reply, somebody grabbed him, too, and swung him around.

It was Bjorn, a tight frown on his face. "What on earth are you doing?" he demanded. "How can you think of sailing with Harald?"

Peer's gaze slid past Bjorn's shoulder to where Hilde was standing with Ralf. "I'll be all right, Pa," she was saying in an earnest voice. "I really, truly want to go."

"Ah," said Bjorn. "So this is Hilde's idea, is it? I might have known."

"Not entirely," said Peer, blushing.

Bjorn shook him. "I thought we were going to work together. I thought you wanted to build boats, like your father."

"I do." Peer touched the silver ring he always wore, his most treasured possession. It had been his father's, and it never left his finger. He added earnestly, "And I do want to work with you, Bjorn. When I come back—"

"*When* you come back!" Bjorn exploded. "*If* you come back! Peer, this is no fishing trip. Whatever they say, Gunnar and his men are Vikings, and that ship is—is like a spark from a bonfire that goes floating off, setting trouble alight wherever it lands." He added wryly, "Well, I'm not usually so poetical. But you see what I mean?"

"Yes," said Peer. "But your brother's going, isn't he? This is a trading voyage, not a Viking raid. Gunnar has his wife with him. He's not going to fight anyone in Vinland, he's just going to cut down trees for a cargo of timber. Besides—"

He broke off. *Who am I trying to convince?* And yet he still felt the unexpected longing that had squeezed his heart yesterday evening as he looked westward from the stern of *Water Snake*. "Bjorn," he said awkwardly, "the very last ship my father worked on, the *Long Serpent*, she's in Vinland now. Think of it, she sailed all that way! He'd have been so proud of that. I'd like to follow after her, just once. I'd like to find Thorolf and say, 'Remember me? I'm the son of the man who built your ship.'"

Bjorn began to speak, then shook his head. They stood

looking at each other for a moment, while the gulls screamed and circled, and the men shouted on the jetty.

"One thing you should know," Bjorn said at last. "Gunnar's own men have been gossiping that he and Harald killed a man in Westfold and had to run for it. No wonder they're on their way back to Vinland."

"But that's no secret," said Peer. "He told us about it. That's when he lost his hand. It was self-defense. The other man started it."

"You mean, the same way you 'started' that fight with Harald yesterday?"

"You might be right," said Peer after a pause. "But I won't back out now."

Bjorn sighed. "Arnë won't change his mind either. He's always been crazy, but I thought you had sense. Well, stick together." He caught Peer's expression. "You can trust Arnë. You know him. But keep out of Harald's beautiful hair." He clapped Peer on the back. "Maybe you'll come back rich! And now we'd better go and lend a hand—before Gunnar decides you're nothing but a useless passenger."

"Don't touch the sail," Astrid said to Hilde. "That red color comes off all over your clothes."

"Where shall I go?" Hilde looked around, wondering where she could sit. The ship was full of scrambling seamen.

"Just try and keep out of their way." Astrid perched on a barrel, forward of the mast, and began to tie her hair up in a head scarf. "It'll be better when we're sailing."

"Mind out, miss." One of the men pushed past Hilde. "Here, you, son"—this was to Peer—"give me a hand with these oars."

Hilde craned her neck to see if Ma and Pa were still watching. Of course they were. She gave them a desperate little wave. *This is awful. If only we could just get going.*

A rope flipped past her ears. Arnë jumped down into the ship and pushed off aft. Bjorn tossed another rope down to him. Harald took the tiller. A gap of water opened between the ship and the jetty. Hilde stared at it. It was only a stride wide. She could step over that easily if she wanted.

With a heavy wooden clatter, the oars went out through the oar holes—only three on each side, but *Water Snake* was moving steadily away. For a moment longer the gap was still narrow enough to jump—then, finally and forever, too wide.

Pa's arm lifted. Sigurd and Sigrid waved, and she heard them yelling, "Good-bye, good-bye!" Even Eirik opened and closed his fingers, and Sigrid was flapping Elli's arm up and down. But Ma didn't move. Hilde raised her own arm and flailed it madly.

Too late to say the things she should have said. *I love you. I'll miss you all so much.* Too late to change her mind. *Ma, please wave. . . .*

And at last Gudrun's hand came slowly up. She waved, and as long as Hilde watched she continued to wave across the broadening water, till the jetty and all the people on it dwindled with distance to the size of little dark ants.

Hilde blinked, carefully, so as not to spill tears down her cheeks. Her throat ached from not crying. She turned a stiff neck to look around at the ship: her new world, her new home.

And there was Peer, wrenching away at one of the oars. He looked up and caught her eye, and gave her an odd lopsided smile, and she knew that he knew just how she was feeling.

It's going to be all right, she thought, comforted.

"Oars in," Gunnar bellowed. "Up with the sail!"

Thankfully Peer dragged his long oar back through the oar hole. *Water Snake* began to seesaw, pitching and rolling over steep, choppy waves. He laid the wet oar on top of the others in a rattling pile, and went scrambling down to the stern to help haul up the sail.

"Hey—up! Hey—up!" Each heave lifted the heavy yard a foot or two higher. When it was halfway up the mast, Arnë yanked the lacing to unfurl the sail, and swag upon swag of hard-woven, greasy fabric dropped across the ship. "Haul!" Up went the sail again, higher and higher, opening out like a vast red hand to blot out the sky and half the horizon: a towering square of living, struggling, flapping cloth. The men on the braces hauled the yard around, fighting for control. The sail tautened and filled, and the ship sped forward so suddenly that Peer had to catch at the shrouds to keep his balance.

"Good work!" shouted Gunnar. He seemed glad to be at sea again: His face had a healthier color; he straddled forward, his good hand on Harald's shoulder to help his balance, bad arm tucked under his cloak.

"Right, lads, listen up! Some of us are old friends already. Magnus, Floki, Halfdan ..." His eye roamed across the men, who grinned or nodded as he named them. "Anything you others want to know about me, ask them—but don't believe more than half of it. The way I like to run things is this: You jump when I say jump, and we'll get along fine. We're going a long way together, and if you don't like the idea, you'd better start swimming." He bared his teeth ferociously, and the men laughed. "I lost my hand a few weeks ago. But if anyone thinks that makes me less of a man, just speak up now." The men glanced at one another. No one spoke. "We're going to Vinland, boys, and we'll come back rich! That's all, except—we're the crew of the *Water Snake*, we are, and there isn't a better ship on the sea!"

The men cheered. Even Peer felt a stirring in his blood. *The crew of the* Water Snake—*sailing to Vinland, across the world!*

Waves smacked into the prow. Spray sprinkled his face. The dragonhead nodded and plunged. They were out of the fjord already, and the wind was strengthening.

He looked back. There was the familiar peak of Troll Fell, piebald with snow streaks, but behind it other mountains jostled into view, trying to get a good look at *Water Snake* as she sailed out. As the ship drew farther and farther away, the details vanished, and it became more and more difficult to pick out Troll Fell from among its rivals, until at last they all merged and flattened into a long blue smudge of coastline.

CHAPTER 6

The Winter Visitor

Kwimu is wide awake suddenly, and wonders what has woken him. He's lying in the wigwam, feet toward the fire, which still burns enough to warm the air. He can tell by how low it's burned that it's the dead of night. All around him, his family breathes quietly, lying like logs wrapped in their warm furs.

Cautiously he raises himself on his elbow, listening. Behind and above him, his shadow rears against the sloping birch-bark walls, as if looking over his shoulder. Everything seems well. He scans the sleeping faces near to him: Sinumkw, his father. Kiunik, his mother's brother. Beside him, the pale face of Skusji'j, the Little Weasel. Across the fire on the women's side, his mother, grandmother, aunt, and sister sleep. Even the dogs are fast asleep, noses buried in their bushy tails.

Out in the woods, an owl calls sadly: *koo koo!* Perhaps it was the owl that woke him. He settles back, arranging himself on the springy fir boughs that layer the floor, breathing in the green smell and the faint scent of the fire. He draws the warm beaver-fur robe up to his chin, and folds his arms behind his head, staring up to where the slanting poles of the wigwam come together high overhead, a rough frame holding a patch of black sky. Sometimes you can see a star.

Outside, the snow is still thick, the cold is strong. His stomach grumbles a little, but he's not truly hungry. It's been a good winter for the People, with plenty of game. No need to kill the dogs, as they had to do in the famine three winters back. Dog is good to eat, but moose is better. Besides, Kwimu likes these dogs. They are good hunting companions.

Yes, the worst of the winter is over. This is Sugar Moon, the forerunner of spring. Soon the sap will be rising in the sugar maples, and it will be time to collect it and boil it into thick, sweet syrup. Kwimu is looking forward to showing Skusji'j how to pour little coils of hot syrup into the snow, where it cools into chewy candy. Then the thaw will come, the rivers will melt, and it will be time to move down to the seashore again. He glances again at Skusji'j. Hard to believe that nearly four seasons have passed since he and his father took the Little Weasel away from the deserted houses of the Jipijka'maq People. It hadn't been easy. The child had fought like a weasel, too, biting and scratching so fiercely they'd had to tie his hands and bundle him into the canoe all trussed up—till he realized they meant him no harm.

And he'd been quick to pick up words—a gruff greeting, a *yes* or a *no*. Still, it was months before he could tell in stumbling sentences who he was and how he came in his people's ships from a land across the ocean, a journey of a moon or more. Everyone there has pale skin. It sounds like the Ghost World. But the Little Weasel is certainly not a ghost. "He is my little brother," Kwimu murmurs, and his heart is warm.

He reaches down to touch Fox, who doesn't stir, even though Kwimu runs his hand over the pricked ears and sharp, pointed nose. Kwimu yawns, shifts position. Why can't he sleep? He's not even drowsy. Outside, everything is still. The owl has stopped calling. Perhaps it has killed.

His mind roams back over a year of changes. He'd thought, after the Jipijka'maq People had gone, that they could move down to the bay as usual. But Sinumkw hadn't liked the idea. "How do we know if the Jipijka'maq People have gone for good? What if they come back?" The rest of the men, after discussing it, agreed with him. They arranged with the Beaver Clan to share their shoreline and fishing grounds for the season.

But what will happen this year? Grandmother says those dark earth houses are haunted. "Angry ghosts sing songs there now," she says. It is a place of bad memories, best avoided.

Kwimu lies thinking of it: The river where they built the fish traps, the shore where he's dug for clams and oysters, the river packed with salmon, the marshlands where ducks and geese gather in the hundreds, and where huge brown moose sometimes wander out of the forests to splash through the boggy pools. *Is it all lost forever? Will we never go back?*

A branch cracks with the cold: a sharp, splintering, tearing sound. Kwimu starts. Of course, though, branches break all the time. They snap like pipe stems, weighed down with snow or split by frost.

All the same, he holds his breath. The cold intensifies, the fire pines and dwindles, darkness creeps up the walls. Just as he has to let his breath go in a cloud of vapor, he hears it again: another crack. And then heavy, slow footsteps in the snow. *Crunch. Crunch.*

Beside him, Fox twists into sudden life. All through the wigwam the family wakes, eyes flying open, breath caught. No one speaks. Even the dogs know better than to yap. No one wants to attract the attention of what is outside. Skusji'j sits up. He looks tensely from face to face. *Muin?* he mouths to Kwimu. Bear?

Kwimu shakes his head. All the bears are asleep. They won't wake, hungry and bad-tempered, till late spring.

Crunch. Crunch. Something shuffles about the wigwam. Kwimu's heart beats so hard he is afraid it will burst. Quietly, Sinumkw stretches out his hand and grips Kwimu's arm above the elbow. The touch calms him.

The framework of the wigwam jerks and shudders as the thing outside jostles it, and then picks at the walls, patting and fumbling. Kwimu's little sister is panting with terror. Any moment now the frail birchbark walls will be torn away, exposing them to the bleak wind and icy stars, and to—

Skusji'j cries out loudly in his own language, and as Kwimu turns on him in furious anger, repeats it in the language of the People: "See! See there!" He points upward.

Something is blocking the opening at the top of the wigwam—something round and dark and glistening—something that rolls about with quick, jerky movements, showing a yellowish-white rim, fixing for a malevolent moment on each person below.

An eye as big as your hand.

Sinumkw seizes his lance. Kwimu's mother shrieks. But Grandmother springs nimbly to her feet, shaking off her covers. She catches up two of the fir branches that line the floor, and thrusts them into the fire. They crackle and catch, and she waves them upward, streaming hot smoke and burning sparks.

The eye vanishes. From high above the wigwam a terrible scream rings across the forest. The sound crushes them with its weight of cold anguish. They huddle flat, clutching each other, expecting any moment to be trodden and trampled. But the frozen ground shudders to the impact of huge feet running away.

Before his father can forbid it, Kwimu dashes to the door of the wigwam, Skusji'j at his heels. He peels back the hide flap and scurries out into the bitter night. Around him the peaceful village is waking in alarm. Men stumble from the doorways of the nearest wigwams. Sleepy voices call out to ask what is happening.

The treetops are dark against a sky hazy with moonglimmer. A few hundred yards to the southeast, something crashes away through the trees, howling, brushing the very tops of the white pines. There are enormous, pitted tracks in the snow.

Kiunik, Kwimu's young uncle, ducks out of the wigwam and races toward the trees, yelling a war cry, his black hair streaming loose. Some of the other young men join in, but the older ones call them roughly back: "It's gone; let it go."

"We've been lucky."

"You can't fight a *jenu*."

"What was it?" The Little Weasel tugs Kwimu's arm. He looks like a ghost in the white darkness. "Kwimu, *what was it?*"

"*Jenu,*" Kwimu mutters. "Ice giant. We have seen the *jenu*— and lived."

CHAPTER 7

Ghost Stories

"There are no trolls in Vinland," said Magnus confidently. Peer sat with his back against the curve of the side, rocking to the steady up and down of the ship. He could see sky, but not sea, and it was comforting to shut out for a while the sight of all that lonely vastness. The sun had just set. The boat was in shadow, but the top half of the sail still caught a ruddy glow on its western side.

The cold northeast breeze had held. *Water Snake* was on the starboard tack, lifting and diving over the waves in a rhythm as easy as breathing. They were far from land—farther than Peer had ever been before. Fishing trips with Bjorn had never taken him past the islands and rocky skerries that lay scattered beyond the fjord mouth. This big ship seemed very small now—a speck of dust under a wide sky.

The day had passed simply. At home there would be a hundred things to do: plowing fields, chopping firewood, patching boats, mending nets. Here there was only one purpose: to sail on and on into the west.

As for keeping out of the way of Harald Silkenhair—so far it hadn't been difficult. The ship divided naturally into separate spaces, like "rooms." There was the afterdeck in the stern, where the steersman stood. Around the mast was the open hold with all the goods and gear, and the ship's boat upside down across it. A narrow strip of decking each side of the hold allowed gangway up and down the ship. And up here in the bow was the foredeck, narrowing to the point where the dragon-neck reared stiffly from the prow.

Like an enormous slewed curtain, the sail almost cut off the front of the ship from the rear. To be heard by someone in a different part of the vessel, you had to shout across the wind. Just now, Harald was steering, and Peer was almost as far away from him as it was possible to get. He hoped to keep it that way.

He leaned back, watching Loki scrambling over the stacks of crates and barrels in the hold, sticking his nose in everywhere, and making friends with the crew. Loki was having no problems adjusting to his new life at sea!

And neither was Hilde. On leaving home this morning, she'd been as close to tears as Peer had ever seen her—but now she was sitting on a crossbeam, cheerfully chatting to some of the men. *Trust Hilde*, he thought with a rueful smile.

She knew the names of half the crew already, and was busy finding out about the others.

"No trolls in Vinland?" she was saying now. "Is that so? Then you've been there, Magnus—you've sailed with Gunnar before?"

"That's right." Magnus was a middle-aged man with a shrewd face, all crisscrossed with tiny lines from screwing up his eyes against sun and weather. He beamed cheerfully at Hilde. "Me and Halfdan and young Floki here, we all went with the skipper on his last voyage. Never saw a troll. Floki's my mate. I look out for him, and he does what I says. Like a father to him, I am, ain't I, Floki?" Floki was a youngish man with curly hair and a rather vacant expression. Magnus dug him in the ribs, and he sniggered amiably.

"Now what the skipper does, you see, missy," Magnus went on, "he splits us into two watches, so we can take turns to sail the ship and rest. There's us three, and your brother here, Peer—"

"I'm not her brother," said Peer, so firmly that Hilde looked at him in surprise.

"Oh, aye, like that, is it?" Magnus showed three missing teeth in a grin. "And in the other watch there's Arnë—"

"We both know Arnë," Hilde interrupted.

"And young Harald Silkenhair and Big Tjorvi," Magnus finished. He frowned at his hands and bent down gnarled fingers, muttering, "Six, seven . . . that's eight of us, counting the skipper, who's in charge but who don't do much hauling and rowing anymore. See?"

"It makes ten of us," Hilde corrected him, "counting Astrid and me."

"Women don't count," said a deep voice. A man ducked under the edge of the sail and straightened up—and up, and up. Big Tjorvi. He was like a white summer cloud, the kind that towers up against a blue sky. His hair and beard were as fluffy as dandelion seeds. He stood, swaying easily to the pitch of the ship, regarding Hilde with a straight-faced, solemn expression.

"Why don't women count?" Hilde demanded.

"Too weak," said Big Tjorvi.

"I like that! We may not be as strong as you, but brains count for something, you know . . ." Hilde's voice died away as she took in the men's furtive grins and nudges. "You're teasing me, aren't you?"

"Wouldn't dare." Big Tjorvi's eyes gleamed.

"Better not," Magnus joked. "This girl took on a whole mountainful of trolls, so she tells me."

"Not by myself," said Hilde hastily. "Peer was there too."

"Did you, now?" Tjorvi looked at the pair of them with interest.

"Tell Tjorvi about that troll baby," urged Floki. "She saw a troll baby, Tjorvi. With a pig's snout and a purple tongue. Like this!" He pushed his nose up with his thumb, and stuck out a slobbery tongue.

"Um, yes," said Hilde, averting her eyes.

"Don't tell that tale to the skipper," said Halfdan darkly.

"Why not?" asked Peer.

Several of the men looked around. But Gunnar was in the stern with Harald and Astrid, and with the wind blowing as it was, there was no chance he could overhear this conversation.

The men were uneasy, vague. "The skipper's a bit—you know . . ."

"Edgy," said Halfdan, a small, skinny man with rather narrow-set eyes.

"Reckon he'd think talking about trolls is unlucky," said Magnus. "Lots of things is unlucky at sea. Like whistling."

"Whistling's unlucky?" asked Hilde, who could whistle nicely herself.

Everyone nodded. "'Cos it brings the wind," said Floki. He pursed his lips and mimed a breathy little whistle. There was no true sound, but Magnus aimed a cuff at his head. "Stow that, you young fool!" he growled.

It could have been coincidence, but just then a strong gust sped over the water. The ship heeled and put her bow hard into the next wave. Several of the men glared at Floki, and a small shiver ran down Peer's back. Out here at sea, maybe these things weren't funny.

"There'll be no good luck this trip," continued Floki, who seemed to have no sense of self-preservation. "Women on ships is unlucky, too, and here we are with two of 'em!" Hilde opened her eyes and gasped indignantly, but the men weren't thinking of her.

"Astrid . . ." There was a sort of general mutter.

"The skipper got a wrong 'un there."

"What's she got in that bag of hers?"

"I reckon she's half a witch."

"You know what I heard?" Halfdan said in low tones. "I heard she's got troll blood in her veins—it runs in the family. But her father tried to hush it up. Who'd marry a troll? Likely the skipper doesn't know. Well, who'd tell him?"

Floki's rather protuberant blue eyes opened wide. Magnus sucked air in through his teeth. Peer tried to exchange a skeptical glance with Hilde, but she was examining her nails. Big Tjorvi stretched. "I reckon that's rubbish," he said slowly. "At least she looks after the skipper. She's got healing herbs in that bag of hers."

"Then why's he still sick?" demanded Magnus.

"What's wrong with him?" Hilde asked. "Not just his hand?"

Magnus seemed to take this as criticism. He glared at her. "The hand? Take more than losing a hand to stop an old sea wolf like Gunnar. No. But he gets awful fevers and black sweats that shake him till he can't hardly stand."

"That's no ordinary sickness what's wrong with the skipper," said Floki in a melancholy singsong. "There's a ghost a-following after him, ah, and it won't rest till it gets him."

"A *ghost*?" Hilde squawked. Peer sat up.

"Shut up! Shut up!" Magnus lunged at Floki. He grabbed a handful of shirt and twisted it up under Floki's chin, shaking a hard fist under his nose. "I told you not to talk about that!" he said.

Floki screwed up his face, flinching and crying, "Sorry, Magnus, sorry. I won't do it again!"

"See you don't. Or see what you'll get!" Magnus dropped him. "Don't listen to him," he added to Hilde. "He's simple, a moon-calf. Believes anything you tell him. The skipper would kill him if he heard. There's no ghost. *There's no ghost!*"

Peer and Hilde looked at each other. Peer got stiffly to his feet. With Loki at his heels, he made his way up into the prow, where the tall neck of the dragonhead divided the darkening horizon. Hilde murmured an excuse and came after him.

"*Well*, Peer, what did you make of that?"

"I don't know," said Peer. "It doesn't sound good." He leaned over the side and Hilde did the same, her left arm almost touching his right. Rank after rank of surly waves slopped up as though trying to reach them. Peer was wishing with all his might they had never set foot on this ship. At the same time, since Hilde was here, he was glad to be with her. He thought of something to say: *At least we're together.* But before he could get the words out, Hilde said crisply, "Not good? I call it very odd indeed. A ghost? Whose ghost?"

Peer sighed. "Well, we know that Gunnar and Harald killed a man in Westfold. Maybe Floki's thinking of him. But that doesn't mean there really is a ghost," he added, seeing she looked disturbed. "I don't think Floki's very bright."

"No, but why did Magnus get so upset? And Astrid said

Gunnar's afraid of the dark."

"Did she?" Peer frowned. It seemed a strange thing for a girl to say about her husband. "Do you like her? The men don't. All that stuff about troll blood . . ."

"I like her—I think," said Hilde. "It's odd, though: She wanted me to come, but ever since we got on board this morning she's avoided me. If I sit with her, she moves away. If I talk to her, she barely answers. It's as though she's hiding something."

Peer didn't really want to talk about Astrid. "Perhaps she's feeling seasick."

"A ghost," Hilde repeated. "How could a ghost follow a man over the sea?" She glanced over the side and shivered. "But then there are all sorts of things out there. Remember the draug boat?"

"Of course I do." The draug: the fearsome sea spirit that roamed the seas in half a boat, with a crew of drowned corpses. He'd caught a glimpse of it one wild, stormy morning last summer—a tattered sail and a dark hull, manned by stiff silhouettes. He looked nervously out across the heaving water, beginning to understand why sailors didn't like talking about such things. That ragged cloud on the horizon—could it be a sail?

"Here you are!" said a voice behind them.

They both jumped. "Time to eat," said Arnë cheerfully. "Astrid wants you, Hilde. Serving out the rations is women's work!" And he winked at Peer, much to Peer's surprise.

"All right," said Hilde mildly. She picked up her skirts and began clambering back along the ship toward the stern.

Peer made to follow her, but Arnë held him back. "A word with you, Peer?"

"Well, what is it?" asked Peer after a moment.

Arnë lowered his voice, fidgeting. "It's just—you know I've always liked Hilde. More than liked her. She's a grand lass, and I don't reckon I could do better when I come to get a wife. No, listen!" He threw up his hand as Peer tried to interrupt. "I know what you're thinking, you're thinking, *Why's he telling me this?* You see, I used to think you'd taken a sort of boy's fancy for Hilde yourself. But after what she said the other night, I saw I was wrong." He gave an embarrassed laugh. "You were children when you met. I should have known you're like brother and sister. Let's shake hands—and if you could put in a good word for me with Hilde—"

"No. Look, Arnë," Peer said in confused anger, trying to ignore Arnë's outthrust hand. "You've got it wrong. She's not my sister. I've never felt like her brother, and I never will."

Arnë recoiled. "So that's your game?" he said in a voice brimful of disgust. "And you told Ralf and Gudrun you were only coming along to protect Hilde!"

"I didn't—I mean, I am!" Peer stammered in dismay and increasing rage.

"Well, *she* says you're her brother. So what's this about? Using her trust to take advantage of her?"

"I—just leave me alone!"

"With pleasure. And you leave her alone." Arnë turned away.

Peer boiled over. *"It's up to Hilde who she spends her time with!"* he yelled, and saw Arnë check and stiffen before ducking under the sail and walking on.

The meal was cheerless: dried herring and cold groute—barley porridge that had been cooked on shore and left to congeal in the pot. The crew sat around, scraping their spoons into the sticky mess. And although Gunnar had taken on fresh water only that morning at Trollsvik, it already tasted odd. When Hilde suggested warming the food up, Astrid said scornfully, "How? Light a fire? On a ship?"

"Oh, of course . . ."

"There won't be any hot food till we touch land."

"And when will that be?" asked Hilde, looking around. "How far is it to Vinland? And how do we find the way?"

"Depends on the weather," Gunnar grunted, through a mouthful. "Three weeks . . . four. As for how . . ." He shrugged.

Talkative Magnus waved his spoon. "See, first we go past the Islands of Sheep, just far enough south that the mountains show half out of the sea. And after that we follow the whales past Iceland. And so, west to Greenland."

"I know how to spot Greenland," said Floki eagerly. "Don't I, Magnus? Remember, last time, you pointed out the old Blueshirt Glacier? I'd know that again."

Magnus reached across and tugged Floki's earlobe. "That's

right, laddie," he said with a grin. Floki squealed and rubbed his ear.

"That'll be our first landfall, Greenland," said Gunnar, ignoring this.

"You'll all be glad to stretch your legs by then," said Magnus, relentlessly joky. "And then off we go west again till we strike a rocky, barren sort of coast, and follow it south with the land on our right, till we get to Vinland."

Peer hadn't realized it was quite so far. His teeth chattered. The wind struck a dash of spray into his face. "Such a long way," he muttered under his breath.

Harald's voice came quietly out of the dusk:

"May the white-armed women of the waves
speed us safely through the sea-kingdom,
through the whales' home and the heaving waters
to the far strand where the sun westers."

For a moment everyone was still. Even Peer was held by the music of the words and the rhythm of the waves.

Then Harald broke the spell he himself had cast. "Worrying again, Barelegs?" he jeered. "Wishing you hadn't come?"

Arnë laughed out loud.

Peer's face flamed. Before he could think what to say, he felt a large hand grasp his arm. "Time to turn in," said Big Tjorvi calmly. "Skipper? Gunnar? Who's for the first watch?"

Gunnar chose Magnus, Peer, Halfdan, and Floki to take first watch. Stringy dark-haired Halfdan took the steering oar. Magnus and Floki propped themselves against the sides, each holding one of the long braces that trailed dizzyingly upward to either end of the wide yard. Peer went off forward for the solitary task of lookout. The rest of the crew unrolled their wide two-man sleeping sacks wherever they could find a bit of empty deck, and scrambled in.

Astrid's sack was already spread out in a spot as sheltered as any, in the lee of the starboard side. She slid into it as neat as a knife into a sheath, and snuggled down without speaking, but Hilde sat for a few more moments, knees drawn up to her chin, biting her fingers. Harald's jeer and Arnë's laugh hadn't escaped her. Peer and Arnë—they'd never got on. Not like Peer and Bjorn. She guessed why, but pushed it out of her mind, flushing uneasily. Blue-eyed Arnë: She'd always liked him. He came and went, tall and handsome, bringing little gifts from Hammerhaven, letting her know he admired her. But Peer—Peer was *family*. Arnë had no right to laugh at him, and especially not to side with Harald against him.

I hope the other men will like Peer. I hope he'll be all right. . . .

The sky wasn't totally dark. It had a deep color tinged with lingering light against which the sail looked black, a great square of starless night hanging over the ship.

Lonely wonder overcame her. Whatever was she doing out here on the ocean, with the brisk breeze chilling her skin, listening to the chuckle and truckle of the water running along the sides and under the bottom boards? She tried to imagine the close, smoky darkness of the farmhouse. *Have they all gone to bed? Has Ma left the dough to rise on the hearthstone? Has she put out the bowl for the Nis? Is she lying awake, missing me?*

A feeble glow kindled in the stern. It flared, flickered, and settled to a bright seed of light. Halfdan had lit a small horn-windowed lantern and put it at his feet.

Hilde pulled off her soft leather shoes and tried to stuff her legs into the sleeping sack without her skirt bunching up. Nobody undressed on a ship, and in any case it was much too cold. She inched her way in like a caterpillar, trying not to disturb Astrid, who lay with her face turned away. It wouldn't be a comfortable night. The inside of the bag was lined with thick, tufted wool for warmth, but she could already feel the hard decking pressing through. The ship tilted and tipped and swung; she heard the mumbling voices of the men on watch, and the coughs and grunts and snores of those who, like herself, were sleeping or trying to sleep.

Her bare feet touched something at the bottom of the sack. A sort of bundle, firm but yielding, with a hairy surface. She prodded it with her toes—and it jerked.

"Ouch!" Hilde twitched her feet away.

And suddenly Astrid was sitting upright. "Hush!" she hissed.

"Astrid!" Hilde seized her arm. "There's something in there. It moved!"

Astrid heaved an exasperated sigh. "I suppose you had to find out sometime. But just *keep quiet* about it, right?" Without waiting for a reply, she ducked deep into the sleeping sack, delving past Hilde's legs, and heaved out her goatskin bag by its long strap.

"Your bag?" whispered Hilde. She remembered Astrid's little buzzing box. What else did she keep in there? Something alive?

"What is it?" She drew back. The bag bulged and bounced, as if something inside it was kicking and punching.

Then came a muffled, furious squeaking: *"Help, he-elp!"*

"The *Nis*?" Hilde gasped.

"You open it." Astrid shoved the bag at Hilde. "It might bite me."

"Oh, you haven't. You couldn't." She wrenched at the buckle, tore open the flap, and then almost dropped the whole thing as a frantic little whirlwind clawed its way out of the bag, fell into her lap, kicked itself away, and shot up the mast with a noise like a cat fight:

"Aiaieiyoooooooooo!"

With a yell of fright, Floki let go of the port brace. He danced about, pointing. "There's something on the mast! An evil spirit!"

Astrid snatched the bag from Hilde and thrust it out of sight into the sleeping sack. "Lie down," she whispered fiercely. "Pretend you're asleep."

"Asleep?" Hilde cried. In the darkness overhead, the Nis

caterwauled and shrieked.

"Shut it up, then! Make it stop!" Astrid lay back and screwed her eyes firmly shut.

Wobbly with shock, Hilde struggled out of the sleeping sack. *Where's Peer? I have to find Peer.* By now everyone was yelling and pointing and rushing about. Loki was barking madly. From the top of the mast, the dreadful screaming went on.

"Peer?" she shouted.

With a noise like a rough kiss, waves slapped into the side, and spray showered on board. Halfdan had accidentally steered *Water Snake* too far into the wind. The sail blew back, clapping and thundering, and the ship hung in the water, tossing helplessly. Hilde lost her balance and staggered into someone tall and slender who caught her and steadied her. It was Peer. She pulled his head down and said urgently into his ear, "It's the Nis—Astrid's brought the Nis!"

Peer gave her one incredulous look, nodded grimly, and disappeared forward. Hilde sank to the deck. Thank goodness! Peer was good with the Nis: He would deal with it somehow. . . .

"Get back on the tack!" Gunnar was bellowing. Arnë and Magnus wrestled with the braces. Young Harald sprang past her, his long hair flying, threw Halfdan off the steering oar, and grabbed it himself. *Water Snake* swung back on course. The terrible screeching stopped. What had happened? Had Peer coaxed the Nis down—or had it fallen overboard?

Big Tjorvi held up the lantern. The tiny flame made the darkness darker, the steep sides of the waves as black and glossy as coal. It gleamed on Gunnar. Hilde saw at once that the story about the ghost was true. Gunnar was staring about as though he expected to see slimy hands clawing out of the sea. His face stretched, eyebrows high, mouth agape, eyes popping.

"What made that noise?" he choked. No one answered. His voice climbed. "By Thor and his Hammer! One of you must have seen it. There's something on board this ship, and I swear, when I find it, I'll cut it into tiny pieces!" Spittle caught in his beard.

"I saw it!" came a cry from the darkness beyond the sail. Everyone froze. Peer came scrambling along the side, skirting the hold. "It's all right," he gasped. "It was only a seagull. A huge one with great flapping wings—must have been attracted by our lantern."

Hilde shut her eyes and crossed her fingers. Gunnar stared; the men broke into raucous disbelief. "A gull?" "Never!" "That was no gull—no gull screams like that!"

"It was just a gull!" Peer shouted. "Look!" He held up a fistful of white feathers, then opened his fingers and let the wind pick them away. "Didn't you see it, Astrid?"

Astrid was on her feet now. "Me? Oh, yes! My goodness, it frightened me, it flew up right in front of my face. Its wings must have been six feet across!"

"It wasn't as big as that," Hilde joined in, scowling at Astrid.

Stupid girl, why does she have to exaggerate? "Maybe four feet."

"You saw it too?" Gunnar said slowly.

"Absolutely." Hilde returned his stare, eye to eye. "How could you miss it?"

"All right. All right!" Gunnar swung around. "Just a bird, lads, a great stupid bird." He clapped his good hand across his eyes, rubbing it to and fro, gritting his teeth as though in pain. "A gull!" he gasped. Was he laughing or crying? His whole body shook.

Astrid untwirled her thick cloak and threw it around him. "Come with me, Gunnar, and I'll give you something to make you sleep. You've done too much. Remember, you haven't been well." He grabbed her and for a moment buried his head against her neck like a child hiding its face. Astrid patted his shoulder soothingly. She led him away.

Halfdan coughed, apologizing to Harald. "I'm sorry, master. I don't rightly know what I was thinking. I had such a shock when that great bird flew right over my head—sort of whirled around me, like, screaming . . ."

Hilde bit down a nervous giggle. Soon everyone would think they'd seen it.

"All right, Halfdan, forget it." Harald strode down the deck and dragged Peer aside. "That was no gull," he said in a low, hard voice.

"You saw the feathers," Peer said, his face unmoving.

"From a distance. Before they blew away. And I happen to remember that we have a white hen on board."

Hilde edged closer. Peer said, "What are you saying? You think I had time to open the coops, grab a couple of chickens, pull out their feathers, and then come and tell a story about a seagull? Why would I do that?"

An uncertain flicker crossed Harald's face.

"Gunnar seems glad to think it was only a gull," Peer pressed on. He added meaningfully, "What else could it have been?"

Harald's eyes narrowed. His fingers tightened on Peer's arm. "Let's leave my father out of it, Barelegs. I don't know what it was, but I think you do, and I hope it's no longer on this ship, because if I find it I'm going to kill it. And it was *no seagull.*"

He glared at Peer and swung away.

"Why does he call you that—Barelegs?" asked Hilde angrily.

"He does it to annoy me." Peer sounded exhausted. "I'd better get back on duty."

"Well done, anyway. Using the feathers was a great idea. Where's the Nis?"

"Hiding in the chicken coop." Peer's voice was suddenly furious. "It's terrified. Miserable. What was Astrid thinking of to bring it here?"

"That's what I'm going to find out next," said Hilde.

The two of them were standing close together. She couldn't see Peer's face very well—he was just a dark shape against the sky—but he moved hesitantly toward her. She had the feeling he was about to say something more. But a second later he just said, "Good luck," and went off forward.

She climbed into the sleeping sack with a lot less care than the first time. Astrid was already there again, lying on her side. Hilde poked her. "You stole the Nis."

"Bravo," said Astrid in a muffled voice, her arm across her face.

"Kidnapped it. What did you do? Drug it?"

"I put a tiny, tiny bit of henbane in the groute to make it sleep," said Astrid indignantly. "That's all. And then I very carefully scooped it into my bag. It simply had a nice snooze, and woke up a little while ago."

"Stuffed away at the bottom of the sleeping sack. How could you? And why did you bring it? It belongs at home. The Nis would never, never want to cross the sea!" Her voice broke.

"I *brought* it because it will be *useful*," Astrid whispered. "Just wait till we get to Vinland, that's all. Who'll be doing the housework? We will, the only women. Cooking? You and me. Collecting firewood, carrying water? Us again. The men will be hunting and trapping for furs—guess who'll be cleaning the hides? Believe me, you'll be glad of some extra help."

"But the Nis is a person, not a thing. You can't force it to help you! And what about my mother? What will she think when she finds it's disappeared?"

"Oh, stop complaining." Astrid sounded sour. "If she's as fond of you as she pretends to be, she'll be glad you've got it. I think it was very clever of me to bring the Nis."

"Clever?" Hilde's voice rose. "What about the fuss we've just had? If it hadn't been for Peer . . ."

"I approve of that boy," said Astrid. "He thinks quickly."

"I don't suppose he approves of you. The Nis should go home."

"So? Try telling Gunnar to turn the ship around."

"I know it's too late for that," said Hilde angrily. "But when I go home next summer, the Nis will come with me."

"But you won't be going home."

"Of course I— What do you mean?"

Astrid gave a brittle laugh. "Well, you *may* go home, of course. Eventually. But it won't be next year, or the year after that, or—"

"What do you mean?"

Astrid stuck her face close to Hilde's. Her breath struck hot against Hilde's lips and chin. "Gunnar and Harald are outlaws. They wouldn't pay the blood price for the man they killed in Westfold, so they've been outlawed for five years. That's why we're going to Vinland. Now you know."

The ship pitched, and Hilde's stomach seemed to pitch sickeningly with it. *Five years?*

"Who else knows about this?" she got out. "Arnë?"

"Arnë? Why Arnë? Oh, you think he should have told you because he likes you? Well, maybe you'd better marry him. Because we'll be living in Vinland for a very long time." She turned away from Hilde with a heave and a flounce, and lay still.

Hilde wanted to spring up and rush to tell Peer. She wanted to grab Gunnar or Harald or Arnë, confront them, shake them till they confessed. She forced herself to lie still, biting her knuckles, thinking furiously.

It could be true. It must be true. But she's lying to me about Arnë. Gunnar would have left Westfold in a hurry. He'd get to Hammerhaven ahead of the news. He wouldn't tell anyone about being outlawed, or no one new would sail with him. Five years!

She became aware of a fine tremor running through Astrid from head to foot.

She's crying.

Let her cry.

But after a while she put out a quiet hand. Astrid flinched and froze. "What's the matter?" Hilde whispered, knowing it was a stupid question.

"I suppose you hate me," Astrid muttered.

Hilde was still very angry. "You should have told the truth."

"You were warned." Astrid twisted around like an eel. "I told you I'm part troll. Of course I tell lies and steal things. How else can I get what I want?"

"And you've got it, have you? Is this what you wanted?"

"I never get anything I want," said Astrid bitterly. "It's always the same. If I like someone, I lose them."

"Don't feel so sorry for yourself," Hilde began, but then she remembered how Astrid had hinted before at someone she'd loved and lost. She said more gently, "Was there really someone you wanted to marry before your father made you marry Gunnar?"

"Yes," Astrid sniffed.

"What was he called?"

"Erlend," said Astrid. "Erlend Asmundsson. But now he's dead."

"Dead!" Hilde fell silent. Something in Astrid's gruff voice suggested an awful possibility. "Astrid, was Erlend the man Harald killed in Westfold?"

For a couple of heartbeats Astrid was very still. It was too dark to see her face. At last she sighed: a long, silent, stealthy breath. "You've guessed," she whispered softly. "He was. Yes, he was. That's exactly what happened."

CHAPTER 8

The Nis at Sea

N is!"
Peer crouched, uncomfortably balanced on the cargo, trying to see into the chicken coop. His blood was racing. *I faced down Harald.*

More than that—standing next to Hilde in the dark, he'd nearly kissed her. It had seemed so easy and natural, but at the last moment he'd lost his nerve. What if she protested, shoved him away? Everyone would know.

He was furious with himself. So much for those bold resolutions to behave as he felt. Well, he couldn't cope with it now. He bundled the thoughts away to the back of his head and tried to concentrate on the Nis. *I have to get the Nis out of this coop.* In the darkness he could only make out a whitish frill of feathers here, the glint of an eye there. The hens crooned and clucked softly, weird burbling sounds. But he thought he could also detect quick, shallow breathing.

"Nis, it's me, Peer. It's all right."

Loki lurked behind him, interested and suspicious. Peer pushed him. "Go and lie down," he whispered sternly. Loki and the Nis had never really tolerated each other. "I can't have you upsetting the Nis now. Go on!" Loki backed reluctantly away.

"Nis, do come out," Peer pleaded. "If I stay here much longer, someone will notice me, and we need to talk. I have to explain what's happening."

No reply.

"All right, come and find me. I'll be in the prow, by myself—that's the pointed bit with the dragonhead," he added. "But don't leave it too long, or they'll change the watch, and somebody else will be there."

Before he could move his cramped muscles, a sliver of a voice whimpered, "Wait...."

"I am waiting," Peer said after a moment, as patiently as he could.

"Has there been a flood?" the voice quavered.

"A flood? What, you mean all the water? That's not a flood, Nis, it's the sea. We're at sea."

No answer, though a hen rustled and squawked, as though someone had startled it with a sharp movement.

"In a boat," Peer added. "Listen, I know it's very frightening for you, but come out and let me tell you how it happened."

A moment later, the hens shifted and clucked again. From under their feathers a thin little shadow scuttled on all fours. It slipped between the bars of the coop.

Peer led the way up into the windy bow. Up here it was like standing on a high seesaw. Every so often, spray flew past the dragon-neck, and the decking was wet. He tucked himself into the angle below the dragon, next to the anchor, and the Nis actually climbed into his lap. Loki pressed jealously against Peer's knees, grumbling. Peer gently rubbed the little creature's thin shoulders, feeling the tiny knobs of its backbone under its ragged gray clothes. Its heart was jumping in its sides. The wind messed its wispy hair, and it had lost its little red hat.

"Where am I?" it wailed. "Why is I here? One minute I was supping up my groute, Peer Ulfsson—nice warm groute with butter and a bit of cream—and the next, I wakes up in the dark bag, all hot and smothery, and then I gets out, and there's no house and no hills. Where's Troll Fell, Peer Ulfsson? Where's home?"

"Good question," Peer muttered. He braced himself and tried to explain. "We're a long way from home, Nis. How much did you overhear last night? This ship is going to Vinland...."

The Nis listened fearfully. At last it interrupted. "But how did I get here, Peer Ulfsson?"

"Well . . ." Peer hesitated; he knew the Nis wouldn't like this. "I'm afraid Astrid stole you. I think she must have put something in your food."

"In—my—food?" the Nis repeated slowly, swelling up. In the darkness its eyes were two angry sparks. "Something in my food, my lovely food that the mistress gives me?" Peer nodded.

The Nis took a deep breath, but at that moment Loki lost control of himself and lunged at it excitedly. With a terrified shriek, the Nis hopped up to the base of the dragon-neck, where it crouched precariously, holding on by the forestay.

"Get down from there," Peer cried. "Look out!"

"Keep that dog off me," panted the Nis, "or . . . Oooh!" It screamed and leaped for the deck as the prow lifted and plunged over a big wave, and spray soaked them.

The Nis curled on the planking like a drowned spider, a bedraggled, pitiable figure. Loki tried to pounce on it. Peer grabbed his collar. "Sit!" he ordered angrily.

He looked at the Nis. What on earth could he do? It needed to get dry and warm. Above all, it needed to feel good about itself again. And then he heard a voice and saw someone clambering toward him from the waist of the ship. By the size of the silhouette, it was Big Tjorvi. There wasn't a moment to lose. Peer tore open his thick jerkin and the linen shirt under it, scooped up the limp Nis, and stuffed it out of sight against his skin. He'd done the same thing with orphaned lambs in bad weather, and the Nis was not much bigger.

"Off you go, son." Tjorvi patted him on the shoulder. "Your chance to sleep." Peer was grateful for the friendly tone. He would have stayed and talked for a while, but he was afraid Tjorvi would notice the lump he was clasping to his chest. And the Nis wouldn't keep still; it squirmed about and clutched him with cold froggy fingers. Trickles of seawater ran down under his clothes.

He unrolled his sleeping sack one-handed, clumsily, and slithered in, cold and damp. What a good thing he had a sack of his own and didn't have to share with another of the men. He made a space for Loki, who crept in and turned around. The Nis crawled out of his jerkin. It wrung out its beard, sniveling. Loki growled. Peer grabbed his muzzle. "Bad dog!" he said in a low, fierce voice. "From now on, you and the Nis have got to be friends." Loki flattened himself in shame.

Peer shut his eyes, wondering what he could say to the Nis. It had been drugged, kidnapped, made to look a fool, and finally drenched. How could he salve its wounded pride?

"Nis, I'm really sorry this has happened, but I can't tell you how glad I am to see you." As he said it, he realized he meant it. The whimpering quieted. The Nis shook itself and seemed to listen. "Hilde will be glad, too. We're going to need all the friends we can get," Peer went on. He added, hoping the Nis would be pleased, "Do you know you just scared everyone on board nearly to death? They all thought you were some kind of—I don't know—ghost or evil spirit or something."

But the Nis took offense. "I was never bad, Peer Ulfsson, I was always good. I never does anything but sweep the house and help the mistress, and I doesn't deserve to be taken away and put in a bag. And I doesn't like ghosts, Peer Ulfsson. All stiff and cold, they are, and they make nasty sliding drafts."

Icy fingertips tickled Peer's neck. He said hastily, "Oh, come on, Nis, you know you enjoy playing tricks. I'd have thought you'd be glad to scare the people on this boat. Astrid kidnapped you, and Gunnar's certainly hiding something, and Harald—I don't have to tell you about Harald, do I? You dropped beans on him, remember? That was so funny."

The Nis sniffed.

"You know something?" said Peer. "I bet you're the first Nis in the world who has ever gone to sea. Imagine that, the very first!" Inspired, he added, "You should have a special name. People who do important things always get given special names. Like Thorolf. They call him 'the Seafarer' because he's such a good sailor."

The Nis stared at him, dewdrop eyes luminous with excitement. It drew a trembling breath. "Could I really, Peer Ulfsson? Could I really be called that?"

"Nithing the Seafarer?" Peer asked. "Yes, why not?"

"Nithing the Seafarer," the Nis breathed in ecstasy. It cracked its knuckles and did a little hop.

"That's right," Peer said, smiling. "And when we get to Vinland you'll meet Thorolf, and you'll see he's a real hero, a real sailor—and you'll be a hero, too. But listen. You mustn't let Harald or Gunnar or the others on this ship see you. Harald's dangerous, Nis. If he finds you, he'll try and kill you. He told me so."

"Don't worry, Peer Ulfsson." The Nis had completely re-covered its spirits. "They can't catch me," it boasted. "Nithing the Seafarer is too quick, too clever."

Peer said no more. He didn't want to frighten the Nis, and he reckoned it could keep out of sight if it tried—there were plenty of hiding places on board. He yawned. With three of them in it, the sleeping sack was beginning to feel warm, and was reeking of salty wet dog. He was dropping asleep, when the Nis jerked and wriggled. He forced his eyes open to see why—and held his breath. The disgraced Loki had wormed his way so close to the Nis that he was nosing its fluffy hair. His tongue flicked out in an apologetic lick—and another— and to Peer's utter astonishment the Nis cuddled contentedly against Loki's side and allowed the dog to go on washing him.

Friends at last! Deeply relieved, Peer sank back and closed his eyes. A moment later, he was fast asleep.

"Lee-oh! Let go and haul!"

A soaking wet rope whipped through a hole in the gun-wale, scattering icy water into Peer's hair. Someone jumped over him—he got a good view of a pair of boots just missing his head. Up in the sky, the yard changed angle as the men on the braces hauled it around. Peer felt the deck tip slightly as the ship heeled and the sail filled. Gunnar was putting *Water Snake* onto the port tack.

Peer levered himself out of the sack and got up. He hadn't slept for more than a few hours, but it was too uncomfortable to lie there any longer. There was no sign of the Nis. He dragged a reluctant Loki out of his warm nest, rolled up the sack, and looked around.

Dawn was in the sky. *Water Snake* rode over broad gray swells, leaving a wake like a long furrow drawn across the sea. Most of the crew were awake, but no one seemed inclined to talk. Magnus stood at the tiller. He nodded to Peer and spat over the side. "I hate the first night at sea." He yawned. "And that one was worse than most." Peer grinned wanly. Gunnar stood bundled in his cloak on the port side, brooding.

Peer moved away and leaned on the wet gunwale. The sun climbed out of the waters behind them, and the shadow of the great square sail streamed ahead of them across the waves.

"G'morning," said Hilde. He turned. She looked pale and moved stiffly. Her hair was tousled. She had wrapped herself up in a brown shawl, and the tip of her nose was pink with cold. He wanted to put his arm around her, to hug her to his side and warm her up. But would that be loverlike, or brotherly, or just plain affectionate? He didn't know himself. And suddenly he didn't care.

"You look frozen," he said. "Want to share my cloak?"

Hilde leaned against him and shivered. "What wouldn't I give," she said through chattering teeth, "to be standing over a nice hot fire?"

"Sorry you came?" said Peer, half teasing.

"No," she said after a second, but she didn't sound too sure. "Here—have some nice cold breakfast." She passed over oatcakes and a piece of dried fish.

Loki sat promptly, eyes glued to the food, and Peer broke an oatcake and dropped it into his greedy jaws. "Loki and the Nis actually made friends last night," he told Hilde in a lowered voice. "And you know what? They have a lot in common. They both love food!"

"The poor Nis; how is it?"

"It was very upset last night, but it's fine now. It's got a new name it's terribly proud of." He grinned, wanting to share the joke. " 'Nithing the Seafarer!' "

Hilde's laugh sounded hollow, and he glanced at her. "Is something wrong?"

She nodded, staring out to sea. "Something I found out last night. I'd better just tell you quickly. You know Gunnar said we'd be coming home next summer? Well, we won't." She stopped. "Where's Astrid? Is anyone listening?"

Peer looked over his shoulder. "I don't think so. Astrid's combing her hair. Why? What's happened?"

She began to whisper. "Oh, Peer, it's an awful story. The man Harald killed in Westfold was someone Astrid really liked. He was called Erlend, and she'd wanted to marry him, but he was too young and poor, so her father wouldn't agree. He made her marry Gunnar instead. But Gunnar was jealous of Erlend, and when they met he picked a quarrel with him, and Erlend defended himself, but he was alone and Gunnar had Harald and it was two against one. So Erlend died. Poor, poor Astrid!"

Peer thought of Harald's long steel sword and winced. *Poor, poor Erlend!*

"But what's it got to do with us?" he asked.

"Harald and Gunnar were blamed for the killing. They've been outlawed for five years. That's why they're running for Vinland. Five years, Peer. And there's no way of telling Ma and Pa. They'll think we're never coming back."

Peer's heart dropped like a stone. "I *knew* Harald and Gunnar couldn't be trusted. Bjorn even said they were running from justice. He didn't say they'd been outlawed, though."

Hilde said miserably, "It's my own fault. I wanted to come so much, I didn't let anything put me off. Now I keep thinking of that story Sigrid was telling, about the boy who sailed across the sea. Remember it? East of the sun and west of the moon, and he was away for so long his mother and father thought he was dead. And I was mean to Sigrid and wouldn't let her finish it—and now who knows how long it will be before I see her again?" She dashed a hand across her eyes.

"Hilde, it'll be all right. We're fine. They won't start worrying for ages, and by then we'll have found a way to get home." Peer scowled suddenly. "But Astrid—she should have told you about this."

"I know," said Hilde. "She wanted a friend. It was selfish of her—like kidnapping the Nis, I suppose. She wants it to help with the housework in Vinland. But she's really sorry now, Peer. She was crying last night."

115

She cried to make you feel sorry for her, thought Peer, but there was no point in saying so. "What about the crew?" he asked. "Are they all in on this?"

She said despondently, "They know about the killing. Everyone does. Harald joked about it, remember? He made it sound funny. It didn't seem real. But the five-year sentence . . . Well, I'm sure Arnë doesn't know, Peer, or he'd have said."

"You're right," Peer conceded. He looked at Hilde's forlorn face and felt a rush of angry determination. "I promised Ralf I'd bring you home, and I will, even if I have to build a ship with my own hands," he swore. Then his eyes opened wide. "Wait, Hilde, there *is* another ship. The *Long Serpent*! We've forgotten about Thorolf. He's no outlaw. He'll help us."

Hilde's face cleared. "Thorolf! Of course!"

"Thorolf's a good man." Peer stopped and thought. "He'll be there. He settled in Vinland. Why should he leave? Even if he went away for the winter, like Gunnar, he'll be heading back there for the summer to cut more timber, just like us. One way or the other, we're bound to meet him."

"And maybe we could come home on the *Long Serpent*. On your father's ship, Peer. Funny to think it might rescue us!" Hilde looked far more cheerful. She added rather shyly, "You always think of a way out."

The sun seemed to be shining twice as brightly. It was a beautiful morning. Peer put his arm around her shoulders and said gaily, "You see? Nothing to worry about. On to— where? West of the sun?"

"East of the sun," Hilde corrected him.

"Oh, that won't do; we're sailing west—"

"Would you like to know where we are, Hilde?"

It was Arnë, cutting across him in a loud, rude voice. Hilde turned, startled.

"Can you see those clouds?" Arnë took her elbow, deftly detaching her from Peer, and pointed to the northwest, where some vague, steamy, ghostly clouds lay above the horizon. "That's where the Faroe Islands are, the Islands of Sheep. We'll be passing them later."

"Land," breathed Hilde. "I'm already missing it."

"We won't be setting foot there, alas," Arnë laughed. "Just passing by, on our way west." He gave her one of his wide smiles. His beard was already growing through; the glittering stubble gave him a raffish, attractive air. Peer's hand went to his own smooth chin. Arnë put a foot up against the side timbers and leaned there. *Posing deliberately,* Peer thought.

Several white gulls with long black-tipped wings had appeared out of nowhere and were flying above the ship. Ignoring Peer, Arnë said to Hilde, "See those gulls? That's a sure sign we're not far from land. Maybe it was one of those that was screaming last night." Hilde flicked a humorous glance at Peer—and the gray surface of the sea shattered without warning. Out shot three, four, five dark curving bodies, and plunged back in wings of spray. Arnë's pose slipped, and he grabbed at the gunwale to steady himself. There was a shout from Magnus at the tiller: "Dolphins!" Harald raced along the starboard side, shoving Peer out of his way.

"Dolphins!" Hilde leaned out over the side. "Look at them go!"

The dolphins were springing out of the water again, traveling faster than the ship.

Something like a long black needle flashed out from *Water Snake*'s bow and sank into the waves.

Hilde whirled around. "It's Harald. He threw a harpoon!"

"Missed," came a disappointed yell. Harald leaned over the side, hauling in the line and retrieving his dripping harpoon.

Astrid picked her way over the deck behind them, stepping daintily as a disapproving cat. "He just likes killing things." She eyed Harald as he scrambled lightly back toward them, harpoon in hand. He was laughing, and his long golden hair hung loose to his waist.

"I'm out of practice," he said to the two girls.

"Yes, Harald, we noticed," said Astrid sweetly.

"I think I grazed one, though."

"Why did you do it?" Hilde demanded. Harald gave her an impertinent grin. "Sweetheart, when I'm at sea, I take every chance to amuse myself." He examined the tip of his harpoon. "Ooh, do you think that's blood?" He waved it under her nose, and laughed again as she drew back.

"Fool," said Peer, not quite under his breath.

"What did you say?" Harald jabbed the harpoon at Peer. "Did I hear you speak?" He jabbed again, and Peer had to twist aside to avoid the point. "What did you say to me, Barelegs?"

"If you must know," began Peer, breathless—

"Yes, I must. I must!" With blank, bright eyes Harald sliced the harpoon toward him. Peer tried to dodge again, but there was nowhere to go.

"Stop it!" screamed Hilde, and Arnë's arm flew out to deflect the stroke. A heartbeat later, Arnë was gripping his forearm tightly and cursing. Bright blood ran liberally between his fingers and dripped onto the deck.

"Arnë!" Hilde gasped.

Harald stepped back one dancing pace, lowering the harpoon. "Sorry, my friend. You shouldn't have got in the way."

"Shame on you, Harald!" Astrid spat like a wildcat. She raised her voice, "Gunnar, Gunnar, see what Harald's done! Look what's he's done to Arnë!"

Harald glared at her and threw the harpoon down. Gunnar came striding over. His eyebrows curled together in a thick frown, but all he said was, "Can you use the hand?" Arnë opened and closed his fingers. "Good. Take him away, Astrid, and tie that up."

"It's only a cut," said Arnë, grimacing. He looked up at Peer, who was standing shocked by the suddenness of it all. "Get out of my way! Just clear off and keep out of trouble," he burst out in a hard, exasperated voice, adding softly, "This was going to be a good trip till you came along."

Peer turned abruptly and went forward, ducking under the sail.

For the rest of the long morning he kept to himself, doing

his share of the work in silence, or sitting in the bow away from the others. When Hilde came to tell him that Arnë's wound was only a long deep scratch, he turned his shoulder on her. She stared at him. "What's the matter with you? Arnë saved your skin, and you haven't even thanked him yet." She marched away.

He doesn't want my thanks. He doesn't even like me. He told me to keep away, and I'm doing it. I was trying to stand up for you. . . . It sounded thin and childish, but he was too angry to care. He waited for Hilde to come back, so that they could talk properly, but she didn't.

Loki stayed with him until noon, and then abandoned him for Astrid and Hilde in the stern, hoping for scraps.

In the mid-afternoon, the long low shapes of mountains became visible along the northern horizon, grayish scarps and knobs protruding from the sea, dark or faint, some near, some farther away. Peer began to come out of his self-imposed isolation. He looked around. Floki, Magnus, Halfdan, and Big Tjorvi were sitting together under the taut arc of the sail, throwing dice and talking.

"Are those the Islands of Sheep?" he called.

"That's right." Tjorvi got up and leaned on the rail beside Peer, looking northward. "Bare, bleak places, but good enough for sheep. Nary a tree to shelter under. Narrow waters and dangerous currents."

"You've been there?"

"I'm *from* there," said Tjorvi quietly. "That's home. Got a wife there, and a little daughter. Haven't been back for years. Always meaning to; never make it. Maybe next time. . . ."

Many more seabirds were now flying alongside the ship. One of them swooped past and scanned Peer with its fierce, yellow-rimmed eye. It seemed to consider him once, coldly, as a possible source of food, and then discard him.

"How they stare," said Halfdan, looking up at the gracefully wheeling birds.

"Aye," Tjorvi rumbled. "Gulls are strange things. Have you seen them after a storm, turning and circling over the place where a boat's gone down? And that's because they're tracking the drift of drowned corpses on the seabed."

"Is that so?" said Halfdan with a shiver, watching the gulls keeping easy pace with the ship.

Floki said, "I've heard how the souls of dead sailors put on the form of seagulls, and go flying after their shipmates, a-crying and a-calling . . ."

They all turned their heads to look at Peer. "Was that really a gull last night?" Tjorvi asked.

Peer hesitated. He didn't want to reinforce the fears about ghosts. But he couldn't afford to have news of the Nis reaching Harald. "It seemed just an ordinary bird," he said lamely.

"Ordinary?" Magnus growled. "It may have looked like a gull, but it didn't act like one. Nor sound like one, neither." Remembering the Nis's screams, Peer couldn't blame him for thinking so.

"It'll be back, you'll see," said Floki with a mournful shudder.

"The skipper knows. Did you see the look on his face?"

"Will you shut up, Floki," said Magnus. "I've told you before." But he sounded irresolute, as if his heart wasn't in it, and this time Floki was unabashed.

"Now wait a minute, boys." Tjorvi glanced around and put the question Peer was longing to ask. "If there's really a ghost, then whose is it?"

Magnus got to his feet. "I don't want to talk about it. I'm out of this." He glanced at Floki, who sat stubbornly where he was. Halfdan looked at his feet.

"Don't tell 'em," said Magnus. "I'm warning you, all right? Just don't say." He marched off.

Floki licked his lips. "I'll name no names," he muttered. "It'd be asking for trouble, that would—naming a ghost. But there was a man the skipper killed . . ."

"It was young Harald finished him off," Halfdan put in somberly.

Erlend, thought Peer.

"And he cursed him as he lay dying. I wasn't close enough to hear him myself, but Magnus was. Magnus heard the curse. He said"—Floki's voice dropped to a hoarse whisper—"'*A cold life and a cold death to you, Gunnar. A cold wife and a cold bed. Look out for me whenever you close your eyes. For I'll follow you wherever you go and bring you to a cold grave.*' And he'd have cursed Harald, too, Magnus says, but Harald was too quick for him. He dealt him the death blow."

Though he knew that what they'd heard last night was no

ghost, but only the Nis, Peer was glad of the sunlight on his face, and the bright spray blowing.

"And it's working, isn't it?" added Floki. "That Astrid— she's a cold piece, all right."

"If I'd ha' thought a ghost was following this ship, I'd never have joined her," said Tjorvi heavily.

Peer said guiltily, hoping to change the subject, "Where did you join the ship, Tjorvi?"

"In Hammerhaven, lad, like your friend Arnë."

Peer couldn't help himself. "He's not my friend. Not anymore."

The three men stared at him. "Arnë stopped a harpoon on its way to you," said Halfdan. "And you say he's not your friend?"

"Yes, but . . ." Peer went hot to his ears.

"Anyone's a friend that stands up for you against Harald," said Tjorvi firmly. "He's not one to cross."

"Right," Halfdan agreed. "You never know where you are with Harald."

"He's a natural-born fighter," Floki said with pride.

Peer was quiet. The men went on talking about Harald with an odd mixture of horror and admiration. As usual, Floki's tongue chattered most freely, dropping "Magnus says" into almost every sentence. Magnus had started out as one of Gunnar's farmhands in Westfold, and had told Floki lots about Harald. At nine years old Harald had almost killed another boy, a playfellow who'd tripped him in a ball game, by pounding his head with a rock. At twelve years his mother,

123

Vardis, had given him his first sword. He'd killed a man with it before his thirteenth birthday. Since his mother died, he'd accompanied his father on all his voyages. It was said he was a berserker, who lost all control when he fought.

"A berserker?" Peer's skin crawled.

Berserkers could fall into a kind of mad fury. They might go red, or even dark blue or black in the face. They would howl like wild beasts and hurl themselves, screaming, at anyone in their way. A warrior who went berserk would have terrible strength.

"Magnus says Harald's mother fed him raw wolf meat to make him strong," Floki whispered, wriggling with gruesome delight. "So when the fit's on him, he's as wild as a wolf. We've seen it, haven't we, Halfdan? We've heard him howling. Enough to scare you to death!" He laughed suddenly, stupidly. "Didn't they all run!"

"Shut up." Halfdan looked half angry, half sick, as though he didn't want to remember something. "Magnus is right, Floki. You talk too much." He got up and moved restlessly away. Floki stuck out his bottom lip like a child.

"I'd follow Harald anywhere," he told Peer defiantly. "Magnus is Gunnar's man, see, but I'm Harald's. I'd like to put my hands between his and swear to serve him. That's what real warriors do!"

"Floki, Floki!" Tjorvi suddenly burst out laughing. He put out a big hand and ruffled Floki's tight curls. "You don't want

124

to be a warrior, son, believe me. Stick to being a sailor. It's safer."

Floki's rough, red face flushed even redder. He went off in a huff, leaving Tjorvi and Peer alone.

"I guess I'd better be more careful," said Peer gloomily. "Gunnar doesn't think much of me. Harald hates me, and he turns out to be a berserker. Floki thinks Harald's wonderful. Arnë's angry with me . . ."

"Angry?" said Tjorvi. "Angry's nothing."

"I used to really like Arnë," Peer cried. "I used to . . ." He remembered how much he'd admired Arnë when he first met him years ago. Arnë and Bjorn had seemed like heroes to him then, brave enough to stand up to his bullying uncles when no one else dared. "If he won't be friends with me, there's nothing I can do."

Tjorvi looked shrewdly at Peer. "No wonder they say women on board ships is unlucky. It's that young lass that's causing all the trouble, isn't it? And is she fond of you?"

"I don't think even she knows," said Peer.

"Ask her and be done with it," said Tjorvi.

CHAPTER 9

Lost at Sea

B ut Peer didn't take Tjorvi's advice. He thought about it constantly—but there was no privacy on the ship. If ever he found himself alone with Hilde, someone always pushed in before he could say anything important, and it wasn't just Arnë. Hilde's sunny disposition made her a favorite with the entire crew. Everyone wanted to talk to her, or sit beside her. As far as Peer could see, she liked them all, and never minded the interruptions. And so he put it off. *When the voyage is over,* he thought, *when we strike land—then I'll have more of a chance. That's when I'll tell her how I feel.*

Day after day passed, and the crew of the *Water Snake* grew used to the hard boards under them, the cold air always around them, the movement of the long waves rolling under the ship. They were resigned to eating cold food and drinking stale water. On bright days they were grateful for the growing strength of the sun warming their aching limbs. On wet days the lucky ones donned waterproofs—supple capes of fine oiled leather. Those who had none wrapped themselves up in double layers of wool, and blew on their cold red hands.

There were no more fights. Peer kept away from Harald and Arnë, and didn't speak to them even at mealtimes. Once or twice he saw Arnë watching him with an odd expression, half sorry, half annoyed. But if Arnë wanted to say something, he could. Peer wouldn't be the one to begin.

Harald ignored Peer completely, unless to give some order about the ship. Peer guessed Gunnar had spoken to Harald. Arnë's wound had been slight, and was healing well, but Gunnar wouldn't want to risk any of his able-bodied men.

The Nis adapted surprisingly well to life on board. The mast and rigging became its playground, and there were all sorts of nooks and crannies where it could hide. The apple barrel in the hold was one of its favorites, but it often curled up with Loki in a patch of sunshine, hidden from view behind the coil of the anchor rope. If anyone approached, it shot for cover. The men thought there was a big rat somewhere on board.

Late one evening, Peer was standing in the bow, keeping ice watch. They'd passed a big iceberg at around sunset—a scary thing like a chunk of white mountain. Gunnar yelled at the helmsman not to pass too close—the high sides of the berg towered over *Water Snake* and would steal the wind from her sail. Once safely behind, the berg remained in sight for an hour or more, the low sun turning it to warm amber and blue shadow, and finally to a dark tooth against the southeastern horizon.

It was a warning they couldn't ignore. So Peer stood through the long twilight, straining his eyes for the telltale gleam of looming ice castles, and listening to the Nis bouncing about in the rigging. Now it was sitting in the crosstrees at the top of the mast, thin legs dangling, wispy hair blowing in the north wind—just visible against a patch of sky where a few stars burned.

Peer was hungry. He hoped that Hilde would bring him his evening meal—she sometimes did when he was on watch, and stayed to chat for a while—but this time he was surprised and rather disappointed to see Astrid. She handed over his food, and then didn't go, but leaned back against the steep curve of the prow and looked up at the masthead.

"There it sits," she said, and her fingers drummed on the planking. "There it sits, and it won't speak to me."

"The Nis?" Peer asked through a mouthful of crumbling oatcake. He'd forgotten that Astrid could see it. "Why should it speak to you? You're lucky it hasn't done something in revenge."

"It wouldn't dare," said Astrid coolly, and it occurred to him that she was probably right. There was something about Astrid that would make even the Nis think twice. She moved closer to him. "It would talk to me if *you* asked it. Why don't you call it? Ask it to come down."

"Why should I?" demanded Peer. He neither liked nor trusted Astrid, and saw no reason why he should do anything for her. "Besides, someone might hear."

"They won't hear," said Astrid. "They're all listening to Hilde telling about some of your adventures under Troll Fell." She put a slim hand on his shoulder. "It's a shame you're up here by yourself, especially when it's your story too."

Peer couldn't help secretly agreeing. With a pang of loneliness he imagined the gathering back there on the afterdeck, Hilde's animated face, her hands gesturing as she described their adventures.

"Do ask the Nis to come down," Astrid wheedled. "I'd like to make friends with it. And look! Here's its little red cap. It'll want that back."

She opened her hand and showed him the tiny cap, dark in the darkness against her white fingers. It was true that the Nis would be glad to have that back. And where had she found *it*? Peer wondered. Probably inside her goatskin bag.

"All right," he said gruffly, "I'll try, but I don't know if it'll come."

He chirruped gently, and saw the Nis's humped outline go tall and thin as it sat up like an alarmed squirrel and looked around.

"It's only me," Peer called. "And Astrid," he added, in case the Nis thought he was trying to deceive it. "She wants to say sorry to you. Come on down."

He didn't truly think the Nis would come. However, it skipped onto the forestay and came sliding cleverly down. Astrid jumped as though half afraid, then stretched out a coaxing hand.

The Nis grabbed the cap from her fingers and crammed it on its head. It made a rude noise with its lips, and jumped away to crouch on the iron fluke of the anchor, where it deliberately turned its back to her, fiddling with something it held in its skinny lap, and chanting some odd-sounding gibberish:

"Half hitch, clove hitch, bowline, sheep-shank.
Sheet bend, double sheet, reef knot, splice."

Peer leaned over. "Whatever are you doing?"

"Practicing knots," squeaked the Nis. Its long nimble fingers flickered like spider legs. "Make a little hole," it muttered to itself. "*Out* pops the rabbit, *around* the tree it goes, and *back* into the hole again." It held up a piece of looped string in triumph. "See! Bowline." It undid it busily and tried another. "Reef knot!" It held out the end. "The harder you pull, the tighter it gets," it explained importantly. "Pull that, Peer Ulfsson."

Peer pulled, and the knot slid apart. "That was a slipknot," he said.

The Nis snatched the string back. "*Over* here and *under* there . . . No, it goes *around* here and over *there*. . . . Pull!" Peer tweaked, and the knot came apart again. The Nis scrunched the string up. "I could do it before," it said crossly.

Astrid laughed. "Why are you learning knots?" she asked.

The Nis wouldn't answer, but Peer guessed. "They're all knots that sailors use. The Nis is turning into a real seafarer!"

Astrid caught on fast. "Goodness, yes. Why, I'm terrible at knots. I'm nothing but a landlubber. However did you learn so quickly?"

The Nis could not resist flattery. Flicking her a sideways glance, it said with shy pride, "I watches, and I listens, and I sees Magnus showing Floki. And I thinks to myself, *I am a ship Nis now, I must learn the things that sailors know.*"

"How clever," Astrid praised. The Nis swaggered its thin shoulders, spitting a tiny white speck over the side in uncanny imitation of Magnus. "I knows all the right words, too," it bragged. *"Ahoy there! Haul, me boys! Lee side! Luff!"*

"That's wonderful," said Peer in a shaking voice.

The Nis nodded complacently. "Now I must go up to the masthead, like I does every night, and keep lookout. Every evening I goes *aloft*"—it looked sharply to see if they had noticed the nautical term—"I goes aloft and I can see lots from up there, much more than you can see down here, and I keeps a good lookout for icebergs, Peer Ulfsson, so no need to worry. And I looks out for storms, too, and rocks, and sea serpentses and whales . . ." Its voice trailed off as it sprang for the forestay and scampered rapidly back up, hand over hand.

Struggling not to laugh, Peer and Astrid caught each other's eye.

"Well, it's forgiven me!" said Astrid.

"Maybe," said Peer. "Just keep buttering it up."

"You're fond of it, aren't you?"

"Of course I am." Peer discovered that he also felt very proud of the way the Nis was coping with its sudden uprooting from everything it had ever known. "I think it's doing better than I am," he added soberly.

"You're a nice person, Peer," said Astrid softly. "Why doesn't Hilde notice?"

Peer stiffened. "I don't know what you mean."

"Yes you do." A gleam of mischief came into Astrid's eyes. "I expect I could get her interested in you. Want me to help?"

"No!"

"You're afraid of me, aren't you?" she teased. "Why? A handsome boy like you shouldn't be afraid of girls."

Peer was blushing so hard, he was glad of the darkness. Astrid stepped closer. Before he knew what she was going to do, she slid one hand up over his neck and kissed his cheek. "There! Now you can say a girl's kissed you."

"Astrid!" Peer felt his whole skin scalding. "You'd better go," he said furiously. "What if someone—"

"What if someone sees us?" Astrid made her eyes go big. "Oh, yes, Gunnar would kill you, wouldn't he?" She laughed. "Don't worry, Peer, you're safe with me. I won't frighten you anymore. I like you. I really do. And I can't say that about many people."

Her voice was half sad, half mocking. Peer remembered what Hilde had told him about the young man Astrid had loved. *Erlend*. The name rose to his lips, but he bit it back. He looked at Astrid. She was staring up at the stars, her white skin luminous against the darkness of the vast sail. Did she know the story of Erlend's curse? He pitied her.

"Hilde told me your secret," he said gently.

"What secret?"

She rapped it out so sharply, Peer wished he had said nothing. "About . . . having to marry Gunnar, and then Harald killing Erlend," he stammered.

"That!" To his amazement, she sounded relieved. After a moment she said, "Well, it was dreadful. But I'm married to Gunnar now. I don't want to think about it anymore." She was suddenly in a hurry, pulling her cloak around her. "I don't want Gunnar to miss me. I'd better go." And she whisked away, stumbling over the curved wooden ribs of the ship's side.

Peer shook his head. His hand went to his cheek, and he rubbed the spot where she'd kissed him. Did she love Gunnar? Had she loved Erlend? He couldn't make her out at all.

"Floki!" Magnus yelled the next morning as a line came apart in his hands. "I thought I'd shown you how to do a sheet bend." He waved the loose end under Floki's nose. "Call yourself a sailor? That slipknot came undone as soon as I pulled on it, you—you landsman, you!"

Floki examined the line, as though somehow it could tell him what had gone wrong. "I'm sure I did it right," he grumbled.

"Never mind who did what. Pull that sail in!" bellowed

Gunnar. The corner of the sail had blown free and had to be recaptured. All day knots fastening the shrouds, stays, and sheets came mysteriously loose, or undone, or were found retied in the wrong way, until Gunnar was driven nearly crazy, cursing his crew for a nest of unhandy landlubbers. Tempers rose so high that Peer began to fear fights would break out again—but luckily, after a day or two of turmoil, the Nis finally got all the knots figured out, and peace was restored. Floki muttered that *Water Snake* was an unlucky ship. When Magnus heard, he threatened to throw Floki overboard.

A few days later, just after daybreak, Peer heard an excited shout from Halfdan in the bow: "Land ahead! There's old Blueshirt! Greenland, me boys!"

Everyone who was free rushed forward. Peer was holding the starboard brace and couldn't join them, but by shading his eyes and leaning out over the side, he caught a glimpse of it: a jag of bluish white on the iron horizon.

With a satisfied grunt Gunnar ordered Magnus, on the tiller, to alter course south of west. It was a freezing cold morning, with the wind gusting almost dead north. As those white, unfriendly mountains drew a little nearer, snow began to scud down the wind. Moments later, a snarling squall enveloped the ship. The horizon in all directions vanished. Great gray snowflakes plastered themselves against the sail and whirled away again. The bow disappeared as if into an unseen future, and the ship reared and rolled like a frightened horse.

"Reef!" Gunnar screamed. Peer could hardly hear him over the noise of the wind.

They shortened sail. Peer sat jammed against the starboard side, hanging on to the sheet and the braces, holding his breath each time the ship rose among the shouldering waves. Like gray monsters they rolled down on *Water Snake*, foam spilling greedily down their fronts. They threw her up and snapped at her sides. Spray came overboard in white arcs.

For a second the snowstorm cleared. He could see forward, under the sail, the dark line of the dragonhead with seas bursting around it. Then hail rattled across the deck boards, bouncing and rolling, knocking against his skull like elfin hammers and numbing his face and hands.

Someone shook his shoulder. It was Arnë, shouting into his ear. *What? Something—the steering oar?* "Broken," Arnë bawled. Half crawling, Peer clawed himself along to the stern, where Magnus was clutching his wrist and waving a splintered peg leg of wood—the remains of the tiller. A wave had wrenched the whole thing out of his grasp, twisting the steering oar upward and snapping the tiller like a stick of firewood. Peer clung to the side and looked over at the steering oar, which was lifting and falling uselessly in the waves. "It's not broken," he yelled. "The withy's snapped."

The withy—the rope that pinned the steering oar against the ship—had gone. Only a broad leather strap kept the oar from floating away as the ship tossed and dropped at the mercy of wind and waves.

Gunnar appeared out of the gale. He put his face close to Peer's. "Can—you—fix—it?" He bellowed each word separately.

"Not in this weather," Peer shouted back. He was afraid Gunnar would argue, but Gunnar nodded as though this was what he'd expected, and disappeared again.

"Let's get it in," Peer yelled. "Get me a line." Magnus brought a length of cord, which Peer knotted tightly around the top of the steering oar. He lashed the other end to one of the crossbeams so that the oar couldn't wash away when he loosed the leather strap. "When it comes free, haul!"

Magnus nodded. At Peer's other side, Harald leaned over the gunwale. The steering oar was a heavy blade of oak, as long as a man, scything about in the strong waves, capable of breaking an arm or crushing a hand between it and the ship.

"Now!"

They grabbed for the oar. Magnus heaved on the line. Peer caught the middle of the oar and was nearly tugged over the side by the deadweight as the ship rolled and the water sucked away below. For a second he stared into boiling froth, then the water rose to engulf him. But the oar rose with it, and together Harald and he dragged it over the side and fell to the deck boards with the oar on top of them. Magnus lifted it clear.

Soaked and breathless, arms nearly torn from their sockets, Peer and Harald exchanged glances. Harald was gasping,

136

his hair plastered to his face in rattails. He bared his teeth in a savage smile of triumph, and Peer found himself grinning back. Harald got up. He pulled Peer to his feet, and clapped him on the arm.

It wouldn't last. But for a moment, Peer almost liked him. He was ruthless, selfish, dangerous—but enjoying the danger, twice as alive as most people, with a glow to him that you wanted to be part of. *And he knows it, and he uses it.*

They moved apart, the bond already breaking. Already Harald's eyes turned indifferently away. You couldn't be friends with him. There was no warmth to his brightness. He was in love with action, and with himself.

"Peer!" Magnus yelled. Gunnar was gesticulating angrily. "Port side—get over to port!" Peer flung himself across to help balance the ship.

"Got to keep her straight," Magnus shouted in his ear. "Got to run before the wind. Or else—" He didn't finish. Peer nodded. If the ship turned broadside to the waves, they would be overwhelmed—sucked down without a trace.

Now Peer saw Gunnar for the shipmaster he was. With no steering oar to help him, he took his ship in a crazy ride over the rolling hills of water, bellowing orders to haul in or slacken off the braces—twitching the sail this way and that—until Peer's palms blistered and the touch of the harsh, soaking ropes was raw agony. With the others he staggered to port or starboard as Gunnar yelled at them—clutching for balance at the shrouds and the gunwale, bruised and frozen. In vivid flashes between periods of dazed exhaustion Peer saw his shipmates—Floki being sick, Tjorvi hauling the yard around like a giant, Astrid and Hilde steadily baling, their sopping skirts spreading around them like puddles. Loki crept to his feet, and Peer stroked his cold wet ears.

At long last dawn came. The seas dropped into heaving, sullen swells, as though the tempest had got over the worst of its tantrum and was sobbing itself to sleep. Then the sun came up on the port side, its disc hidden behind broken clouds, poking white rays upward like gigantic wheel spokes. The mountains of Greenland were nowhere to be seen.

Peer mended the steering oar. He threaded a new rope through it, with a thick knot against the outer side. The tiller, which slotted into the end of the steering oar, was too damaged to reuse, but he made a new one by trimming down an oar handle. As soon as it was ready, Gunnar put the ship about. At last they were sailing west again.

The crew cheered. Tjorvi slapped Peer on the back. Gunnar gave him an approving nod. Even Arnë produced a faint smile. Peer felt he truly belonged. It was a good feeling. As he put his tools carefully away, he heard Magnus say, "No sense trying to reach Greenland now. But where are we? That's what I'd like to know."

A brisk discussion broke out:

"May as well keep going west."

"Aye, but we could be anywhere. Did anyone see the stars last night?"

"Never a break in the clouds. But we've come a fair way south."

"We know that," Magnus said with a sneer.

"What if we miss Vinland altogether and sail over the edge of the world?" Floki piped up, conjuring in every mind a vision of the endless waterfall plunging over the rim of the earth.

"Showing your ignorance, Floki," said Magnus. "The world is shaped like a dish, and that keeps the water in. Ye can't sail over the edge."

"That's not right," Arnë argued. "The world's like a dish, but it's an upside-down dish. You can see that by the way it curves."

Magnus burst out laughing. "Then why wouldn't the sea just run off? You can't pour water into an upside-down dish."

"It's like a dish with a rim," said Gunnar, in a tone that brooked no arguments. "There's land all around the ocean, just like there's land all around any lake. Stands to reason. And that means so long as we keep sailing west, we'll strike the coastline."

The crew's worn faces broke into smiles. This was a good explanation, which everyone liked. There was no chance of getting lost, or of sailing over a precipice. Peer looked around at a collection of bloodshot eyes, bruises, cracked lips, and dull, salt-soaked hair. More than half of the crew had been seasick. Loki's coat was sticky with salt. Astrid was hollow-cheeked, with purple shadows under her eyes: the storm had blown away her beauty. Hilde's looks were more robust: the wind whipped roses into her cheeks and tousled her yellow hair. Gunnar looked terrible, gray under his red, chapped skin. His good hand shook, and he clenched his fist to disguise it.

Yet almost against his will, Peer found he trusted Gunnar to get them to Vinland safely. Rough and tough Gunnar might be, but he knew how to sail a ship, and how to put confidence into his men.

And so did Harald. "Here's a riddle for you all!" he called out. "Guess what this is:

> "I know a stranger, a bright gold-giver.
> He strides in splendor over the world's walls.
> All day he hurries between two bonfires.
> No man knows where he builds his bedchamber."

The men's faces brightened; they pushed one another.

"Go on."

"You go first."

"A king!" shouted Floki.

"Wrong." Harald cocked an eyebrow. "Guess again."

"An earl?" ventured Halfdan. Harald shook his head.

"What are the two bonfires?" Arnë wondered aloud.

Halfdan let out a whoop. "I've got it! The two bonfires are sunrise and sunset, and nobody knows where the sun goes to bed. It's the sun!"

"But the sun's not a stranger," Tjorvi objected.

"It has been for the last two days," said Harald, and the men laughed and clapped.

"Give us another!"

Astrid came up behind Peer and draped her arm over his shoulder. Peer knew she was only doing it to tease, but he wished she wouldn't. He saw Hilde's eyebrows go up, and tried to move aside. Astrid took her arm away with a comical pout.

"We were talking about your husband," said Hilde pointedly.

"Really?" said Astrid. "What about him?"

"Just that he knows what he's doing," Peer said. "He's a good skipper."

The corner of Astrid's mouth lifted. A faint gleam appeared in her eyes. She threw a glance at Gunnar, where he sat against the port side. He happened to look at her, and his bristly, hard-eyed face softened for a moment.

"He doesn't look well," Astrid murmured. "He hasn't slept more than a snatch since the storm began. Thank goodness you got the steering oar fixed, Peer. You're so clever." She tucked her arm through Peer's, and pinched him playfully. "Don't you think he's clever, Hilde—this brother of yours?"

"He's not my brother," Hilde contradicted—then frowned, as if wondering what she'd said.

Astrid smiled. She dropped Peer's arm and went on, "But I came to ask you: How's the Nis?"

"The Nis!"

Hilde's mouth opened in horror, and she and Peer stared at

each other. "The Nis! How did it manage in the storm? Where is it?"

Astrid looked at them with scornful amusement. "Really! You two are the ones who are supposed to look out for the Nis. I'm just the wicked woman who dragged it on board. I suppose neither of you fed it, either?"

"If you were clever enough to remember it, why didn't you do it?" Hilde snapped.

"Nobody had time to think," Peer said. He imagined the Nis lying in some cold corner, wet, seasick, and frightened; or clinging to the masthead in all that wind; or being blown off into the sea.

"We'd better try and find it," he said anxiously.

Most of the crew still clustered around Harald on the afterdeck, calling out riddles and answers. Peer made his way along the ship, tugging at knots and knocking on beams and joints as if examining them for strain after the storm. "Nis ... Nis," he called softly whenever he dared. Astrid and Hilde looked into barrels and crates, pretending to take stock of the provisions.

The Nis wasn't in the apple barrel. It wasn't in the chicken coop, though all three of them checked it, even moving the bedraggled, seasick chickens to make sure it wasn't huddling among their feathers. In growing dread they searched across the big cluttered hold. It was impossible to be sure the Nis wasn't hiding there somewhere, but it didn't answer their calls.

They met in the bow, confirming with pale faces their lack

of success. Loki plodded after them, poking an inquiring nose into the cranny behind the anchor. No sign of the Nis. With the nagging worry growing into real fear, Peer even lifted the loose deck boards to look into the dark triangular space under the foredeck, though he couldn't imagine why the Nis would ever go there. There was nothing to see but a little black water spilling about.

"Oh, where can it be?" said Hilde in despair.

"Lost something?" Arnë took them by surprise.

Peer jumped and clattered the boards back into place. "No," he answered. "Just making sure we're not leaking."

Arnë gave him a close look. "You seem worried." His eyes were watchful and concerned, and for a fleeting moment he looked and sounded like his brother. He turned to Hilde: "Something's wrong, isn't it? Why don't you tell me?"

Hilde began to speak, stopped, and flung an unhappy look at Peer. Peer squared his shoulders and lifted his chin. "Everything's fine," he said brusquely.

Arnë turned on his heel and went off.

"That was convincing," Astrid murmured.

"We should have told him," said Hilde. "He could have kept an eye out for it. He might even have seen it."

"Well, you go after him if you want," said Peer. Arnë's expression had made him feel cross and guilty. "As far as I know, he's never seen the Nis in his life. And what if he tells Harald?"

Hilde raised a cold eyebrow. "Why should he? Why do you always think the worst of Arnë?"

"Children, don't quarrel," said Astrid wearily. They looked at each other, ashamed.

Hilde dug the heels of her hands into her eyes, rubbing hard. "Oh, Nis, Nis, where are you?"

No one answered her. *Water Snake* rocked over long swells, nodding into wave after wave with a fresh splatter of spray. The sun was slipping down into yellow haze. "I'm so tired of this ocean," said Hilde, with a dreary little laugh. She looked at Peer with red-rimmed eyes. "We've looked everywhere. Let's face it. It's lost, isn't it? The Nis is lost."

CHAPTER 10
Landfall

They searched till long after dark, hoping the Nis would wake and come creeping out of some forgotten hidey-hole. Even after they'd all given up, and were sitting with the crew over the evening meal, one or another would get up restlessly, and wander off to try again. Everywhere he looked, Peer missed seeing the Nis's skinny little silhouette hopping in the shrouds or outlined against the sunset.

At last he crawled into his sleeping sack, all hope gone. He thought of the storm, and the way the ship had leaped like a spurred horse. He imagined the Nis swept over the side like a little scrap of cloth, perhaps crying out in a thin voice, then lost in the cold, limitless waves. *The poor little Nis. After being brought all this way, and after it tried so hard to be a sailor.* A lump rose in his throat. "The Nis is gone, Loki," he whispered, and Loki whined. He tried not to think of the Nis anymore, but what else was there to think about? The ship was a hateful place, a trap, a coop.

He lay staring up at the great swaying sail, listening to the creak as Halfdan twisted the steering oar, the hoarse whistle of wind in the shrouds, and the slap and tickle of water running along the sides. He knew all the sounds of the ship now. That loud snoring was Tjorvi. The irritating little cough followed by a sniff was Floki. But tonight there was a muttering undercurrent. Peer lay half sleeping, half waking, hearing it running on: somebody talking, low and rapid and feverish, and then a great sobbing shout: "Keep him off! Keep him off! Keep him off!"

Peer sat up fast, dislodging Loki, who sprang up barking. All around him startled men struggled out of their sleeping sacks.

"The skipper's gone mad!" yelled Halfdan at the helm.

The sky flashed. From unguessable heights, silent streamers unrolled across the heavens. Like the folds of some enormous garment, they trailed overhead, then twisted into ropes and went snaking over the northern horizon. The ship gleamed and flickered: Every upturned face reflected a pale green. "The Northern Dancers!" cried Hilde.

"Help me! Help!" Gunnar crouched against the rail, panting with terror. His eyes goggled; he seemed beside himself. Astrid threw herself down, trying to clasp him in her arms, but he flung her off, catapulting upward with a jump as sudden as a grasshopper's. He grabbed the backstay with his good right hand and swung from it, pivoting and peering this way and that, poking out his chin. "D'you hear him? D'you hear him?" he mumbled.

"Gunnar, Gunnar, there's nothing to fear," cried Astrid.

"There is. I hear him splashing after us, splashing, splashing . . ." Gunnar began to choke.

"Father." Harald's long hair shone an elfin green in the weird dancelight. He trod forward warily, hand outstretched as if approaching a wild animal. Which was what Gunnar resembled, Peer thought, horrified by the change in him.

Astrid got to her feet. "Harald, he's ill again. He needs medicine."

"Medicine? He doesn't need *your* medicine," said Harald fiercely. "Who knows what you've been giving him? Father, wake up. You're dreaming." He edged forward. Peer wondered why he was being so careful, till he saw Harald keeping an eye on the knife at Gunnar's belt. "Wake up, Father. It's me, Harald. It's your son."

Gunnar quieted. He dropped to his knees and began rocking to and fro, arms clasped across his chest as if in an agony of grief. "Oh, oh," Peer heard him groan. "Oh, oh." But when Harald tried to touch him he screamed, "He's climbing over the side!"

He scrabbled away on all fours, cramming himself into the angle of the stern.

"Help me. Quick!" Harald snapped at the men. But they hung back, and not just because of Gunnar's knife.

"He's here!" Gunnar's hands were over his face and he peeped between his fingers. "I heard him, I heard him s-s-splashing after the ship, and then he climbed on board, black and blue and dripping. He's hiding somewhere. Arrchch!" With a retching cough he stuck his tongue out as far as it would go, shaking his head from side to side as if he had bitten something unbearably bitter.

Prickles raced across Peer's skin. He twisted his neck, trying to see behind his back. The men were doing the same. Gunnar's terror was catching. The dark sea burned with a million green glints.

"The ghost!" Floki burst out.

Harald spun around and struck Floki a ringing crack across the cheek. "A ghost, is it? Where? Have you seen this ghost, Floki?" Floki reeled back. Harald followed. "What ghost? Whose? Do you want to give it a name? Do you want to call it up? Because if there's a ghost on this ship, I'd like to meet it. *Hoo-ooo!*" He flung his head back with a howl. "Come on, ghost! My name is Harald Silkenhair, what's yours?

"My name is Harald Silkenhair.
I am not afraid of death or darkness,
Of white ghost or black ghost,
Of night walker, or barrow-dweller."

Floki fell over, sobbing. With one eye on Harald, Magnus sidled in, grabbed Floki's arm, and dragged him out of

Harald's way. The other men backed off.

"*Hoo-ooo!*" Harald began to slap his thighs and swing his head from side to side, tossing his hair. "Come on, ghost!"

"He's running berserk," muttered Magnus.

"Do something!" wailed Halfdan, trapped at the tiller.

Peer felt a quick hand grasp his arm. "This is ridiculous!" Hilde hissed. She had a bucket in her hand, attached to a length of rope. "Help me!" She dropped the bucket over the side, and Peer helped her drag it up again, slopping full. Before he had time to think what she would do, Hilde seized the handle, stepped forward, and threw the whole pailful over Harald.

As the icy seawater hit him across the chest, there was a collective gasp. Peer balled his fists and moved forward, ready to spring on Harald if he went for Hilde. For a long second of stillness Harald looked down at himself. He spread out his dripping arms. He lifted his head slowly and looked at Hilde. He started to giggle, uncontrollable high-pitched giggles that raised the hair on Peer's scalp.

Hilde dropped the bucket, which rolled, clattering. She turned her back on Harald and stamped her foot. "*Will* you men stop making fools of yourselves? Floki, get up at once. There isn't any ghost, Gunnar is just sick. Tjorvi, instead of standing there like a big lummock, help Astrid get him into his sleeping sack. As for you, Harald, Gunnar *does* need medicine, whatever you think!"

The men obeyed like children. Harald took a few gasping breaths and stopped giggling. He sat on a thwart and put his head in his hands. Peer gave him a wide berth and went to find Astrid's bag. Astrid delved into it and brought out a small linen pouch. Gunnar seemed semiconscious, and was tossing and twisting. Sweat coated his face. Astrid shook a dark, gritty-looking powder into her hand, threw it into a small cup, and mixed in some water.

"Willow bark," she explained briefly. "To quench the fever." She propped Gunnar's head against her shoulder and brought the cup to his lips. Gunnar coughed, drank a little. Dribbles of blackish liquid ran down his beard.

The men stood around in a nervous cluster. "Never seen the skipper this bad. What if he dies? Who'll give the orders?"

"Young Hilde, I guess," said Tjorvi, attempting a joke.

But no one laughed, and Floki said with dogged loyalty, "Harald." His lip was bleeding. Heads turned to look at Harald, who sat limp and motionless a few feet away.

The sky was paler. The flickering Northern Dancers had burned themselves out. Peer hadn't noticed them go, but now he saw that the mast and sail were distinct again: Dawn was approaching; the waves around the ship were no longer black and green, but gray. He shuddered in a comfortless world.

Arnë came and stood a few feet away. He stared gloomily out over the sea, shoulders hunched. With his untidy hair and sprouting beard, he looked more than ever like Bjorn. Peer felt a wriggle of remorse. If only things were different. If only they could be friends. He cleared his throat. "It's not good, is it?" he tried.

Arnë gave him a discouraging glance.

Peer's heart thumped. He said suddenly, "I'm sorry we fell out. I ought to have thanked you—that time Harald got you with the harpoon—"

Arnë interrupted. "Just tell me one thing. What *were* you looking for this evening?"

Their eyes met. Arnë's eyes were blue as the sea on a summer afternoon. Blue as Bjorn's, but Bjorn had never looked at him with such cool suspicion. This was it, then—the price of Arnë's good opinion. Trust him, and tell the truth.

"The Nis," he said after a moment. "Haven't you heard Bjorn talk about it? It's Gudrun's house spirit. It's my friend. It used to live at the old mill. Astrid stole it—stuffed it into that bag she carries. The first night at sea, remember all the noise? I said it was a seagull, but—"

"It was the Nis?" Arnë's eyes widened. He shook his head, laughing under his breath. "Why didn't you say so instead of scaring everyone stiff?"

"How was I to know a seagull would scare everyone? Would you have told Harald about the Nis? Besides, it likes— liked—to be secret. No one usually sees it, only me some-times."

"But if you know the Nis is on board, why look for it?"

"It's missing," said Peer bleakly. "None of us has seen it since the storm. I think it got washed overboard."

"Oh."

They stood together. Peer drummed his fingers on the rail.

Presently Arnë said, "Well. Thanks for telling me."

"Hilde wanted to tell you," said Peer.

"Maybe." Arnë sounded rather bitter. "She didn't, though, did she? Not without your say-so." He looked sideways at Peer. "Of course, a sister would back up her brother. Don't you think?"

There was no need to answer that. Peer rewrapped his cloak, pulling it higher around his neck. *Why is it always colder at dawn?*

Tjorvi joined them. "Look at the sunrise," he said quietly. "It's like gold leaf across the sky. I saw a picture once of a sky like that. In a book, it was."

"What's a book?" Peer asked.

"A book . . ." Tjorvi held his hands apart, squaring off a bit of the air. "With leaves of calfskin, all painted and covered in runes. One of the lads on my last ship showed it to me. We'd been down to the Southlands and he got it in a raid. And there was this picture, bright as a jewel. A woman, and a child, and a golden sky . . ." He gave up, shaking his head. "I can't describe it."

"What happened to it?" asked Arnë.

"Oh, he burned it," said Tjorvi. "Didn't know what the runes said. Could have been spells, see? All he wanted was the boards—set with goldwork and stones, they were. But I always remember that picture. And there's the sky now, just like it."

They all stared in subdued silence. Behind the high sternpost, the whole eastern sky gleamed pale, chilly gold.

"My wife and child's back there somewhere," said Tjorvi. "Wonder if I'll ever see 'em again?"

"We've come a long way," said Arnë.

Maybe it's time to turn around. Nobody said it, but it was what everyone was thinking. No one had slept properly for days. *Floki's right. This is an unlucky ship. Weeks at sea, out of sight of land.*

"I'd give a lot to step on dry ground," Tjorvi sighed.

"Light a fire," agreed Arnë.

Hear birdsong. Smell grass. Walk up the fell and see the lambs being born...

"Land ho!" a shrill voice sang out from the bow.

"What?" Peer's world fell into bits and rearranged itself. He knew that voice....

"Land! Land ho!"

Hilde whirled past, smiling from ear to ear. Peer joined the general rush. "Where?"

"There—dead ahead!"

The men crowded together. Far, far to the west, a long uneven line lay on the horizon. It wasn't much. It was everything.

"Land!" They hugged one another, stamped their feet, pounded one another on the back.

But Peer, after one irresistible glance, tore himself away to find Hilde. "That was the Nis!"

"I know! Where's it *been*? And why didn't it come when we called? Just *wait* till I get my hands on it." Tears came to her eyes. "And now where's it gone? I'll put out some food. Oh, I'd better not look too happy—people will wonder why."

"They won't," said Peer. "We all look happy now." It was true. Everyone on board looked different, faces washed clean by joy and relief.

All through the long day *Water Snake* cut her pathway toward the land, straight at first and then in long loose tacks as the wind shifted into the northwest. No one minded: At last they could see they were making progress. Magnus swore he smelled forests, and got everyone sniffing. Seabirds sailed over, the first for days. Seaweed floated in the current. On the afterdeck, Gunnar slept, and then woke, weak but clear-headed. By late afternoon he was shakily on his feet.

The foredeck was no longer a private place. It was where everyone wanted to be, to see the land growing out of the sea until the sinking sun obscured it in a haze and a glory.

Peer caught the Nis as evening fell. It was bobbing in and out of the crates forward of the mast, chirping happily.

"Where *were* you?"

"Me, Peer Ulfsson?" It bounced and sprang like a kitten, immensely pleased with itself.

"Yes, you. We were worried sick! We looked all over for you. Didn't you hear us calling?"

"Did you hear *me*?" the Nis asked. It rubbed its long fingers together, full of self-satisfied glee. "'*Land ho,*' I called. I saw it first, Peer Ulfsson. I found it!"

"Right," said Peer drily. "They'll probably call it Nisland. *Listen* to me. We were terribly worried. We thought you'd drowned."

"I didn't," said the Nis indignantly. "I worked very hard in that storm, Peer Ulfsson, holding on to the forestay and the backstay, so that the mast wouldn't fall down. And the wind blew me, and the rain rained on me, but I didn't let go. And after that I was very, very tired."

Peer cast a glance at the stout, thick cables running from masthead to prow and stern, and then at the Nis's fragile, twiggy arms.

"You would be," he agreed. "So where did you go?"

"To my nice den. My nice secret place where nobody else can go. Watch how I get there."

It reached the base of the dragon-neck in one flying leap, and swarmed up the crisscross carvings to the head. It perched for a second, poised over the ocean—and vanished. Peer sucked in his breath. But the Nis hadn't fallen. A moment later it swung back up onto the top of the dragonhead.

"The dragon's mouth?" said Peer. "You've been sitting in the dragon's mouth?"

The Nis nodded. "Nithing the Seafarer can go anywhere," it squeaked. "After the storm, I curls myself up in there, and I goes to sleep. And then I wakes up, and I smells land. And I sees it, too. And so I calls out, 'Land ho,' for everyone to hear. Am I famous now? As famous as Thorolf? Will they really call it Nisland, Peer Ulfsson?"

Peer hadn't the heart to tell it the land was already named. "As far as I'm concerned," he said solemnly, "that bit of the coastline will always be Nisland."

The Nis frisked and preened itself.

Next morning the land was in plain view: forested hills, and beyond them the white smears of mountains like the ghosts of clouds. Everyone stared hungrily as Gunnar altered course to run south, with the mountains on the starboard side. Every hour brought new sights and sounds. The yelling clamor of a seagull colony on one abrupt limestone rock could be heard for miles. A flight of ducks passed over the ship, quacking loudly. Whales were everywhere, heaving gray or black bodies between the waves and snorting like bullocks. The day was full of mild sunshine, with a gentle haze over silver water.

Hilde looked over the side. Down in the shadow of the ship, pale frilly blossoms floated past—jellyfish, like ghostly baby's bonnets, flowing through the cold clear water. Millions of them. It made her sleepy to watch.

At noon Magnus shouted at the helm. "The Wonderful Beaches!" Hilde raised her eyes from the hypnotic water and saw an unbroken white line running along the coast. Sand. Wonderful white sand. She longed to run on it.

"Now we know where we are," Magnus told her, satisfaction in every crease of his face. "The Wonderful Beaches. Go on for miles, they do; there's no mistaking them. And you know what that means? Only a few more days, and we'll be there."

Serpent's Bay! How long ago it seemed, the night she'd first heard of it, sitting at home in the snug, warm farmhouse. *And soon we'll be there. Won't Thorolf be glad to see us!* A thrill of happiness ran through her. *Oh, Ma, Pa—if only you could see me now!*

CHAPTER 11
Spring Stories

"Kwimu! Go, Kwimu!" Skusji'j yells.

The young men are playing the ball game. Stripped to their loincloths, they shout and jostle, throwing and catching, leaping through shafts of dusty evening sunlight. Dots of white and yellow paint flash on their faces as they follow the shifting patterns of the ball.

It flies across in a shallow arc, and Kwimu snatches it. He twists and darts, evading pursuit, racing for the tall pole at the edge of the glade.

"Go on, Kwimu!" shouts Skusji'j from the sidelines. "Run! Ow!" He winces. Another player has tackled Kwimu. It's Kiunik, his young uncle. Seizing a handful of Kwimu's glossy black hair, he jerks him off balance. Kwimu hooks a foot around Kiunik's ankle. They fall to the ground, wrestling, and a third young man grabs the ball and reaches the post. His friends cheer, and as Kwimu and Kiunik pick themselves up, the game is over.

"That looks like so much fun," the Little Weasel says as they come over, disheveled and panting, to collect their things.

"Very rough fun," Kwimu complains, laughing, slinging his soft moose-hide jacket over his shoulder, and retying his belt. "Did you see Kiunik? He nearly pulled my head off."

"Good practice for war." Kiunik adjusts his great necklace of curving bear claws and slyly tweaks Kwimu's long hair. "This stuff is too easy to grab. Wear it like mine." He passes a hand over his own head—shaven on both sides, with a stiff black crest running down the middle.

"Ha!" Kwimu retorts. "If I wore it like you, I'd always be changing it. When Kiunik sets a fashion, he likes to think everyone will copy him," he adds to Skusji'j. "But not me. When I'm as tall as he is, I'll rub his face in the dust."

"You can try," says Kiunik amiably, disappearing into the wigwam.

Kwimu sits down outside and offers Skusji'j a lump of balsam gum to chew. The boy accepts it cautiously—he's still not used to the strong flavor. Fox settles down between them, tail outspread, nose between his paws. Smoke from the cooking fires hangs over the village, keeping away the insects that have started to arrive.

Spring is here. The rivers are melting: Geese and ducks are flying in from the south. Children chase around the wigwams, laughing and calling. And the woods echo to a shrill piping. Skusji'j cocks his head.

"What's that noise?" he asks.

Kwimu looks at him. It often worries him how much the Little Weasel does not know. This is Frog-Croaking Moon. In the boggy hollow down the slope thousands of mating frogs keep up a constant, deafeningly loud shrilling. "That noise is frogs," he explains. "Don't you have frogs where you come from?"

"*Sqoljk?*" The boy looks puzzled. He doesn't know this word. Kwimu hooks two fingers in his mouth and pulls a wide frog grin. He tries to make his eyes bug out. He croaks and hops. Skusji'j falls over, laughing. "Oh, now I get it. Frogs!"

Kwimu laughs too. Fox grins. The boys chew companionably.

After a while, Skusji'j says, "What are the little ones playing?"

The small children have formed a long line, hands on one another's shoulders. The leader calls out, "Look out for Swamp Woman!"

Kwimu's little sister, Jipjawej, is creeping up on them. "I'm so-o-o-o lonely," she wails. "I'm coming to get you!" She runs at the line, which swings away from her, shrieking, but trying to stay joined.

"There they go!" says Kwimu. The line breaks up as Jipjawej grabs one of them, and the children tumble over one another to get away from her. "Now *you've* got to be Swamp Woman!" she cries.

"Who is Swamp Woman?" asks the Little Weasel.

Kwimu wriggles his shoulders. "One of the Old Ones. She walks in the woods, especially in the boggy places. You know the curved fungus that grows on tree trunks? The children think those are her dishes. Some evenings she wanders around the edges of villages singing, trying to lure people away, because she's lonely. She doesn't mean to harm you, but she comes from the Ghost World, where the dead people go."

"It's like a game we play at home," says Skusji'j cheerfully. "Only in our game it's not Swamp Woman who does the chasing, it's a wolf."

"It isn't just a game."

"I know." Skusji'j hesitates, stiffens. "Kwimu—when we move from here, where will we go? Has your father decided?"

"I don't know. Not to the bay, this year. Perhaps to the lake instead."

Skusji'j spits the gum into his palm. "I'm not a baby, Kwimu. You don't have to pretend to me. I know what everyone's saying."

Kwimu is silent. Everyone used to speak of the bay as *we'kowpaq*—"the bay where we go in summer." Now people are calling it *skite'kmujue'katik*—"the place of ghosts."

"I've heard people talking." The boy bites his lip. "Your father and Kiunik went back there, didn't they? And they say—"

Kwimu sighs. "They say there is a great stir of the Other Ones in that quarter of the woods this spring. They heard strange singing, and the tree cutter, Kewasu'nukwej, striking

161

at the trees with his invisible ax. Grandmother thinks the Other Ones are angry because of your foreign ghosts."

The Little Weasel says with a shiver, "And is that why the *jenu* came? You never told me anything more about it."

"I know," says Kwimu slowly. After the terror of that midnight visit, no one wanted to speak of it. Speaking of such things may give them power. But now—

"Is that why it came? Will it come back?" Skusji'j fixes anxious eyes on Kwimu's face.

Kwimu shifts uneasily. He scoops up Fox and strokes his head. In fact, he shouldn't be telling stories now the thaw is here. Wintertime is the storytelling season. But Skusji'j needs to know these things. He lowers his voice. "Well, the *jenu* comes with the cold. . . ."

And, of course, his grandmother hears him. "Kwimu! Come inside right now, and bring your younger brother, too. You know what happens if you tell stories outside in springtime? The snakes all come and listen. You want that the camp should be full of snakes?"

The boys jump up—Skusji'j red with pleasure at being called Kwimu's younger brother—and go in.

It's warm inside, with a good smell of roasting meat. Grandmother has hung a big piece over the fire, suspended on a doubled cord that twists and untwists, first one way, then the other, so that it will cook evenly. Sinumkw and Kiunik are playing dish-dice at the back of the wigwam—banging the bowl down to make the dice jump, and laughing over the scores. Kiunik's young wife, Plawej, sits beside him, tickling the baby on her lap.

"Grandmother," Kwimu begs, "tell Skusji'j about the *jenu*."

Grandmother looks at the Little Weasel. Her eyes are shrewd, and her hair, bound back with strings of painted eel-skin sewn with shells, is almost as thick and black and strong as a girl's. She has just a few ash gray streaks at the temples.

"Why should the Little Weasel need this story?"

Kwimu's little brother screws up his face. He says in a rush, "Nukumij—Grandmother—why did the *jenu* come? Did it come like the Other Ones in the woods—because of what happened down at the bay?"

"Ah." Grandmother nods slowly. She reaches out a wrinkled hand and brushes his cheek. "Don't worry, little one. Don't worry, *nuji'j*. That was not your fault."

"Then it was the fault of his people," Kiunik interrupts sharply, looking up from the game. "I still say we should camp there this year. Pull down their houses and drive out their ghosts."

Sinumkw shakes his head. "Then they would wander loose in the woods. People should not interfere between Other Ones and ghosts."

"Ghosts don't frighten me," Kiunik declares. He rubs his hands over his scalp, flattening his black crest and letting it spring up again. He steals a sideways glance at Plawej, looking for her approval. She smiles at him and goes on singing softly to the baby:

"Let's go up onto the beautiful mountain
  And watch the little stars playing follow-my-leader,
  While Grandmother Lightning lights her pipe,
  And Grandfather Thunder beats his drum."

The baby gurgles, and Kiunik suddenly leans across and picks up his little son, tosses him into the air, catches him, and kisses him. He rolls back onto the fir boughs and lets the baby play with the big bear-claw necklace on his chest.

Grandmother shakes her head at him. "Those ghosts are not angry with us, Kiunik. The Other Persons are not angry with us. But they are disturbed, like bees swarming when a bear breaks into their nest. Keep away, and you will not be stung. But the *jenu*, now. The *jenu* is different, and I will tell you how."

Instead of beginning, though, she prods the meat to set it spinning again. Her face is troubled. At last she takes out her slender-stemmed pipe and hands it to Kwimu. "Light it. The smoke will help me."

Kwimu fills the pipe with a pinch of red willow bark mixed with lobelia leaves. He lights it and hands it respectfully to his grandmother. After drawing on it, she fans a little of the sweet smoke over the boys and says quietly, "This winter has been easy. There has been plenty to eat, plenty of game. Last winter, too. But we all remember the winter before that when it was not so good. There were many blinding snowstorms. The moose and the caribou were scarce. Everyone was hungry.

164

Some of the children died." She pauses. "Kwimu's little brother died."

Kwimu closes his mouth hard, shutting his tongue behind his teeth. He forces his face to remain steady, emotionless. The Little Weasel shoots him a sudden round-eyed glance.

Grandmother nods. "Yes. It's good for Kwimu to have a little brother again."

She smokes thoughtfully for a while. "And that's how life is: good winters and bad ones, times of hunger and times of plenty. But in the very worst winters, *Eula'qmuejit*, Starvation, comes tiptoeing through the villages, lifting the flaps of the wigwams, blowing his icy breath to chill the people's hearts.

"So long as we care for one another and share what food and warmth we have, he cannot harm us. But sometimes, if the winter is very hard, we may begin to see a terrible change creeping over one of our neighbors. He will not speak, or join in the songs we sing at the fireside to help us forget the hunger. He sits in the cold at the wall of the wigwam, glaring at the others with red-rimmed eyes, gnawing on his own knuckles, dreaming of human flesh. His heart is hardening into ice."

The thin smoke rises from Grandmother's pipe, ascending to the ghosts and the ancestors. "They say this happened to my mother's uncle. Perhaps, at first, he was afraid of himself— afraid of what he might do to his kinfolk. He ran off into the night, crazy as a wolf. At sunrise his brothers went after him, following his trail."

Everyone is quiet now, listening very seriously to Grand-mother's story.

"First they see his moccasins, kicked off, and the neat marks of bare feet running through the snow. Then they find his coat tossed into the bushes. He has pulled off his clothes to run naked in the biting wind that makes his brothers shudder and pull their faces deep inside their fur hoods. Soon they notice blood in his tracks. The sharp, broken crust of the snow has cut his feet, but instead of limping and stumbling, he's running faster and faster, till at last his footprints are so far apart he must be leaping like a moose. And it's then that the brothers see that the bare foot tracks are changing. Growing longer, larger. Broad and shapeless, like a bear's, with great gouging marks at the toes."

Kwimu's neck prickles, even though he's heard the tale before.

"Deep in the woods the brothers stop, half frozen. Around them the branches rub and squeak in the cold wind. They stare at the tracks, which are no longer the marks of human feet, and the hair rises on their necks.

"From far ahead, the wind carries a bone-chilling scream. It is too late to save their brother. They stand, afraid to go on, afraid to follow those great clawed marks. What if their quarry has already turned, racing back down the trail with terrible speed? What if he has begun hunting them? He will tear them apart and eat them raw.

"And that is what a *jenu* is, little son. Not a ghost, not one

of the Other Ones at all, but a man who has lost his human-
ity. Inside every *jenu*, they say, is a frozen heart, a little man-
shaped core of ice. Nothing else is left."

"Then what was it doing?" Skusji'j asks in a whisper. "What
was it looking for when it came to our village?"

"Food," says Grandmother simply. "A *jenu* is always hungry. It prowls in the woods all winter, looking for fat. If it finds
a village, it rips the bark from the wigwams and drags us out
as we would break open a beaver dam. It comes with the snow
and retreats with the snow. Only fire can harm it, because its
heart is made of ice."

"And is there more than one?" the Little Weasel asks.

Grandmother shrugs. "Never many. One winter when my
father was a boy, he heard two *jenu* calling to each other from
two blue mountaintops. 'Cold heart crying to cold heart,' he
told me. A dreadful, lonely sound. They are drawn to each
other, and yet they hate each other. If two *jenu* meet, they will
fight till one eats the other up."

"They eat each other?" asks the Little Weasel.

"A *jenu* eats anything," Kiunik says as he sits up, frowning.
"See what you've brought on us—you and your people."

"That's not fair," says Kwimu hotly. "It wasn't his fault that
the *jenu* came. It was bad luck. And good luck that
Grandmother knew what to do."

"Did I say it was the Little Weasel's fault?" Kiunik's dark
eyes flash. "I only say that the Jipijka'maq People came, and
the *jenu* followed. Yes: It was bad luck. Bad that his people

came to the bay. Bad that they killed each other there. I think bad luck breeds bad luck. And things like the *jenu* are drawn to it—like moths to a flame."

"You may be right," Sinumkw agrees. "That's why I don't want to stay there this year. We'll go to the lake instead."

"The lake's a good place, but so is the bay. We shouldn't abandon it," Kiunik argues.

"Kiunik," Plawej pleads softly. "Remember, it's the Place of Ghosts now."

"I'm not afraid!" Kiunik hands the baby back to his wife and swings to his feet. "And I'll not be driven out. Those are our hunting grounds, our traplines. I'll go there whenever I like."

He pushes out of the wigwam into the twilight.

"What a hothead," Sinumkw complains, pretending to be annoyed. But he looks after the tall young man with affectionate approval.

Grandmother lays her pipe aside and looks at the Little Weasel's worried face. "The *jenu* has gone now," she says soothingly. Her eyes are very kind and bright. "Gone far away into the north to live upon mosses and grass. Now is the hungry time for the *jenu*, while we grow fat. It can't endure summer. In the summer we are safe."

"Wonderful summer," says Kwimu, smiling, and he stretches his arms wide, and wider, as if to embrace the whole green, growing world.

CHAPTER 12

Serpent's Bay

Water *Snake* glided in over the shallows. Peer looked
down through clear water at thickets of groping weed,
and pale undulations of sandy gravel.

"Serpent's Bay!"

It was late afternoon. With four oars out, they were rowing
into the mouth of a river. It ran from a tuck in the hills and
flowed across meadowlands and a shelving gravel beach to
empty into the bay.

A black cormorant flew over. The trees made a dark fringe
around the bay, rising into wooded slopes. The clear voices of
Astrid and Hilde echoed off the shore.

"There are the houses!"

"I see them!" Then, after a pause: "But . . . they look empty."

Peer cupped his hands around his eyes. The two houses

he'd heard so much about squatted side by side on rising ground behind the meadowlands. They looked just like Ralf's farm: small and homely, with thick grassy roofs. The doorway of the nearest seemed to have been left half open.

Nothing moved on the shore. No dogs ran out, barking. No smoke rose from the houses, no voices called in excited welcome. Where was the busy, bustling settlement Peer had imagined, with Thorolf's little boy waving cheerily from the roof?

And there was no ship drawn up on the beach or moored in the river. "Where's the *Long Serpent*?" he asked.

Arnë heard, and twisted to look over his shoulder as he sat rowing in the bow. "Where's Thorolf, skipper?" he sang out. The oars swung raggedly as the other men tried to look, too. "Where's Thorolf?"

"Keep rowing," Gunnar grunted. "How should I know where he is? I'm not his master."

"They've gone." Hilde's voice was hollow. Peer knew what she was thinking. *Five years.*

"They'll be back," he said, as much to comfort himself as Hilde.

"I thought you said Thorolf had settled here," Tjorvi called to Gunnar.

"He must have changed his mind," Gunnar said shortly.

Tjorvi snatched a quick glance shoreward and his oar clashed with Magnus's.

"Watch your stroke," Magnus snarled.

170

"Concentrate, boys," Gunnar bawled. "We'll put her aground on the beach. Harald, steer for the houses. Pull!"

Harald leaned on the tiller. The men heaved. *Water Snake* slipped toward the shore. Her prow grated into the shingle.

The crew broke into cheers. The noise was oddly thin, rebounding off the shore. The dark line of trees seemed to advance, one marching step. Startled waterfowl clattered off across the tranquil river, honking alarms.

But the air was sweet, smelling of earth and forest—rich soil, black bog, fresh water. Peer filled his lungs and forgot about Thorolf. *We're here! We made it! We're in Vinland!*

"First one ashore . . . !" Arnë vaulted into knee-deep water, whooping. Peer leaped after him. Floki came tumbling after. Magnus methodically shipped his oar and clambered down. They splashed up onto the gravel. Land! Solid footing for the first time in weeks! It rocked under Peer, and he stumbled. Magnus laughed. "Aye, you'll be unsteady for a while. . . . Odd seeing the old ship from the outside again, ain't it?"

It was. Peer stood back, taking in *Water Snake* with new eyes. How huge she'd seemed coming into the jetty at Trollsvik. Now he just wondered how on earth he'd crossed the ocean in anything so cramped and small. Her paintwork looked even more faded than before. Her sail was down, an untidy crumple of sea-stained fabric. Ropes trailed everywhere. But the dragonhead glared inland with all its old, stiff-necked arrogance.

Loki's head and two front paws appeared over the side. He

jumped, hitting the water with a crash of spray, then swam steadily to shore. As soon as his paws touched, he bounded out and shook himself all over Magnus and Floki.

Hilde leaned out, looking down into the water. "Is it deep? Shall I jump?"

"Your dress will get soaked. I can carry you." Peer reached up to her. "If you sit on the edge, I'll take you on my back."

"Don't trust him, Hilde," said Arnë, wading up. "He'll drop you. Better come with me, I'm stronger." He flashed his wide, charming grin and flexed his arms in a mock show of strength.

"How strong do you think you need to be?" asked Hilde, laughing.

"Here's an easier way," Tjorvi called. He and Halfdan were manhandling a long gangplank. Once it was firmly settled between ship and shore, Tjorvi swept off his cap. "Would the Lady Hilde care to descend?"

"Thank you, Tjorvi." Hilde caught Tjorvi's hand and he walked her down. At the bottom she dropped him a curtsy. Tjorvi bowed. "See?" he said over his shoulder to Peer and Arnë. "She likes me best." He went back to help Astrid.

"Vinland," breathed Hilde. She staggered, and Peer saw her eyes widen. "I feel as if I'm still on the ship. Oh, that's strange."

"You'll soon get your land legs back if you walk around a bit," Magnus told her.

"Walk?" Hilde picked up her skirts. "Ha! Who'll race me to the houses?"

"Not me," said Astrid, stepping cautiously down the gang-plank. "I'm not running anywhere. Oops!" She checked as something small and light rushed past her skirts. With a patter of feet, a disturbance of the gravel beach, a swishing movement, it dashed into the grass.

Tjorvi's head jerked around. "Did you see that damn great rat come ashore?" he exclaimed. Peer smothered a smile.

And Hilde was off, too, tearing up the slope toward the houses, plaits flying. "Wait," yelled Peer. "It might not be safe." He plunged after her. On legs that seemed hardly to obey them, they ran across spongy meadows patched with bright green moss and pocked with boggy holes. Birds whirred up everywhere. Loki streaked ahead.

Hilde reached the nearest house and promptly disappeared inside. Peer flung himself at the door. It opened inward, protected by a rough wooden porch sticking out of the turf roof.

It was cold inside. The thick turf walls cut off all sound. The house smelled of frost-bitten earth and old smoke, and it was so gloomy Peer could hardly see. There were no windows. A little light splashed through the smoke holes in the roof, gleaming on Hilde's pale hair as she stood looking around. The only other light came from the doorway. Gradually Peer made out two lines of wooden posts supporting the rafters. Down the middle of the house ran the fire pit, edged with stones. At either side long sleeping benches lined the walls. At the far end, another doorway led into a small second room. That would be for Astrid and Gunnar, Peer guessed.

Or had this been Thorolf's house? He squinted about, but there was no clue to show who had been living here, no personal possessions, or bedding, or stores.

He jumped. Something bounded through the rafters like a squirrel, caroling, *"Ooh, a house, a house, a lovely house!"* It fetched up on a crossbeam just overhead, and peeped at Peer upside down, wispy hair trailing like old cobwebs.

"You like it?" asked Peer.

"A house!" the Nis sang.

"Where's the Nis?" Hilde squinted up, but the Nis had scuffled into an angle of the rafters. "I likes it, Peer Ulfsson," came its muffled voice, "but it needs—a spring-cleaning!" And it flung a bird's nest down at them, giggling.

"Well, the Nis approves." Peer brushed twigs out of his hair. "What do you think?"

"I can't wait to light the fire," said Hilde. "Hot food tonight!"

"Sleeping under a roof, warm and dry!" said Peer.

They looked at each other and laughed.

"I can't wait to explore. It looks so wild and beautiful. No farms, no fields. No sheep, no cows, no villages . . ."

"No Thorolf."

"He'll turn up," said Hilde optimistically. "You know, that first night on the ship when Astrid told me about Harald and Gunnar being outlawed, I thought I'd made a terrible mistake. I thought we should never have come. But I like all of the men now, don't you? Even Gunnar."

"Except Harald," said Peer.

"Except Harald," Hilde agreed. "Come on, we've spent long enough in here. I wonder which house we'll use. Shall we look at the other one?"

"Hey!" Peer raised his voice. "Nithing—want to see the other house?"

With a scuttle and a rush, the Nis was at the door. It scampered outside, and Peer was surprised to see that dusk was falling. The sun had sunk below the hills, and the wooded slopes looked dark and mysterious. Down by the ship, the men had lit a fire on the shore. Around the flames, the evening turned a deeper blue. One side of *Water Snake* gleamed, her red and black strakes warm in the firelight. On her other side was a black shadow double. The shadows were confusing, Peer thought. There seemed too many people crisscrossing in front of the fire.

"We should go and help," said Hilde. "Look, they're bringing things up already." Someone was coming slowly up the path, as if stiff from weeks at sea. His face was indistinct in the dusk. He turned aside, heading for the other house. Hilde called out, "Hello! Is that one ours?"

Whoever it was made no reply, but turned into the porch of the second house. Hilde shrugged. "He didn't hear me. It must be that one."

They walked across. Flat stones made a short path outside the door, which was shut. Peer lifted the latch. The Nis darted between his feet—and sprang back like a startled cat, all arched spine and splayed limbs. Peer saved himself by clutching at the doorpost. "What are you doing?" he cried.

The Nis was creeping backward, bristling. "Not nice," it squeaked. "Not a nice house at all, Peer Ulfsson. The other one is better!" It shook itself and shot decisively away.

With an odd feeling under his ribs, Peer shoved the door wide open and looked in. He didn't step over the threshold. Hilde craned over his shoulder.

It was just like the first house. Same long fire pit, same smoke holes, same dusty-looking benches and line of dim posts leading to a doorway at the far end.

This house was colder than the first. The air felt disturbed, as though someone had recently passed through. But it was completely empty.

Peer's skin crawled.

"Surely we saw—" Hilde broke off. "Or is he in the room at the far end?"

"In the dark? Hiding?" Peer looked at her. "Do you want to find out?"

"No," said Hilde hastily. "Let's go."

Peer nodded and tugged the door shut. "I think I agree with the Nis. I like the other house better."

Not quite running, they hurried back past the first of the houses. The fire crackling merrily on the beach looked like a beacon of safety.

Magnus and Halfdan were struggling up over the rise, carrying a big chest. They put it down, wiping their faces, and Magnus sat on it.

"That looks heavy," Hilde called. No one but Peer would have noticed the slight quaver in her voice.

"Women's stuff," Magnus sniffed. "Bed linen and clothes." He looked past the houses at the steep woods, and shivered. "I'd forgotten the forest was so close. Looks like it's got nearer. Looks like—" He stopped.

"What?"

"Like it's watching us." Magnus laughed to show he didn't really think so, but Hilde and Peer both turned to look back at the dark rampart of trees. Hilde froze.

"Peer. What's that, by the second house?"

In the gloaming it was hard to be sure—a blackish blur that could be a tall shrub or a forgotten woodpile. But it looked like a man, standing silently beside the door of the farthest house. Magnus sucked air through his remaining teeth.

"I see what you mean," said Peer with dry lips. "But I think it's just the shadow of the porch."

Floki arrived, bent double under a sack. Behind him came Gunnar and Astrid walking together, Gunnar stumping uphill with a seaman's straddling walk, Astrid stepping daintily, holding up her skirt.

"Aye, aye, it all looks much as it did," Gunnar said to her, sniffing at the air like an old dog. "I remember—"

He stopped, and seemed to choke. Astrid caught his arm. "There . . ." he croaked, staring up the slope. "Who's that—in the doorway?"

The man was gone as he spoke. Peer was sure now it was

only the shadow of the porch. Yet the house door was slowly opening, swinging back in a gesture of invitation. *Come in.*

"Peer, you didn't shut that door," said Hilde, alarmed by Gunnar's face. Gunnar turned straining eyes on Peer.

"Yes I did," Peer blurted. "I latched it."

Gunnar stumbled like a deer with an arrow in its heart. He clutched Astrid's shoulder. Her breath hissed as she braced him.

Mist had formed over the bay. A white moon was rising out of the sea. The temperature was dropping. Down in the marshes a duck quacked sharply. From somewhere in the shaggy hills came a distant, thin howl. *Wolf?*

Loki pricked his ears. Magnus and Halfdan stood tensely by the chest. They made no move to pick it up again. Their breath came in clouds. Floki, who had dropped his sack, looked around as if wondering whether to run back to the ship. Harald came loping up toward them. "What's wrong?"

Gunnar's teeth clacked. "I–I'm not well."

Harald pushed Astrid aside, dragging his father's arm over his shoulders. "You heard!" he snapped at the others. "I'll get him indoors. You women—make a fire in the house. Our own house, the first one," he added roughly, seeing Hilde about to ask. "The rest of you bring the stuff up from the ship."

Peer lay on his back, unable to sleep. Odd to lie on a bed that didn't move—odd to look up at a roof—odd to smell smoke after weeks of cold fresh air.

Gunnar and Astrid had retired into the little room at the end of the house. They had a grand bed, which had been brought up in pieces from the ship and slotted together. Astrid had covered it with linen sheets, a goosefeather bolster, and woolen blankets. Hilde was shut in with them, away from the men, in a small closet bed paneled off from the rest of their room. She had gone reluctantly, and Peer felt sorry for her. He was glad to be out here in the hall where the fire had a chance of warming the air.

The house was so cold. They'd piled branches and logs in the hearth and kindled an enormous blaze, but it would take days for the thick sod walls to warm through. The smoke hung in the rafters, drifting aimlessly as though it couldn't remember the way out. Around him his shipmates talked in whispers:

"... the skipper looks bad ..."

"... what d'you think he saw?"

"... any door can swing open ..."

"... aye, but it's odd it happened just then ..."

"... he does look bad ..."

"... the cold curse ..."

"... d'you think it's the skipper it's after, or all of us?"

"... shut up, Floki, I keep telling you ..."

At last the whispers died and the snores took over. Peer turned on his side and watched the long hearth, where the fire sank to a blue and yellow flicker over whispering embers. Every so often the powdery gray wood ash tumbled, opening gashes of glowing red. Then, across the hearth, apple green eyes gleamed. The Nis crept out on the hearthstones, warming its spindly hands.

It was a comforting sight. *At least we got here, all of us, alive and well.* He tried to keep watching the Nis. But sleep pounced on him like a hunting cat, and tossed him away into oblivion.

CHAPTER 13
Seidr

Hilde lay awake in her cramped little closet. It was hardly more than a hole in the wall with a wooden lining. The bed—a straw mattress on planks—wasn't long enough to stretch out on. If her legs were straight, she had to sit propped against the hard wooden panels. If she lay down, she had to curl up. The bedding, like the mattress, had come from the ship. Both were slightly damp and smelled of seawater.

It was pitch-black, not a scrap of light, and her toes were freezing. She envied Peer, asleep in the fire hall. She lay rubbing her feet together and wondered if she dared creep out to warm herself at the hearth. Surely the men would be asleep by now? But what about Astrid and Gunnar?

She fumbled for the edge of the panel and slid it back a few inches. It was as dark out there as it was in here, and just as cold. She listened for the sound of quiet breathing that would tell her Gunnar and Astrid were asleep.

Only they weren't; they were muttering together. Hilde tried to drag the panel closed again, but it stuck. She tugged at it, hearing Astrid murmur, "Gunnar, you mustn't fret. I'll look after you."

Gunnar said unsteadily—it sounded as if his teeth were still chattering: "How c-can you protect me?"

Hilde paused silently. She knew she shouldn't, but she had to listen to this.

"You men never know how to do things," said Astrid. "You should have run needles into his feet after he was shrouded. That would have stopped him walking."

Hilde went cold all over. *Is this Erlend we're talking about?*

Gunnar's laugh turned into a cough. "We didn't bother with shrouds," he said hoarsely. "Besides, it's too late now." He was silent for a moment, shivering—Hilde heard the air hissing between his teeth.

"I saw him on the ship," he whispered suddenly. "All swollen up and black."

"Hush!"

"If—if anything does come, Harald's sleeping in front of the doorway."

Is he indeed? Hilde thanked her stars she hadn't gone creeping out.

"And what can Harald do?" Astrid said softly. "You need me."

"I can't sleep. I daren't sleep."

"You can, and you will. Let me help you. There are ways. If you trust me."

"You're—my wife," said Gunnar. Then came an odd sound that puzzled Hilde, till she realized, her fingers curling, that it was a kiss. There'd been no intimacy on the ship. She'd never seen Gunnar kissing Astrid, or Astrid kissing Gunnar. But in private, of course they would. Frantically she wrenched at the panel. It wouldn't budge.

"Gunnar," said Astrid on a deep, purring note. "Give me your soul."

Hilde's heart almost stopped. Gunnar mumbled something. It sounded like "How?" or "Why?"

Astrid whispered rapidly, "Because I can take it from your lips with your breath, and keep it safe. I'll hide it away where no one can find it, I'll lock it all around with charms. No ghost can touch you then. You'll sleep safe. No dreams. Nothing will harm you...."

Her voice sank away. There was a long, busy silence. At last Astrid murmured, "Hush. Sleep. Sleep."

Gunnar didn't answer. Soon afterward Hilde heard a gentle snore.

She waited, damp, cold, and not at all inclined to sleep. The bedroom was still dark, but she heard the bedclothes stir, and a quiet footfall on the earth floor. She held her breath. In a moment she heard Astrid whispering very softly, *Those who sleep, sleep on still. Those who wake, wake.* The outer door creaked. A rosy glow of firelight brightened the room, and

Hilde caught sight of Astrid's dark shape slipping through the door. She must be stepping right over Harald, if he lay across the threshold. Moments later she returned, carrying a smoking stick with a glowing end. She pushed the door shut, and stopped.

She's seen the open panel.

But all Astrid could see would be a black gap in the wall. Hilde shut her eyes and breathed evenly. Brightness shone through her closed lids. She felt the heat of the glowing stick very near her face. She kept still—not afraid, but intensely curious.

The stick was withdrawn. Darkness and cold returned. Hilde's eyes flew open. Astrid was on the other side of the room, using the stick to light a shallow oil lamp. Now a single flame twinkled starlike in the gloom.

Astrid sat on the bed, and glanced down at Gunnar. From under the bolster she pulled out her goatskin bag, and hugged it to herself. She reached in, and drew out something small and square that gleamed bone yellow.

Hilde thought she knew what it was. She wriggled a little closer to the panel. *Yes. The little buzzing box.*

But Astrid set it aside and reached into the bag again. This time she came out with a package wrapped in linen. Inside was a mass of sheep's wool. From the middle of the sheep's wool she picked out something small and held it to the light. A hollow bird's egg that gleamed half transparent against the flame. With gentle fingers Astrid lifted the egg to her lips. She blew into it, a single puff. Pattering out some charm under her breath, she pulled the wool around the eggshell, and rewrapped it in the linen. Briskly now, as though everything was complete, she popped package and box back into her bag and slipped the bag back under the bolster. She reached for the lamp and pinched out the flame. Blackness flooded back.

Hilde knew what she'd seen. It was *seidr* magic that Astrid had been practicing. Hilde didn't know if she believed in it or not, or whether Astrid did. The important thing was that if Gunnar believed his soul was safely hidden, he'd be less afraid—of ghosts, or whatever other danger he thought was threatening him.

She curled up, shivering. Why shouldn't Astrid look after Gunnar? But it was all so black and secret. *You should have run needles into his feet after he was shrouded.* Hilde shuddered. *How can she talk like that? Especially about Erlend. How does she even know such a thing?*

She remembered how Astrid had said, "There's troll blood in me," and "Of course I tell lies—how else do I get what I want?"

What *did* Astrid want? Could you ever trust somebody with troll blood?

Hilde woke with a jerk of panic. Why was it so dark? She flung out a hand and felt it knock against wood.

Someone knocked back. "Did you sleep soundly?"

It was Astrid. She was carrying the oil lamp, and its beadlike flame reflected little points of fire in her eyes.

Hilde sat up, noticing that Astrid was fully dressed. She was about to say, *Not very well.* Then she thought Astrid might have reasons for asking. "Yes, thanks," she said cautiously, rubbing a cricked neck. "Is it early? It's so dark."

"Only in here," said Astrid. "It's light outside. And the fire's burning well in the hall. Listen, Gunnar's feverish. He should stay in bed. Boil some water, will you? I'll make him another drink of willow bark."

Chilled and stiff, Hilde shoved back the panel and swung her feet out of her little cubbyhole. Hot, fresh water sounded good. She longed for a wash. *And if I have to sleep in here, I need warmer bedding,* she thought as she pulled her dress on over her linen smock.

The fire hall smelled of warm smoke and salty, sweaty men. Harald, Peer, and Tjorvi were up. The rest were still in their blankets. Harald was combing his hair and barely lifted his head as Hilde came out. Tjorvi sat cross-legged on the bench, spooning groute from a wooden bowl. Peer was putting more wood on the fire. He looked up at her, his fair hair ruffled, a streak of charcoal on his jaw, and his face lit with sweet, uncomplicated pleasure.

Hilde was used to people being glad to see her. Back home, Ma, Pa, the twins, even the babies greeted her every morning with warmth and love. Even the quarrels were loving quarrels. She'd never thought much about it. She'd taken it for granted.

Now, after a night spent in Astrid and Gunnar's cold dark

room, here was Peer, simply happy to see her, and showing it. It was like stepping into sunlight and fresh air. A strange thought crossed her mind. *We belong together.*

"Hilde." He kicked a log farther into the flames and came toward her. His lanky frame was filling out: He was broader across the shoulders than she'd thought. He moved lightly, with grace. *I once said he looked like a heron. Not anymore. . . .*

"Hilde?" he asked, puzzled.

She jumped. How long had she been staring at him, dumb as a post?

"Is something wrong?" He threw a glance at the dark doorway behind her, ready to tackle anyone who might have upset her.

"I'm fine." She pulled herself together. "I'm fine, but Gunnar's not well. Astrid says he shouldn't get up."

"Still ill?" Harald looked up sharply. "You should have said so immediately!" He vanished into the far room with a swirl of his cloak. Hilde and Peer crowded around the door.

Gunnar sat facing them, leaning against the headboard, red-eyed and pale-faced, wrapped in his wolfskin cloak. Astrid sat on the bedside, singing softly.

Harald gave her a dark glance and knelt on the other side of the bed. "Father." His voice was full of tender respect. "Can't you get up?"

"He'd much better not," said Astrid.

"I didn't ask you," said Harald with a snap. "Father?"

"I—I tried." Gunnar lifted his hand to his throat as if it

hurt. "Dizzy. Listen, son . . ." He muttered hoarse instructions. *Water Snake*'s boat should be unloaded for use in the river. Some of the men should go hunting. . . .

"Yes, Father. But get up! Don't lie in bed like a woman. Fight it off. Get out into the sunshine."

"Fight it off?" said Astrid scornfully. "How can he do that? There are things you can't fight with a sword, Harald." Her voice dropped into a sinister singsong. "Bodiless things. Insubstantial things. Things you had better leave to me."

"*What . . . things?*" said Harald between his teeth.

Astrid's face was a mask of innocence. "Fever, of course. What did you think?"

They stared at each other across the bed. At last Harald said, "Just cure him quickly." He strode out. Peer and Hilde hastily drew back to let him pass.

Astrid turned back to Gunnar, stroking his forehead. "I'll sing to you again."

Gunnar nodded wearily. His head rolled back under her fingers; his eyelids flickered shut. Peer and Hilde tiptoed back to the fire.

Peer was laughing. "I think Astrid won that bout," he whispered.

Hilde nodded impatiently. "Peer, I have to tell you about last night."

But before she could begin, Magnus sat up and stretched. With his arms widely spread, he used one foot to prod Floki in the ribs. "Wake up, Floki, you lazy young brute." He gave

Hilde his gap-toothed grin. "Morning, Hilde, my lass. What have you got for a starving man's breakfast? Or has Tjorvi scoffed it all?" Then he cocked his head to one side, and his brow furrowed. "What's going on in *there*?"

Astrid's voice floated out of Gunnar's room, half singing, half chanting:

> "*I know a black stone, out in the sea.*
> *Nine waves wash over it, three by three.*
> *Out, sickness!*

> "*I know an oak tree, out in the wood.*
> *Nine crows sit in it, croaking for blood.*
> *Out, sickness!*

> "*From breast, from body, from hand, from heart,*
> *From eyes, from ears, from every part—*
> *Out, sickness!*"

"Troll girl. Witch woman," said Magnus darkly. "Brrr! It makes you shiver."

CHAPTER 14

Disturbances and Tall Tales

Gunnar was ill for days. Astrid and Harald clashed constantly over his care till Peer wondered if it was more about curing Gunnar or scoring off each other. Mostly Astrid won, but Harald became dangerously sullen. When Gunnar recovered enough to get out of bed, he was very weak, and spent his days shivering over the fire with Astrid in attendance. Harald kept urging him to go outside, but he seldom set foot beyond the door, though the weather was now gloriously hot. Summer seemed to arrive all at once. Wild roses, a curious bright pink, flowered in tangles around the salty marshlands, and down on the shore purple pea blossoms twined over the dry sandy stones above the tide line.

There was food everywhere. Flocks of ducks and geese nested in the marshlands, and more flew in every day. Harald and Arnë took bows and shot down dozens. Salmon were spawning, running upstream in such numbers that Tjorvi joked, "You could almost walk across the river on their backs." Strange birds sang in the bushes. Strange animals were glimpsed in the woods. At night, flashing fireflies wandered silently in the air. The Nis found them too tempting to resist. It went out every evening and caught handfuls, releasing them indoors to drift among the rafters like bright sparks. Tjorvi put one in Hilde's hair, where it winked off and on like a green jewel.

Summer drew on. The settling in was over. With the house roof steaming and smoking, and chickens running in and out, and Loki sleeping in the sunshine, Vinland felt almost like home.

But at home it would be harvest time. Here there were no fields to tend. Peer wondered when they'd start felling trees, but Gunnar seemed in no hurry. For much of the time, the men just sat about, sunning themselves or talking.

And Thorolf's house remained empty, a cold, silent reminder of how alone they all were, how far from other people. Every morning Peer gazed across the bay, hoping to see a square sail making its way in from the gulf. Where were they, Thorolf and his son Ottar and the crew of the *Long Serpent*? When would they come back?

One evening as they sat around the fire the latch flew up. Hilde burst in from outside, eyes wide and black. She doubled over, gasping. "There's someone out there! I was filling my buckets at the stream, and I heard something moving in the trees—farther up the slope. And I'm sure I heard singing."

Harald leaped up, grabbing a bow and a fistful of arrows. He ran outside, and everyone but Astrid and Gunnar followed him.

It was nearly dark. The wooded slope behind the settlement was a wall of shadows, full of creeping sounds, sleepy birdcalls, snapping twigs—all strange, all mysterious. As they approached the trees, the mosquitoes came out to meet them in stinging clouds.

"There's something there all right. Loki knows," said Peer. Loki was staring into the trees, hackles up. He backed off, whining and growling.

"Skraelings, perhaps," Magnus muttered. "Lurking there, watching us . . ."

The slope was almost as steep as a cliff. The stream cascaded down a deep cut between mossy banks, cluttered with fallen branches. The sound of rushing water filled their ears—and then the sound of something crashing and sliding downhill.

Peer's hair stood on end. Would he see Skraelings at last?

"Bear!" Tjorvi yelled. Out from the trees plunged a shambling, sloppy-coated black bear. It saw them and reared up, paws loosely dangling. Peer saw its curved black nails, the white spot on its chest, and its small, narrow-set, blinking eyes.

Harald's bow sang. His arrow flew just as the bear shook its flat head and dropped onto all fours. The arrow vanished, and Harald swore, fumbling for another. But the bear was gone, melting into the dark bushes as swiftly as any deer.

"Well now," Tjorvi said to Harald. "If you'd stung that bear, young master, it would have charged us. And then what would you have done?"

Harald's teeth gleamed. "I would have stepped back and let you deal with it, Tjorvi. You look like a bear yourself. It would probably mistake you for its mother."

Halfdan and Magnus snickered. Tjorvi pretended to scratch his head and said, "I've always fancied a bear-claw necklace."

"But I heard singing," Hilde said. They all looked at her.

Arnë put his arm across her shoulders. "I don't think you could have, Hilde. Bears don't sing."

"I know that, Arnë. And I know what I heard."

"Mosquitoes," suggested Tjorvi helpfully after a moment.

"Don't be silly!" Hilde bent crossly for the buckets she had dropped, but Peer picked them up for her.

"Whatever it was, Hilde, please don't fetch water by yourself again."

Harald's voice sliced through the dusk. "Why don't you fetch it? You look a proper milkmaid with those buckets."

Magnus choked and slapped his thigh. A hot flush crawled under Peer's skin, but he knew it wouldn't show in the dark.

"What a shame we didn't bring any goats," Harald mocked. "Can you milk, Barelegs? I'm sure you can."

He wants a fight. With difficulty, Peer controlled his temper. "Of course I can. If I meet the bear, I'll milk it for you, shall I?"

There was a split second of silence, and he knew he'd shut Harald up. Tjorvi burst out laughing. He threw his arm around Peer's shoulders, roaring, "Milk the bear! Excellent! That was very good, young 'un. Here, give me one of those buckets. Bear's milk! I like it."

With a quick, dancing step, Hilde caught up with Peer. "Good for you. That showed him!" But Peer's flash of triumph was already fading.

He'll make me pay.

Was there no way of dealing with someone like Harald and winning?

Whizz! Whizz! Whizz!

A metallic rasping sound greeted Peer's ears as he and Floki came out of the house together the next morning, heading for the fish traps on the shore. Harald sat on a cut log near the porch, sharpening his sword. He hissed between his teeth, tilting the blade this way and that so that the sun flashed off it in brilliant winks.

It was an ominous sight. Peer was going past without speaking, but Floki stopped in delight. "Your sword, Harald! Bone-biter. You've got her out again. My, what a beauty." He stared at the bright, dangerous thing, obviously longing to touch the sword, just as obviously not daring to ask. "I suppose it cost a lot, a sword like that," he added wistfully.

Harald glanced up, shaking his hair back. "Yes, it cost my father a pound of silver."

Floki gasped like a fish, and Peer just managed to keep his own jaw from dropping. *A pound of silver!* More than the price of a really good horse. *A pound of silver!* He looked at his own little silver ring, the most valuable thing he had. How much silver was in that? A fraction of an ounce. How long had his father scrimped and saved to buy it?

Harald laid the whetstone down. He lifted the blade, shutting one eye to look down its length. "My father always gets me the best," he said to Floki. "Pattern welded, see? Gilded crossbar. And the hilt's bound with silver wire. But the balance—that's where the skill comes in." He reversed it neatly and offered the hilt to Floki.

Floki flushed till even his ears turned scarlet. He took the sword reverently, one hand clutching the hilt, the other palm out under the blade.

"Try her," said Harald. "Go on, give her a swing." He gave Peer a bright look. "Not too close to Barelegs, though. We know what happens if he gets a fright."

With sly glee, Floki prodded the sword at Peer's ankles. Peer stepped back. "Stop it, Floki."

"He's scared!" Floki grinned. "How do I look?" He bared his teeth in a ferocious snarl.

"Floki," said Harald lazily, "with a sword in your hand, you frighten even me."

Peer's lips tightened. But Floki didn't notice the mockery. He raised the sword and slashed it through the air. "Hey, look at me!" he cried. "Magnus, Tjorvi, look at me."

"Mind you don't take your own leg off," growled Magnus from the porch.

Tjorvi emerged, ducking low under the lintel, his shock of hair white in the sun. Yawning and stretching his arms, he watched Floki chop down invisible enemies, yelling, "Ya! Hey! Take that!"

Hilde came out with a pail of dirty water and stopped to stare. Encouraged by the audience, Floki whirled ever more wildly till his toe caught on a loose turf, and he fell flat on his face. Everyone burst out laughing. Harald strolled forward. Floki scrabbled for the sword on all fours, and handed it back. He knelt in front of Harald, gazing up with an expression of raw adoration on his silly red face. Peer stopped laughing. This wasn't funny anymore.

"I'm your man, Harald." Floki pawed at Harald's knees. Harald stood, hand on hip, smiling easily down at him, the picture of nobility. Peer's toes curled. There was still a scar beside Floki's mouth where Harald had hit him. Didn't he have any pride?

"'F only I could have a sword like that," Floki mumbled. "But I never will."

"If we make our fortunes, you can buy one," Halfdan suggested.

"A lad like him doesn't need a sword," said Magnus scornfully. "He's got a knife and an ax. What more does he want? Better spend his money on a cow."

"Or a wife," said Halfdan, grinning. Floki looked downcast.

"Here's some advice," said Tjorvi solemnly. "If you do get yourself a sword, Floki, there's something else you ought to get first."

"A shield?" Floki asked.

"Na, na." Tjorvi winked at Peer. "You ought to get yourself a life-stone."

"What's one of them?"

"A life-stone? Ah, it's a wonderful thing to have. If you've got a life-stone, no matter what happens to you, you won't die. Sickness, battles, wounds—no matter. Haven't you ever heard of one?" Tjorvi sounded amazed. He looked around. "*You've* all heard of a life-stone, haven't you?" The men grinned, smelling a joke.

"A mate of mine had one once," Tjorvi went on. "He went to an awful lot of trouble to get it, too. He knew where to look—in an eagle's nest."

Floki listened, wide-eyed. Several of the men were chuckling.

"So my mate shins up the cliff to the nest and grabs the life-stone. There's a terrible fight, the eagle squealing and slashing him with its claws—but with the life-stone in his fist, he slithers safely down. Then he has a proper look at it.

"*My,* he thinks, *that's a bit small. How'm I going to keep it safe? I know—I'll get the wife to sew it into my armpit.*"

"And did she?" asked Hilde demurely.

"She certainly did," said Tjorvi, straight-faced. "Sewed it into his left armpit. He was right-handed, you see. And after that, my mate was as safe as houses. His lucky life-stone got him through all sorts of adventures without as much as a single scratch."

"Has he still got it?" demanded Floki excitedly.

Tjorvi sighed. "That's the sad part. He went on a long voyage, you see. Well, there was a terrible storm, and right out in the middle of the ocean, the ship was wrecked. Every soul on board drowned. Except him. He couldn't drown, could he? He had the life-stone."

"What was sad about that?" Peer asked.

Tjorvi opened his eyes wide. "He had to walk home along the bottom of the sea, and it took him years and years. Oh, a horrible time he had—with sea monsters trying to swallow him, and the fish nibbling at him all the way. At long last he staggered out on shore, and the first thing he asked was for one of us to open his armpit and take out the stone. We did it, of course—anything for a friend—and as soon as it was out of him, the poor fellow crumbled into dust."

They were still laughing at Tjorvi's tall tale—and at Floki, who wanted to know where the life-stone was now, and whether Tjorvi had it—when Halfdan cried out, "Listen! D'you hear that?"

And then they all heard it—the unmistakable ringing chop of an ax, far away in the forest: a flat clap followed by an echo.

It repeated and repeated.

"Someone's cutting wood. But who?"

"Skraelings at last." Harald was on his feet, his eyes bright and narrow, the sword swinging in his hand. "Let's go and find them."

"Let's kill 'em!" Floki yelped. Magnus cuffed his ear. No one else paid him any attention. The prospect of doing something was attractive.

"I'll come!" said Arnë.

"And me," Tjorvi rumbled. He patted his hard, flat stomach. "Too much food and too little exercise. I'm getting fat."

Everyone wanted to come, and Harald had to choose. "Halfdan, Tjorvi, Arnë . . . Not you, Barelegs," he said to Peer, who hadn't offered. "Floki, you can come if you like."

They set off into the trees in high spirits. Magnus stood at the house door and shook his head. "There goes a lad who needs to be kept busy."

"Oh, I wish I could go with them," Hilde exclaimed. "I wonder what the Skraelings are really like? Do you think they'll find them?"

Magnus scratched his stubbly chin. "If not, let's hope young Harald finds another bear or something. 'Cos he hasn't got enough to do."

It was oddly quiet around the houses with half of the men missing. By sunset, they had not returned. Magnus stood outside, wafting away mosquitoes and staring at the woods.

"Shoulda thought they'd be here by now," he kept muttering. "P'raps I shoulda gone along. Floki's got no sense. Still, Tjorvi'll prob'ly keep an eye on him. Don't you reckon?"

Gunnar kept sending Astrid and Hilde to the door to look for Harald coming back. No one could sit still. Peer and Hilde and Magnus walked up to the spot where they'd met the bear, listening for the sounds of their friends coming out of the forest. The chopping had long since died away. Branches cracked, birds cried in strange voices. On the edge of hearing, some creature wailed, a wordless, wistful call. It dragged on Peer's nerves. *Find me. I'm lost, I'm lonely.*

And then: "Ahoy, there!"

This time it was a real shout. Magnus sighed in relief. "That's them. Here they are, look, coming from the river. This way!" he bellowed.

Exhausted, swearing, and plastered with mud, the expedition limped out of the bogs beside the river and up onto the firmer ground below the trees.

"Gods!" said Arnë. "I'm glad that's over. We've wandered for miles." He looked back and shuddered. "I've felt eyes on my back all day."

"And insects!" exclaimed Tjorvi. "Phew!" His eyes were almost swollen shut with mosquito bites. "Everyone got bitten, but they seemed to like me best."

"It's been horrible," Floki whined, scratching at an angry lump on his face.

Tjorvi gave Halfdan a shove. "It was Halfdan's fault. He

kept seeing things." Peer had never seen Big Tjorvi in such a bad mood.

"What things?" asked Hilde.

Halfdan looked unhappy. "Someone slipping between the trees. With long hair covering the face. Sort of . . . greenish. Arnë saw it, too. He thought it was a woman."

"I was never sure," said Arnë quickly.

"So we followed this 'person' till we lost it," Tjorvi growled, "and ended up in a stinking bog, and floundered around for hours. Finally we stumbled across a stream—"

"He means that. Floki fell into it," Arnë added.

"Which led us down to the river. And thankful I am that it's the right river." Tjorvi still seemed unusually angry. "I thought we'd never get back."

Harald had said nothing so far. He was wiping his sword in the long grass. His hair trailed over his shoulders in long muddy draggles, and his legs were mired to the knee. A spirit of mischief rose in Peer. "So you found no Skraelings after all. What a pity!"

Harald glanced up. "Oh, but we did. That was the only thing that went right."

"You found Skraelings!" Peer felt sudden deep alarm.

"Just two," said Arnë. He sounded rather odd. "Camped a mile or so back along the river, under a sort of bark shelter. We saw the fire they'd lit."

"What happened?" Hilde cried. "Could you talk to them? Were they friendly?"

"We didn't have time to find out," said Tjorvi carefully, "before Harald killed them."

Harald finished cleaning his sword and rammed it back in its sheath. "Exciting, wasn't it?" he said cheerfully. "Floki almost wet himself. Look at this." He tapped his chest. Slung from his neck, a rope of splendid white claws gleamed in the dusk, each one as long as a finger. "Skraeling work. A bear-claw necklace: the only thing worth taking. Who said he wanted one of these? You, Tjorvi? Too bad; you'll have to be quicker next time. Come on, it's suppertime, and I'm starving."

CHAPTER 15

A Walk on the Beach

He killed them?" Hilde stared after Harald in disbelief. The thick dusk prickled with stars. Mosquitoes whined about their ears and bit, savagely, drawing blood.

Halfdan muttered, "They might have attacked us."

"Certainly," said Tjorvi with heavy sarcasm. "It pays to be careful with odds like that. Two of them, and only five of us."

"Did they look dangerous?" Hilde asked in a thin, strained voice.

"A couple of young fellows cooking fish over a campfire?" Tjorvi snorted. "They hardly had time to look around, let alone go for their weapons."

"Couldn't you do something?" Hilde cried. "Arnë!"

"It was so quick," said Arnë glumly. "I mean, Harald wasn't fooling around. The one with the bear-claw necklace stood up—maybe he thought we were going to say something. I thought so too, but Harald just—he just . . ." He stopped and looked down.

"They were Skraelings!" Halfdan shouted. "Outlaws, for all we know. Spies, even. Harald did the right thing. He kept us safe."

Tjorvi pushed him aside and stamped past. Halfdan ran after him, arguing. Magnus smacked Floki around the ear and said gruffly, "Come along, lad, and clean up."

Peer held back. He didn't want to go in with them, to the noise and the smoke and the smells. He didn't want to be anywhere near Harald. "There'll be a breeze on the shore," he said to Hilde. "Fewer mosquitoes. Let them get their own supper. Come for a walk with me and Loki."

"All right," she said quietly.

Arnë glanced over his shoulder, but Tjorvi said, "That's right, get along with the lad, Hilde. We can manage to ladle stew out of the pot by ourselves." He dropped a swollen eyelid at Peer and hustled Arnë ahead of him through the door.

Peer looked at Hilde. "Are you upset?"

She folded her arms and hunched her shoulders. "He killed two men and stole from the bodies. I can't believe none of them stopped him . . ."

"It wouldn't be easy to stop him," Peer said gently. He put his arm around her, and she turned to him with a small sob.

The door reopened, and out came Astrid. "Heigh-ho!" she yawned. "Gunnar's all over his darling boy. Have you heard what he did? Horrible, isn't it?"

"It's awful," said Hilde passionately.

"That's what I said." Astrid eyed her. "Were you surprised? You ought to know Harald by now. He's killed real people, you know, not just Skraelings."

"Skraelings are people!"

"Yes—well—never having seen one, I can't say. Are you off for a walk? I think I deserve a break. Are you going to the shore? I'll come too."

There was nothing to be done. With poor grace, Peer led the way along the path they'd trodden to the shore. The two girls walked behind him.

"Oof," Astrid sighed. "It's good to get out. I've been cooped up all day."

"You could have got out before," said Hilde. "There are plenty of outside jobs to do. Carrying water, stacking firewood ..."

"I'm busy looking after Gunnar," said Astrid coolly.

The grassland halted at the shore in a sudden edge of turf, a foot or two high, eroded by winter storms and cut here and there by tiny black brooks that tinkled out of the marsh to vanish in the shingle. Peer jumped onto the stones. Astrid teetered on the brink behind him. "Help me down."

"For goodness' sake," said Hilde. "Jump! It's nothing."

"I might hurt myself. Please, Peer," Astrid said sweetly. Biting his lip, he reached up for her and swung her down. She was lighter than he expected, despite being so tall, and her beautiful hair brushed his face. She clung to his arm as they picked their way across oval pebbles to the level beach. Hilde followed. Peer couldn't guess what she was thinking.

The sea was a glimmering curve with a milk white rim. At the edge of the tide they walked in a film of water, where the gravel stirred underfoot, sucked back and forth by advancing and retreating ripples. Pebbles knocked and turned, clattered and shifted, as though a myriad little people were busy among the stones.

"How bright the stars are," Astrid said to Peer. "Do you know their names?"

"Some of them." She was still holding his arm. He couldn't shake her off. He looked up. "Over the headland, that's the Wagon. See? And if you follow up from the two stars on the end, they'll lead you to the Nail. That marks north."

"The Nail's much lower here than it is at home," said Hilde.

"Because we've come south," said Peer.

"I thought we'd come west," Astrid complained.

Hilde rolled her eyes. "And south, too. How can you not know that, Astrid?"

"I leave all that sort of thing to the men," said Astrid, unperturbed. She released Peer's arm. "I think I'll go and sit on that rock."

She wandered off. Peer looked sideways at Hilde, who was staring at the softly splashing sea. "Are you upset?" he asked again.

"A bit." She crossed her arms. "*I leave all that sort of thing to the men*. Astrid doesn't care about anything, does she? She leaves nearly everything to someone else. Cleaning to the Nis. Cooking and fetching and carrying to me."

"She looks after Gunnar," said Peer.

"I thought Vinland would be a wonderful adventure. Remember Pa first telling us about the Skraelings? People with brown skin, he said, and black hair. I've tried to imagine them ever since." She shivered. "And now I'm imagining blood."

Peer was silent.

"I'll never get to see them now, will I? Anyway," she added bitterly, "I was stupid to expect adventures. I'm only here to keep Astrid company. I'm a girl: I belong in the house."

Peer almost laughed. "That's not how I think of you."

"Isn't it?" Hilde asked. "Then how do you think of me?"

"How can you ask? I think you could do anything. I think you're braver than I am."

She gave him a grateful smile, and he glowed. At last, at last, he'd said part of what he wanted.

"I'm not so brave," Hilde said. "These days I'm almost afraid of going to bed at night. . . ." Side by side they walked on, and he listened, entranced by her closeness, her pale flyaway hair silver in the moonlight, her smooth skin and clear eyes. ". . . You don't know what it's like sharing that little room with them. Gunnar has terrible dreams. I hear him waking, and crying out, and Astrid trying to calm him." She stopped and turned. "And there's something I've wanted to tell you for ages, only we've never been on our own, I've never had the chance . . ."

His heart kicked. His blood leaped. Hilde loved him. She was about to tell him so—

Then he heard what she was saying: ". . . and Astrid was working *seidr*. She hid Gunnar's soul to keep it safe. She has a bone box with a little voice inside that tells her things. I've heard it humming." She stared at him, waiting for a reaction. "Peer, are you listening?"

He drew a hand across his eyes. "Tell me that again."

She did so, with dogged patience. "And Astrid does have troll blood. I was supposed to keep it a secret, but Halfdan and Magnus and Floki all seem to know; it's just that they daren't tell Gunnar. You and I know what trolls are like, Peer. I don't know whether to believe anything she says."

The letdown had been severe. Peer's voice shook as he sought for some kind of answer. "Aren't you rather hard on Astrid?"

Hilde choked. "If you'd been there—if you'd heard her telling Gunnar to stick needles in a corpse's feet . . ."

"Yes, it sounds bad." Since they had to talk about Astrid, Peer set his mind to it. "But what about Gunnar? He's not Harald's father for nothing. What has Astrid done that's so wrong? We know what Gunnar did: killed somebody—him and Harald together. And the way they did it must have been pretty dreadful, or why is he so afraid?"

Hilde began to speak, and stopped.

"And you know," said Peer slowly, "the more I think about it, the more I wonder whether Thorolf left because Gunnar and Harald quarreled with him. We've only Gunnar's word for it that Thorolf ever meant to settle here. He might have decided that living with Gunnar and Harald wasn't worth the trouble."

"Do you think he won't come back?" said Hilde quietly.

"I wonder. And I've noticed something else. I've noticed that when we talk about Thorolf, it's always you and me, or sometimes Arnë or Tjorvi. The others, Magnus and Floki and Halfdan, who sailed with Gunnar before—they don't say anything. Maybe they know something we don't."

Hilde thought about it, and shook her head. "Oh, Peer, that can't be right. Why would it be a big secret? Look at Floki, he can't keep his mouth shut about anything. If Gunnar and Thorolf had fallen out, we'd have heard all about it by now."

"I suppose that's true," said Peer. "I hope so. I want to see Thorolf as much as you do."

Hilde started. Something galloped past them, kicking up splatters of wet gravel. "It's only the Nis," said Peer. He could just see it, careering across the beach in happy circles. "Out for a run."

The moon was up, clear of the headland, casting sharp shadows. The beach ticked, clicked, pattered, as though thousands of little people were pecking and hammering among the stones. Peer looked harder. The gravel danced in patterns.

The Nis dashed past again, jinking and skipping, making

little rushes here and there, picking up stones. "What are you doing?" Peer called.

"Playing with the *wiklatmu'jk*," the Nis cried in a high-pitched, reedy little voice like a birdcall.

"What did it say?" said Hilde.

"Look!" Peer pointed. Ahead, on a patch of smooth sand, someone had laid out figures in lines of pebbles. One had legs, one had a triangular skirt. To the side was a comical short-legged animal with a stiff tail. Hilde and Peer bent over them.

"That's us," whispered Hilde. "Us and Loki. Did the Nis do it?"

Peer shook his head. He straightened up, his face alive with delight. "Hilde, the whole beach is covered with *tiny* people."

She stared.

"I've been seeing them all along," he went on. "I just didn't notice. They're everywhere. But I can only see them when I'm not looking straight."

Hilde half shut her eyes and peeped out of the corners. Nothing. Wait, there was something scurrying through the gravel. "It's crabs," she said.

"It isn't," Peer insisted. "They're all over the place, knocking and chipping at the pebbles. Don't try so hard. Try looking at them the way you look at a faint star."

The moonlit beach didn't change at all, but something happened behind her eyes. For a second she was doing something very difficult: seeing the stones alive with hurrying, busy little creatures, all tugging and pushing and rearranging the pebbles, making patterns and scattering them again. She saw their little black shadows, the size of her thumb.

She lost the way to do it, and they were gone. The picture of the girl and the boy and the dog was gone, too. In its place was a serpentine curve, with four little lines descending from it, and one tall line sticking up from the middle.

"A snake with legs?"

"It's a ship," Peer said suddenly. "See, the hull and the dragon-head and the mast—and those things that look like legs are the oars. It's our ship—*Water Snake*. They're making pictures of what they see."

"What did the Nis call them? The weeklat something?"

"*Wiklatmu'jk.*"

"The weeklatmoojig," Hilde repeated. "How does it know?"

"It comes out playing every night," Peer said. "It's made friends." He swung around, scanning the bay, forest, and stars with shining eyes. "Ralf was right. This is a wonderful country."

"Let's ask the Nis about them," said Hilde. "Where's it gone?"

They had been slowly walking along the curve of the bay. Ahead of them a line of rocks ran out from the southern headland. The sea had scooped hollows around the bases of the rocks, which the retreating tide had left full of water, almost invisible in the moonlight. The Nis was scrambling about between the tide pools. Peer could hear distant giggles, and the occasional *clop!* and *splash!* as it tossed pebbles into the water.

"Let's run!"

He caught her hand. Leaving trouble behind, they pounded across the beach, Loki racing beside them. They clattered over flat stones that slid and clinked like coins, splashed, shockingly, across a flat shining stretch that turned out to be water, so that Hilde shrieked and laughed as the spray flew. Panting, they ran, their lungs pumping, their hearts thumping—tugging each other along by the swinging clasp of their joined hands, till at last Hilde stepped on the hem of her dress and fell over, pulling Peer after her. Loki pounced on them both, play-biting.

Breathless with laughter, they sat up. Hilde brushed gravel off her dress and flicked the bigger bits at Peer, till she saw that he had stopped laughing and was looking at her in a way . . . a way that made the back of her neck shiver. She got up quickly. *Why am I feeling like this? It's only Peer.*

"Look, we're at the rocks," she said at random. "We'd better turn back. Astrid is miles behind. Let's call the Nis and go."

"Hilde." He was still looking at her. "Please listen to me."

Hilde suddenly saw two things with perfect clarity. The first was that she'd known all along that Peer still loved her. Only she hadn't let herself know, because it was easier— because she wasn't sure how she felt. The second was that Peer was no longer the gawky lad who had kissed her so clumsily last year. He had changed. No, he hadn't, he was the same as ever, he had just . . . grown up. She faced him, twining her fingers into her apron. "All right then—go on."

She wasn't used to being shy with Peer. It came out wrong. It sounded petulant and brusque. Then she felt ashamed, and shyer than before. Peer winced. He drew in a deep breath— she saw his chest heave—but before he could speak, the Nis appeared, prancing over the rocks. It leaped onto the beach, prattling excitedly. "Come and see what I has found!"

The breath left Peer in a defeated whoosh. The Nis skipped about, bright-eyed, cracking its knuckles. It darted back to the rocks. "A present for you, Peer Ulfsson! Come see, come see!" it cried impatiently, springing over a strip of water and frisking away.

"Shall we?" asked Hilde in a small voice. Without a word, Peer followed it. Hilde rubbed her hot face with both hands, and went after them both.

Almost immediately, she wished she hadn't. The rocks were full of inky shadows and unexpected holes. Some were loose, tipping alarmingly. She scraped her palms on barnacles, and snatched her fingers from cold, blobby anemones. There was a reek of salt and seaweed and all the nameless things that the sea swept up and dumped. She cracked her knee and muttered a bad word.

Peer looked back. "Can you manage?" he asked curtly.

"Yes." The last thing she wanted was for him to help her. She hoisted her skirts and clambered grimly on.

Cheeping with excitement, the Nis led them farther along till they reached a long pool. Repeated tides had pushed up sand and gravel into a ridge blocking the entrance, so that although waves broke against the rocks a few yards away, only a few ripples ran in over the sandbar to disturb the pool itself. An old black log was jammed there too, half buried.

The Nis stopped, its gray wispy hair blowing in the wind, pointing with one long finger. "For you!" it announced proudly. "Nithing the Seafarer found it!"

Hilde heard Peer say softly, "Oh, no."

"What is it?" she asked, bewildered. "What—Peer, what are you doing?"

She scrambled after him as he flung himself recklessly down the sharp rocks and jumped into the water. It came up to his thighs; he waded madly through it, arms flailing, thrashing up spray. He stumbled up the slope where the bottom rose toward the sandbank, and threw himself upon the old black log, digging the silt away from it with his hands.

"What's the matter?" gasped Hilde, really frightened, though she didn't know why. Had Peer gone mad? There was a bitter taste on her tongue, her heart thudded.

Peer stopped digging. He put both his arms around the log, and heaved. It came out of the silt with a rush, streaming water, and he hugged it to his chest. He turned to face Hilde, holding it. His face was dark against the opal sky, his eyes glittered. She stared, knowing what she was seeing before she could frame it in words.

The black log glistened, slimy as a snail; it was horned like a snail, with two rootlike stumps. It had a savage look, a mockery of life: a twist to it like a neck, a gaping maw like some snarling animal.

"Burned!"

The word burst from Peer. He staggered back through the water and laid the thing on the edge of the rocks. He covered his face.

Hilde crouched. With a finger she gently traced the blackened carvings: the crisscross scales, the round, charred eye.

"A dragonhead."

"It's the *Long Serpent*," said Peer from behind his hands.

"Oh, Peer!" Hilde's voice shook on a sob. She reached out and awkwardly patted his hair. "Oh, Peer!"

"Thorolf's not coming back." Peer looked up. His eyes were dark; his mouth was a white line. A tear fell down his face and he wiped it away with the back of his hand.

Hilde didn't know what to say. "Don't stand there in the water. Come on, get out." She gave him a hand and he clumsily struggled onto the rocks and stood dripping and shivering.

From the peak of a rock higher above the pool, the Nis looked down, its face crinkling anxiously in an effort to understand. "Doesn't you like it, Peer Ulfsson?"

Peer tried to speak. The Nis scuttled down the rocks and laid a knobbly hand lightly against his knee. "Doesn't you want my present?"

Peer bent down. "Yes, Nis, I do. It was very clever of you to

215

find it. Thank you for showing us. Do you know who made this? My father made it."

"Good!" Satisfied, the Nis hopped away.

Peer said to Hilde, "I suppose it's stupid, but I feel as if my father was on the ship, too. I feel as though I just lost him all over again."

He picked up the burned dragonhead and said bleakly, "Let's go."

"What are you going to do with it?"

"Take it back, of course. Show it to the others. Now we know."

"Know what?" Hilde felt slow and clumsy. "What do we know?"

He turned fiercely. "The ship *burned*, Hilde. It wasn't wrecked—it burned. And how do you suppose that happened?"

She hurried after him, fear pecking at her heart. "I—I don't know. How?"

Peer jumped off the rocks. Loki greeted him in relieved delight. "Down!" Peer snapped, striding past.

"How did the ship catch fire?" Hilde had to run to keep up.

Peer flung her a look of disbelief. "How do you think? Gunnar and Harald. They did it, didn't they? All this time they've been lying to us. They know quite well what happened to Thorolf."

"No," Hilde said dizzily. "Surely . . ."

"No?" Peer swung away. "Let's go and ask them."

"Stop! Peer, don't!" Hilde caught his arm. But he broke roughly away, running down the beach toward the low sod houses by the river mouth.

"Peer!" she screamed. He was faster than she was, she'd never catch him. She sprinted after him, and the wind blew tears from her eyes. How quickly everything had gone wrong. Only a little while ago they'd been laughing, running in the moonlight, marveling at the pictures made by the little *wiklatmu'jk*.

Astrid rose like a ghost from a stone in front of her. "What on earth have you done to Peer? Didn't I give you long enough? Has he kissed you?"

"What"—Hilde pressed a hand to her ribs—"are you talking about? We've got to stop him. He's going to—he's found . . ."

Astrid's eyes narrowed. "So it's Arnë after all, is it? What a fool you are. Arnë's quite ordinary."

Hilde nearly screamed at her. "He's found the dragonhead from the *Long Serpent*. Burned. He's going to face Harald."

"Oh, gods." Astrid's face changed. "Get after him, quick. They'll kill him."

"Then it's true? And you knew?"

"Just go!" Astrid shrieked, and Hilde flew on. The surface of the beach seemed to jump at her. Patterns everywhere— patterns. . . .

They danced before her eyes, in her mind, at the back of her head. A boy, a girl, a boat . . . She dashed through the patterns, scattering them. *Watch out, little creatures, for my thumping feet.* Stick figures flew, a leg here, an arm there. *The* wiklatmu'jk *make pictures of what they see.* What pictures had they made a year ago, when the beach was a battleground?

CHAPTER 16

Single Combat

P eer burst into the house like a destroying wind. The door crashed behind him. The men eating around the hearth looked up in amazement. He lifted the dragonhead high, like a standard. Then he hurled it to the floor.

"What's this?" Harald was the first to break silence, in his insolent drawl. "Firewood?"

Big Tjorvi came slowly forward. "That's a dragonhead," he growled in wonder, "a burned dragonhead."

"From the *Long Serpent*," said Peer harshly.

Gunnar half rose, staring at the ruined dragonhead. Harald's lip curled. "And how would you know that, Barelegs?" he sneered.

Peer laughed, a hard, fierce laugh. "Better than anyone, Harald. My father made it. In a way, it killed him. His chisel

219

slipped, and the wound turned bad. . . . You might say he put his blood into that ship."

"And so? Why should I care about your carpenter father?" Harald lounged back, stretching out his legs and propping his heels on a small stool.

The dark, smoky room blurred and narrowed. Peer saw only the pale hated face of Harald. Tjorvi was saying something to him but his voice only boomed and mumbled, making no sense. Peer jerked free of Tjorvi's restraining hand and stepped forward.

"Because my father was a maker, Harald," he yelled. "He put something into this world, instead of taking something out of it. He made a ship, and it was a good ship. It brought Thorolf and his men all the way across the sea, not once, but twice."

He drew a sobbing breath. "And where's Thorolf now? Where's Thorolf and his son Ottar and all his crew? What happened to the *Long Serpent*, Harald? Why did she burn?"

He ran out of air and stopped. Harald hadn't moved. He stared up at Peer with a hard little smile. Beside him, Gunnar bent forward and coughed: short, wet, hacking coughs. Harald's hand shifted to grip his father's arm.

Everyone else remained perfectly still.

Peer shouted, "They're dead, aren't they? Dead, like those Skraelings you slaughtered today. And you know it because you killed them, and then you burned their ship and took their goods and sailed away. Thorolf's in Vinland, you told us.

And like fools we believed you."

The door rattled open. Hilde tumbled in out of the night, her hair coming down, her breath shrill. "Peer, come outside. I . . . I need to talk to you."

Peer didn't look at her. He laughed again, painful racking laughter that tore its way up through his throat. "You murderer, Harald. You bloody murderer. Ships don't burn by themselves. Thorolf's not in Vinland. Thorolf's in Valhalla."

Harald still didn't move. "You're crazy," he said lightly. "I'm flattered, of course. You think I killed how many men, all alone?"

"Of course not alone. You and Gunnar, and—and your crew. . . ." Peer looked around and swallowed.

"You mean Magnus and Floki and Halfdan?" Harald mused, flicking out fingers. "At least five of us here?" He twisted around. "What about it, men? Remember killing Thorolf?"

Floki's ready mouth opened, but Magnus's elbow caught him in the ribs. He doubled over, wheezing. Magnus turned a dark look on Harald and shook his head.

"No, Magnus doesn't remember. What about Halfdan? Can you remember killing Thorolf, Halfdan?" Halfdan pinched his lips together. "Nope," he said quickly.

Arnë and Tjorvi looked at each other.

"Oh dear, Halfdan doesn't remember either." Harald put his head to one side. "It can't have happened, then."

"Peer, leave it," said Hilde. Her voice crackled with fear.

Only his anger was supporting Peer, a fragile scaffolding over a pit of terror. He clung to it. "They're lying. I know you did it."

Harald stood up. "Prove that."

Peer pointed at the dragonhead on the floor. "There's the proof."

"I don't mean that sort of proof." Harald's eyes sparkled. "You've accused me; now let's see if you can prove it—man to man."

"No!" Hilde screamed.

All the men began shouting: "No, no!" "Yes!"

"Fight!" Floki yapped.

The door opened again and Astrid stole quietly in. Her face was white and her eyes narrow: She looked as sharp as a fox. Hilde ran to her. "Astrid, you must know what happened. It's true, isn't it? You know Peer's right. Tell them, quickly." Half pushing, half pulling, she propelled Astrid forward. The clamor died down.

Astrid's eyes flashed from Peer's face to Gunnar's. She hesitated. "Sorry, Hilde." The words were as cold and distinct as chips of marble. "I don't know what you're talking about." And the next second everyone was shouting again.

"Enough!" Gunnar struggled to his feet. He stood, head low, glaring around the room with fierce, red-rimmed eyes. "That's enough. *I'll* say what goes on here." He eyed the blackened dragonhead with a disgusted shudder. "Throw that thing on the fire. And you, boy"—he swung around to Peer—

"apologize to my son and we'll forget about this."

Peer stood up straighter, swaying. He licked his lips. The anger was draining away. He felt he was waking from a dream into a cold daybreak. *How did I get myself into this mess? I've made all the wrong moves. Run straight into the net.*

"Apologize, Peer," whispered Hilde. "It doesn't matter, nothing matters. It's only words. Just do it."

Harald smiled at him, eyes alight with amused contempt. "You heard her, Barelegs. Get on with it. Grovel."

Peer looked at Harald. *I can't,* he thought, *I really can't.* It was a surprise to discover that he'd sooner die than do what Harald wanted. He was almost angry with himself. *Stupid, stiff-necked, stubborn . . .* But his lips wouldn't form the words. He said doggedly, and a chill swept down his spine as he spoke: "No. You killed Thorolf, Harald. I swear it on my father's life."

"All right then." Harald nodded to him. "We'll fight."

"This is crazy!" Hilde's face was white. "How can fighting prove anything? Gunnar, please!"

Peer wished she'd stop fussing: It wouldn't do any good. He watched Harald's sword come out with a grating hiss. Floki was saying, "But what's Peer—I mean, Barelegs—what's he going to fight with? He hasn't got a sword."

"He can borrow my father's," Harald said. He tossed a look at Peer. "Will it do for you? Or would you prefer a hammer?" Laughter bubbled up in his face, and Peer saw in his eyes the memory of that faraway day on the jetty. He remembered, too. He remembered standing there watching the ship come in, wondering if he could hit anyone. Now he'd have to find out. Fear stirred in his belly.

Harald always meant it should come to this.

"He gets to borrow Gunnar's sword?" Floki was saying jealously. "Lucky!"

"Shut your stupid mouth, Floki," Magnus growled.

"This won't do." Arnë slammed a fist down. "Peer can't fight Harald. It's not a fair match." Tjorvi rumbled agreement, but Gunnar picked at his front teeth with a brown fingernail and said, "Two lads, the same age, the same height?" He shook his head. "What's wrong with that?"

"Harald's experience?" said Astrid, her voice like cold water dripping.

Harald laughed. "He doesn't have to fight me, darling Astrid. He can back down."

"Peer," Hilde pleaded.

"But he can't," said Halfdan, shocked. "Only a coward would do that."

Someone—Floki—shoved a sword into Peer's hands. "Here, take it." His red face swam close up to Peer's, round-eyed and curious as a cow's. "You must be mad," he said on a waft of damp, warm breath. "Fancy having a go at Harald."

Peer clutched the sword. It was amazingly heavy: He had to use both hands. He stared at the blade. There were little silver scratches where it had been sharpened, and halfway down, the edge had been turned by some blow. He rested the point on the floor and looked up.

A space was clearing around them. Benches were being dragged back.

I'm going to die. He felt horribly calm, though rather weak at the knees. There was no way out. He had a sword he didn't know how to use, and Harald would kill him. It was as simple as that.

"Right." Harald stepped forward.

"Wait, Harald." Arnë grabbed him. "You can't fight like this—indoors, by firelight. Look around!" He gestured. "There's hardly room to move. What's more, it's unlawful. Night killings are murder: That's the law."

Harald turned. "What law, Arnë? Whose law? This is Vinland," he added cheerfully. "Remember the Skraelings? There are no laws here. That's why we came." He advanced on Peer.

Peer backed away, holding the sword out in front of him. If only he could keep it between him and Harald, like a barrier. He saw Big Tjorvi's troubled face, the firelight shining through his dandelion-fluff hair. He saw Hilde's horrified stare—Floki, twisting his hands together excitedly—Magnus, sour and uneasy. Astrid stood behind Gunnar, gazing at him intently. Gunnar's light eyes blinked at Peer and flicked away. Blink, flick.

Harald was totally relaxed. He shook his sword suddenly and laughed to see Peer jump. He was moving sideways, making Peer turn to face the fire, so that the light would shine in his eyes. He feinted in, a low slash. Everyone went, "Ooh!" and Peer stumbled back before realizing that Harald was playing with him.

Cat and mouse, he thought bitterly. A dog barked outside the door. Loki. Peer's attention flickered. At least Loki was safe out there—

He dodged, barely in time. The sword struck like a serpent, stinging his arm, parting his sleeve. Harald feinted again—high, then low. Peer hopped—this way, that way. Where would the next blow come from? Harald was laughing. *I've got to fight back*, Peer remembered. *Got to use this sword*. He wagged it clumsily.

With a grunt and a cry Harald whirled his sword in an arc toward Peer's shoulder. Peer's reflexes took over. He lashed furiously upward. There was a ringing crash, and the blades clung eagerly together, biting, then slid apart with a tooth-jangling screech and a flurry of blue sparks.

Sweat and terror half blinded Peer. His arm hurt now. There was blood on his sleeve. His fingers were numb with the shock of the blow. He stepped back, blinking, shaking his head. *I'm done for. I'll never manage to ward him off twice.*

Harald was in no hurry. He began to jeer. "Not bad for a carpenter, Barelegs. I can see you've chopped a few trees down in your time. But you'll have to do better than that."

Peer's vision cleared. Past Harald's shoulder he saw Hilde, white-knuckled fists bunched at her sides. Next to her was Arnë. He was staring straight at Peer, as if willing him to look.

Their eyes locked. Slightly but urgently, Arnë shook his head.

Don't play Harald's games. As if a message had flown straight from Arnë's mind to his, Peer remembered Bjorn's warning. *Better to take an insult than a sword in your guts.*

Sorry, Bjorn. I should have listened. It's too late now. Or is it?

Don't play Harald's games. That includes not getting killed. Peer glanced around. Behind him was the door. In front of him was Harald, dark against the fire, his loose hair rimming him in gold. And there on the floor lay the burned dragonhead, with its snarling mouth and blackened eye, like a legless monster creeping into the fight on its belly.

Well, the sword was no good to him. Why shouldn't the dragonhead enter the fight? Shouting, Peer flung Gunnar's sword at Harald. Instinctively, Harald lashed out. His blow sent the loose sword cartwheeling through the air. Everyone yelled and ducked. The sword hit the stones of the hearth with a clang, and skittered toward Magnus's and Floki's ankles. They skipped aside, swearing, colliding with Tjorvi.

Peer hurled himself on the burned dragonhead. He lifted it, holding it up like a club. "You're right, Harald," he panted, "I'm useless with a sword. This'll be better."

Harald's beautiful face contorted. He leaped toward Peer and brought his sword around in a scything sweep at neck level. Eyes screwed shut, teeth bared, Peer swung the dragonhead. There was a thud and a jerk. His eyes flew open. Harald's blade had bitten deep into the wood and was stuck there. Glaring and snorting, Harald wrenched at it.

Peer let go. As Harald went reeling backward, he sprang for the door. The men were roaring. Hilde screamed, "Run, Peer! Run!"

He fumbled with the latch. Harald was up, one foot braced against the dragonhead, wrestling and tugging, working his sword free.

The door came open. Loki rushed in, tail wagging. "No, Loki!" Peer yelled. "*This* way!" He whistled, fierce and shrill, and Loki turned, confused but willing, and bounded after him. Peer banged the door shut and for a second the clamor faded. He was out in the cool night, running for the woods.

Loki raced alongside. Behind them the door opened again, spilling pursuit. Shouts echoed between the trees and the shore. Peer didn't bother to listen. The ground was rough and dark and uneven, scattered with branches, pitted with holes. He ran, staggered, recovered, sprinted on.

Then he was at the foot of the bluff, close to the little cascade where Hilde fetched the water. He threw himself at the rise, pulling himself up. Twigs lashed his face; brambles snagged his skin. He scrambled breathlessly higher and higher, clawing handholds out of the soft leaf mold. Beside him Loki scrabbled and sprang. Sobbing for breath, Peer forced himself to keep climbing on and up.

The shouts faded. The slope lessened, leveled. Still Peer ran, weaving under the trees. Fireflies tacked across the dark: a bright stitch here, a bright stitch there.

He ran on, not thinking, escaping. Something terrible was

following, that was all he knew. And if he stopped, it would catch him. But his legs were weaker and weaker. And his arm was sore, stinging and throbbing. He clapped his hand to it and touched the sharp lips of a wide gash. His sleeve was sticky and warm.

The ground vanished from underfoot. Peer pitched forward. He slithered crazily down a steep slope. Dry branches cracked under him. In an avalanche of dead leaves and small stones, he rolled, fell, and thudded onto rocks.

CHAPTER 17

Losing Peer

R un!" Hilde screamed, as Peer swung the dragonhead at
Harald. Then Peer vanished, and Harald rushed after
him, and all the men followed. Only Gunnar was left behind,
like some crippled old spider that couldn't crawl out of its
web.

Hilde ran out, too. Wildly she looked to the woods, hearing
the men yell as they fought their way up into the forest.

Oh, Peer—get away. Run, hide!

But where? There was nowhere for him to go. Vinland was
a wilderness, a place without places. Hilde gasped as the enor-
mity of the disaster broke over her like a drenching wave. Peer
couldn't come back.

Harald and Gunnar, outlawed for five years for the murder
of Erlend, would never let Peer live to tell of an even worse

crime here in Vinland—the slaughter of Thorolf and all his men. Peer had defied them, accused them outright. So he would die: either slowly in the forest, or quickly under Harald's sword.

There must be some way to save him. *I know as much as Peer does. I could tell everything.* But Harald wouldn't care about a girl's threats. According to the laws back home, a woman couldn't be a witness. Magnus, Floki, and the others were mixed up in it themselves and would say nothing. Arnë or Tjorvi might speak. But Harald had been clever. He'd challenged Peer, asked him to prove his claim through combat. By breaking off the fight, Peer had lost his case.

Hilde ground her teeth. Men! What stupid rules they set up—as though fighting about something could alter the truth!

It was dreadful to be so helpless.

The dragonhead! Gunnar had ordered it to be thrown on the fire. But Peer was right. It was a different sort of proof: it showed beyond doubt that death had come to the *Long Serpent* and her crew. Perhaps, one day, it could be used against Gunnar and Harald. She had to save it.

Quickly. It may already be burning. Silent as a thief, she slid back inside. Gunnar sat at the far end of the fire hall, almost invisible in the smoky gloom, staring into the flames and moodily swigging from his drinking horn. Astrid paced up and down near the door, nervously jingling the bunch of keys at her belt. She jumped as Hilde came in, and whispered,

"Where's Peer? Have they caught him?"

Hilde didn't speak to her. The dragonhead lay in the hearth, where Harald had thrown it after wrenching his sword free. Luckily it had fallen in the ashes. She dragged it out, giving Astrid a searing glare that dared her to say anything, and backed through the door without a word.

The dragonhead was top-heavy and awkward. The ash had stuck to its sea-slimed surface. She hugged it to her chest and thought of Peer. Tears filled her own eyes—but there was no time for that. She looked about. Where to hide it? Nowhere near the house—someone would be sure to find it. No time to run to the shore or the woods. *Quickly, before Harald gets back . . .*

Then she knew. Thorolf's empty house. The perfect place. *Nobody ever goes there.*

She stole up the dim path. The door swung open at a touch, and a chill, damp smell came out. Squatting down, she slid the dragonhead in along the floor. As she let go, it vanished into the waiting blackness so completely that she could almost believe it had wriggled away like a snake. She felt for it, patting the earth floor. If someone did try looking in, she didn't want them to see the dragonhead lying just inside. But she must have pushed it farther than she had thought, for her groping fingers couldn't find it again.

She crouched like a mouse on the doorstep. The silence in the house was tense and emphatic . . . the silence of a roomful of people all holding their breath. And a *tick, tick, tick* of dripping water.

Her skin roughened up in goose bumps. She dragged the door shut. Half running, half looking over her shoulder, she wondered what she'd done. But the dragonhead was hidden, and she couldn't shake off a clinging hope that somehow, if the dragonhead was safe, Peer might be too.

The Nis scampered past her ankles with a swish of air and a heavy patter of feet.

It's still playing. It doesn't know what's happened. Perhaps it can help. She called urgently, "Nis, Nis, I need you!"

No answer. It was probably hiding in the dark porch, hoping to jump out and make her scream.

"Nis, it's serious. There's no time for games. Peer's hurt. Harald fought him. He's run off into the woods. We have to find him."

"What?" the Nis squeaked.

"You heard." Hilde tried to see where it was. "Nis, that dragonhead you found, it means that Thorolf's dead, Thorolf and all his men. We think Harald and Gunnar killed them, and burned their ship. Peer said so, and Harald made him fight with swords. And he hurt him, and Peer's run away." She ended on a dry sob.

The Nis appeared suddenly on the top of the porch. Its eyes glinted like angry garnets. "Thorolf the Seafarer—dead?" it exclaimed. "Dead—my namesake—and Peer Ulfsson lost?"

"Yes, they're hunting for him in the woods. . . ."

"Who is?" the Nis interrupted.

"All of them," said Hilde. "Listen to me—"

"All of them, but Harald Silkenhair is the leader," the Nis chirped shrewdly. "Ooh!" It raised scrawny arms and shook its fists above its head. "I'll make him sorry for this. Nithing the Seafarer will make him pay! I will avenge Peer Ulfsson, my good friend. Avenge!" it repeated grandly.

"Yes, but . . ."

"You thinks I can't, but I can." The Nis bristled. "I can sneak up when Harald's asleep and tie knots in his hair, his beautiful hair he's so proud of. Ha! I can hide his clothes, put stones in his boots. I can—"

"No! I mean, yes, do all that if you like, but the most important thing is to look for Peer! Before he dies in the woods, or gets lost and starves. Please, please, go and find him."

The Nis's eyes widened. It hung its head. "The woods is big, mistress," it quavered. "I am a house Nis, and a ship Nis, but I isn't a woods Nis. I would get lost, too. Then poor, poor Nithing would starve as well, no one to make me nice groute, only mushrooms to eat, and leaves, ugh! No butter anymore, never again . . ." Its voice trembled and nearly broke.

"Never mind, then," said Hilde sadly. "Just do what you can."

The men straggled back into the house empty-handed, as excited and ashamed as a pack of dogs caught doing something disgraceful but fun, like chasing sheep. Even Arnë and Tjorvi avoided Hilde's eyes. Perhaps they'd gone with good intentions, to do what they could. For the moment Hilde loathed them as much as the others, for being part of the dog pack that had hunted Peer.

"Where is he?" she rapped, before even Gunnar could ask.

"Skulking." Harald grinned, clapping Halfdan on the shoulder. Halfdan flinched. "Skulking in the woods. And he can stay there."

Hilde caught her breath. "How? What will he do? How can he survive?"

Harald tilted his head to one side and paused. "By milking bears?" he suggested, and burst out laughing. Floki giggled, but he glanced at Magnus for approval and soon stopped. The others looked uneasily at their feet.

Hilde turned her back on them and marched outside. She sat on the log seat by the porch and folded her arms. Arnë followed. "Hilde, please come in. It's cold out here." He knelt before her, trying to take her hands. "I'll go looking for Peer tomorrow, I swear I will, but it's too dark now, I wouldn't find him. Please."

"Leave me alone."

Astrid stuck her head out. "Hilde, come on. It won't do any good sitting out here." Hilde stared straight ahead. There was no way she was going to shut herself up in the cold little cupboard that was her bed. She heard Astrid say quietly to Arnë, "Come away. Better leave her be." The door shut.

I'll stay here till he comes, Hilde thought. *He'll wait till everything's quiet, then he'll creep out of the woods. He'll see me, and we'll make a plan. We'll think of something. Peer always has an idea up his sleeve. . . .*

The sea hushed and shivered on the beach below the houses. There was a breeze, thin and chill. After a long time, something yapped sharply in the forest, and a thrill of hope brought her to her feet. *Is that Loki? Please, oh please let it be Loki and Peer.*

Nothing happened. No tall figure of a boy with his dog came limping out of the trees.

A terrible conviction settled slowly on Hilde that the worst had happened. She would never see Peer again. She covered her face with her hands. *And we parted so badly. He tried to tell me he loved me, and I was so stupid. . . .*

She saw her behavior from the outside, as Peer must have seen it, and shriveled with shame. *He must have thought I didn't care about him at all. But I did. I do. I'd just—got used to him. I suppose I took him for granted.*

The moon was setting and the sky glittered with constellations. *The Wagon,* she thought, remembering how Peer had pointed them out. *The Nail. Oh, Peer. Can you see them? Where are you now?*

The stars blurred and trembled, and ran together in a luminous smear.

CHAPTER 18
"A Son Like Harald"

Y ou'll have to talk to me again sometime," said Astrid
wearily the next day, "so why not now?"

She wiped her forehead with the back of her hand, leaving
a smear of blood. It wasn't her own, it came from the pile of
dead pigeons lying in her lap.

"And at least Peer got away," she went on. "Harald didn't kill
him."

The girls were alone. The door was open, and the men were
out, either searching for Peer, or hunting or fishing. *How could
they?* thought Hilde. *As if nothing had happened!* Even
Gunnar had felt well enough to walk down to the shore with
Magnus and Harald.

"What do you think I could have done?" Irritably Astrid
tweaked out a handful of feathers. "If I'd rushed in shouting,

'It's all true—Gunnar and Harald slaughtered Thorolf and his men,' do you think that would have stopped Harald?"

Without speaking, Hilde dropped her brace of pigeons into the pot. She threw the refuse and feathers into the fire, and went to rinse her hands in the pail by the door.

"Well?" Astrid insisted.

"It might have helped," Hilde said at last.

"No, it wouldn't," said Astrid flatly. "Harald wanted blood. Arnë tried his best, but he couldn't stop it, and Magnus and Floki and the others do whatever Harald wants. Most of them are too scared not to, and Floki's too stupid."

"Gunnar could have stopped it, and he would have if you'd asked him."

"After everything Peer said?" Astrid's nostrils were pinched and her eyes flashed. "Don't be silly. If I'd taken Peer's side, it would have made Gunnar even angrier. Anyway, he gave Peer a chance to back down, didn't he? And Peer could have taken it."

"No, he couldn't!" Hilde's chest began to heave. "He couldn't possibly, even though I wanted him to, because if he had, he wouldn't have been Peer. You don't know him like I do. Bad things have happened to Peer before, and he's always, always faced up to them, even though he doesn't think he's brave. But he *is* brave. He's the bravest person I've ever met."

Astrid nodded gloomily. "I've always thought so."

Hilde stared at her. "I don't understand you, Astrid. Not one bit. How can you stick up for Gunnar after everything he and Harald have done? And now it turns out they killed Thorolf as well—and all his men, and his little boy too, I suppose. And you knew. You've told me a million lies. You wouldn't risk anything to help Peer. Yet you pretend you liked him."

"You're right." Astrid was icy. "You don't understand."

Hilde's lip curled. "Are you trying to tell me you love Gunnar?"

"Love him? I don't need to love him. He's my husband." Astrid shot out a thin, cold hand and gripped Hilde's wrist so tightly it hurt. "Sometimes I think I'd like you if you weren't such a fool. You don't get it, do you? *I'm married to Gunnar.* It's all right for you, whose father and mother are so soft they'll let you go off on a Viking ship just so you can decide who you really want to fall in love with. It wasn't like that for me. I didn't get a choice. I said I didn't want to marry Gunnar, and my father threw me against the wall till my head bled. There's troll blood in my family. My father would never have married my mother if he'd known about it beforehand, so he was desperate to get me off his hands before Gunnar found out. I'll say this for Gunnar: He's never laid a finger on me."

"You told me that before," said Hilde savagely, "and you spun me that long story about Erlend. So how do you explain what I overheard the first night we came here? I couldn't sleep, and I heard you talking to Gunnar. Telling him how to stop a ghost from walking—by sticking needles in a dead man's feet!"

Astrid's eyes widened. "You heard that?"

"Yes! It didn't sound as though your dead lover meant much to you then."

Astrid went pale. "That had nothing to do with Erlend. We were talking about Thorolf."

"Thorolf?" Hilde felt her head was coming apart.

"Yes, Thorolf." With exaggerated patience, as if explaining to a child, Astrid said, "It's Thorolf's ghost Gunnar's afraid of. He finally told me the whole story, that night on the ship. There was a fight—Thorolf died under Gunnar's spear, but he put his dying curse on Gunnar first. *A cold life and a cold death.* Gunnar's terrified that Thorolf's ghost is after him. They put the bodies into the *Long Serpent* and set her on fire, but she sank before everything burned. That was Gunnar's mistake. That's what you heard me telling him." She added earnestly, "A dead man can't follow you if you sew him up in a shroud and then break off the needle in the soles of his feet."

She saw Hilde's expression, and her own face went rigid. "Don't look at me like that! I can't help what I know! Why should I care for Thorolf? I never knew him. And I cried for Erlend, but even if it *was* his ghost and not Thorolf's, I'd still do what I could to help Gunnar. A live husband is better than a dead lover. I married Gunnar and I decided to make the best of it. What's wrong with that? And I'll tell you something else. Gunnar's all right, sometimes. Often he is. You said so yourself! He's brave, and he's a good skipper, and the men like him. And—"

"Astrid," interrupted Hilde. "He *kills* people. *That's* what's wrong."

Astrid began to sob. "But mainly because of Harald.

Nobody can control Harald, you know that. Harald would have got Peer in the end, whatever we did."

Hilde's voice rose. "And whose fault is that? Who made Harald the way he is? Gunnar, bringing him up to think he can do just as he likes!"

"No!" Astrid shook her head vehemently. "It wasn't Gunnar who spoiled him, it was Vardis—Harald's mother—she must have been an awful woman. I'm not like that. It'll be different this time."

"But Gunnar's so proud of Harald . . ." Hilde trailed off. Her eyes flicked down to Astrid's stomach. Now that she was looking for it, she saw the small bulge at once.

"You're not. Are you . . . ?"

Astrid gave a defiant tear-stained smile. "Yes! I am! I'm having Gunnar's baby."

Hilde was speechless. How had she missed something so obvious?

"Does Gunnar know? Have you told him?"

"Not yet. I wasn't sure, but I am now. I've been very careful. I know you're not supposed to run, or carry anything heavy."

Hilde remembered what she ought to have said. "That's wonderful, Astrid."

"I know." Astrid bit her lip and laughed suddenly. "A little rival for Harald. How annoyed he'll be. I'm so happy, Hilde." Her face shone. "A little baby, all of my own! I've wanted one for ages. Do you remember me cuddling Elli at your parents' house? I was longing to pick her up and take her with me."

Why didn't you? Hilde thought. *You took the Nis.* She looked at Astrid's soft, flushed face, and remembered the weird little nursery rhyme she had chanted then. Something no human mother would sing. A troll's song.

What was it like to be Astrid?

Ma taught me ordinary things—milking and brewing, spinning and baking. Astrid's mother taught her spells and strange songs. She gave her a magic box and told her how to stop ghosts from walking.

What was it like to be Astrid, whose ambitious, violent father regarded her troll blood as a shameful secret, and married her off to a man as violent and as old as himself, instead of the young farmer she'd wanted?

And now she was happy because she was going to have a little baby to love.

"What are you staring for?" Astrid asked abruptly. "Are you still angry?"

Hilde shook her head. Swallowing, she bent down and gave Astrid a kiss. Astrid's mouth trembled. Her arms went around Hilde. They hugged, hesitantly, then tightly.

"I'm sorry," Hilde muttered. "I've been stupid. It wasn't your fault."

"No, you were right. I am a liar. I wish I was like you, Hilde. But I'm all crooked inside . . ."

"No, you're not." They let go, both wiping their eyes.

"But what about Peer?" Astrid sniffed.

All the fear came rushing back. "Peer, oh, gods . . ." Hilde wrung her hands. "And he's hurt. His arm was bleeding."

"Could the Nis help?"

"I already asked," said Hilde bitterly. "It won't go into the woods alone. It thinks it can pay Harald back by playing tricks on him."

Astrid looked momentarily diverted. "So that's why Harald couldn't find his boots this morning."

"Good." Hilde stared miserably at her knotted hands. "Arnë's off looking for him, I think. He wouldn't let me come. But if Peer was anywhere nearby, he'd have come back last night, and he didn't. I waited outside till dawn, and I walked along the edge of the woods and called for him."

"Maybe I could find him," said Astrid slowly.

"You!" Hilde stared. "How?"

"If there's enough time . . . Run outside, Hilde, and tell me what the men are doing."

Hilde ran out into the dazzling sunshine and stared under her hand toward the shore. She saw figures wading with fish spears, and heard distant laughter.

"They're busy on the beach," she reported, coming back in.

"Good." Astrid emerged from the inner room with her goatskin bag. "Leave the door like that—just a bit open. Now then."

She darted her arm into the bag and drew out the little bone box that Hilde had seen before. Hilde's heart began to thump. More *seidr*?

"Keep an eye on the door," Astrid said. "I don't want the men to see."

"See what?"

"Something my mother showed me. When I was little my mother used to make me sit and watch over her while she was away. It scared me. I used to think she might never come back."

"Away? What do you mean?" Hilde's mouth was dry, but she was excited, too.

"Away finding things out," said Astrid impatiently. "No time to explain. You'll see. Here, take the box." She shoved it at Hilde, who nearly dropped it.

"Careful!" hissed Astrid. "Now look. When you see me fall asleep, you have to open it, and *keep it open* until I come back. Understand?"

"Not really." Hilde flicked her plait over her shoulder. "What do—"

"And another thing—don't touch me while I'm away. Don't call my name or try to speak to me. Don't say a word, you understand?"

"What if the men come back?"

"Keep them out." Astrid swung her feet up onto the benches where the men slept, and pulled her blue cloak over her. She lay back, closed her eyes, and began muttering under her breath.

Hilde sat up stiffly, clutching the little box. She remembered the faraway buzzing against her ear, but for now the box was quiet—warm, slippery, and inert. She glanced at Astrid, in time to see Astrid's mouth stretch open in the most enormous yawn. Her eyelids flickered up and her eyes rolled slowly upward till only the whites showed. Her body went limp and relaxed.

Hilde nearly spoke but caught herself. *Quick, open the box.* It vibrated. Hilde bit back a yelp. She prized and twisted with cold fingers, and the lid eased stiffly up. Underneath crouched a large, glittering fly. A work of art, a delicate thing of green enameling, and golden and black wires.

It moved. The wings flirted and blurred. Hilde's hands jerked. The box clattered to the ground. Buzzing, the fly rose, speeding to the open door. It flashed into the sunshine and was gone.

A fly? What was this? Some pointless joke? Hilde turned furiously, but the words died on her lips. She tasted fear, sharp on her tongue. Astrid looked dead. Her eyelids drooped half shut, showing a line of white. Her lips were apart. Was she breathing? Hilde counted silently. At twenty-two she saw Astrid's chest slowly rise and subside.

Subdued, shivering, Hilde picked up the little box. The inside was smooth and empty.

You couldn't keep a fly in a box.

So the fly was a *sending.* She'd heard it whispered of, the power of those skilled in *seidr* to send their spirits out in animal form. She looked again at Astrid, lying like a corpse, except that her fingers sometimes jerked. This was no joke. But could anything good come of it—this troll magic? Could it work? And how long would it take?

She twisted uneasily, sitting this way, then that way. If she faced Astrid, she couldn't see the door. If she faced the door, she couldn't see Astrid. And there was something awful about the way she lay, neither alive nor properly dead. Her teeth showed. Her eyelids twitched occasionally, showing nothing but the whites, like hard-boiled eggs.

It was silly to be afraid. She thought of the child Astrid shivering by her mother's bed. *If a little girl could do it, then so can I.*

Time passed, or crawled. The fire's bright rags fluttered quietly. Nothing else stirred. Hilde rubbed her face with sticky hands. *This has to work. It has to. Peer, we're looking for you. Oh, Peer, be all right. Please come back. Let us find you.*

A glittering green spark whirled in over her head and zoomed around the room, appearing and disappearing through the smoke. Hilde sprang for the little bone box and held it up foolishly, without much hope that the fly would settle. *I'll never get it back.* Surely it wouldn't want to be shut up again in this tiny prison?

But the fly circled down onto the rim of the box. Hilde flinched. It was so big and confident. Deliberately it walked into the middle of the box, cleaned its head with its two front legs, and sidled into a comfortable position. Hilde clapped the lid on.

With a second mighty yawn, Astrid pushed herself up. Hilde flew to her side. "Are you all right? Did it work? Did you find him?"

Astrid's face was still bloodless. Her lips smacked together clumsily. *I saw him,* she mouthed. She sucked in another deep breath. "I saw him. It looks bad, Hilde. I think—"

The door scraped open and Gunnar's shadow filled it. Cursing under her breath, Hilde slipped the box back into Astrid's bag and tried to push the bag behind her skirt.

"Done too much," Gunnar was muttering, standing in the doorframe, puffing. "Where's Astrid? What's this, what's this?" he added roughly as Astrid tried to get off the bench. "What's the matter, woman? Are you ill?" He turned to Hilde. "What's wrong with her?"

Hilde's wits deserted her. She stared at him, blank-faced and dumb. Astrid staggered to her feet. "Gunnar." Groggily she held out her arms. "I've got something to tell you, Gunnar. I'm having a baby."

Gunnar looked stunned. Then a slow smile appeared on his face. "Are you sure?"

When Astrid nodded, he turned around, threw open the door, and bellowed, "You men get in here, and quickly!"

It was his seagoing voice, bound to be obeyed. Looking stronger than he had for weeks, he crossed the floor to Astrid and wound an arm around her. She drooped against him like a snowdrop. "Is this certain?" he demanded again, looking at Hilde.

"She says so." Hilde was grudgingly moved by Gunnar's delight. His chest expanded; his eyes seemed younger and brighter. For a moment it was possible to see that, once, he might have looked very like Harald.

The men crowded in with scuffling boots. Arnë wasn't there. Except Harald, most of them looked apprehensive. Harald wore a slight frown, which altered to a scowl when he saw his father with Astrid.

"Good news, lads!" Gunnar squeezed Astrid's shoulders. "The very best. Astrid's having a baby!"

The men burst into cheers and whistles. They stamped their feet. "Go, Gunnar!" "Good work, Gunnar!" "Well done, skipper!"

Gunnar raised his voice. "So much for the curse, eh?" he shouted joyfully. "So much for Thorolf!"

Hilde nearly choked. Gunnar admitted it! In front of everyone, he admitted responsibility for Thorolf's death. She saw with bitterness that no one looked surprised. Then what had Peer been fighting for?

Gunnar was repeating the curse: "*A cold wife and a cold bed.* Well, that part's wrong, isn't it? So what's the rest of it worth now? Nothing!" He beckoned, sawing his short arm through the air in an excited gesture. "Where's Harald? Here, Harald. Stand with me."

Harald pushed to the front. His face was white as linen, but Gunnar seemed not to notice. He flung his maimed arm around Harald's neck, linking his wife and his son.

"I've beaten the curse!"

He began to cry. Tears trickled down his face and hung glistening in his sandy beard. "I've got it beat. I've a good wife and a fine son, and soon another son to follow him. A son like Harald!"

He squeezed Astrid again. She stood tall beside him, face flushed, eyes bright.

"Give her a kiss!" bawled Magnus.

"Give her a kiss!" The men took up the shout, clapping, as if, swept along by Gunnar's delight, they forgot they'd ever been wary of Astrid.

"Good idea!" Gunnar turned and pulled Astrid against him. He pressed his bristly lips against hers. Smack! Hilde winced, but Astrid was laughing. She cupped a hand to Gunnar's cheek and kissed him back.

"Troll!"

It was a high yell from Harald. The laughter and cheers thinned like smoke, and a bench fell over with a bang as someone backed off. Gunnar turned in amazement.

"Get off my father, troll!" Harald grabbed Astrid's arm and jerked her roughly toward him. Astrid shrieked.

"Tell him." Harald shook her. "Tell my father what you are. Tell him." Again he shook her. "Tell him!"

"Stop it!" Hilde pulled Astrid away just as Harald shoved her aside. Astrid toppled into Hilde's arms. Gunnar stared, bewildered and angry as a baited bear.

"She's a troll, Father," Harald panted. "I found out weeks ago. Couldn't bear to tell you. None of us could. She's deceived you. Troll magic, troll trickery. No wonder you've been ill. And now this. Passing off some troll whelp as your son?"

Gunnar blinked painfully. He seemed to gather his wits. He said in a mild, almost pleading voice, "But Astrid's father is an old friend. Grimolf's daughter can't be a troll."

"No?" Harald snatched Astrid's goatskin bag and upended it, shaking the contents all over the floor. Astrid and Hilde both cried in protest, but everyone else craned to see. Out clattered the little bone box and cracked under Harald's foot. Out fell packages of herbs, balls of red and white thread, a spindle whorl of rock crystal and another of jet.

"Look at this stuff." Harald ripped the packages and threw them down. "Poison, for all we know. Look!" He grabbed the spindles, holding up first the crystal and then the jet. "What does she want two for? For spinning spells. White ones—and black! She's not been curing you, Father. You haven't been getting any better, have you? She wants to keep you ill, weak, womanish. Did you never wonder where she learned all this magic? She sucked it in with her mother's milk. Her mother was a troll, too. Of course Grimolf didn't tell you. It was the shame of his house. But ask any of the men, and they'll tell you. They call her the witch girl, the troll wench. I've heard them talking."

Astrid choked. Hilde sprang to her feet. "Astrid's no troll! I come from Troll Fell, Gunnar, and I know what trolls are like. They're cruel and heartless and selfish. They're the opposite of us. They can't tell wrong from right. They think night is day and black is white." She turned on Harald. "That makes *you* more of a troll than she is!"

Harald ignored her. He stared at Astrid. "You can actually see it when you look at her," he marveled quietly. "Something about the eyes, I think."

Gunnar had turned a terrible color—bluish red like undercooked meat. His pale eyes bulged. Between gritted teeth he said, "Astrid?"

Astrid faced him, bone white. "I'm not a troll."

"And your mother?"

"There was troll blood in her family," said Astrid with difficulty. "Generations back."

"Troll blood will out," Harald sneered. "What will your baby be like, Astrid? Will it have a little . . . tail?"

"Gunnar!" cried Astrid. "Don't let him speak to me like that!"

Gunnar slapped her.

The blow landed with a loud crack and snapped Astrid's face to the right. She reeled and her fingers flew to her cheek. A bright scarlet print sprang out on her ear, mouth, and cheekbone. "You'll be sorry you did that," she said in a low, deadly voice.

They stared at each other. Gunnar looked away first. His gaze fell on the men standing goggle-eyed and openmouthed. "What are you all staring at?" he shouted. "Get out of here!" The men broke for the door, shoving and pushing.

Gunnar turned away. After two steps he stumbled, and Harald was there, supporting him, leading him away toward the bedchamber. Astrid waited till they were in the doorway.

"You'll be sorry you did that, Gunnar Ingolfsson!" she screamed, and folded over on the sleeping bench, burying her face in the sheepskins and uttering gasping sobs. Hilde tried to comfort her. Astrid struck her arm away.

It was dark inside the house, now the door was shut. It must be nearly sunset. Slowly Hilde got down, and on hands and knees began picking up the torn packages and spilled herbs that Harald had strewn across the floor. He came out of Gunnar's chamber while she was doing it and said, "Throw it all on the fire." His face was hard and pale, and Hilde wondered how he was enjoying his triumph. Didn't he realize he'd shamed Gunnar as well as Astrid?

He went out. Then Hilde saw the Nis, peeping down from a crossbeam. "It's all right," she murmured, deathly tired. "It's safe to come out. He's gone."

The Nis ran down the wall. In big-eyed, solemn silence it picked up a few of the broken things. It kept glancing at Astrid, where she lay facedown, with jerking shoulders. It sidled closer—and at last hopped up to crouch beside her. It shook its head, tutting, and timidly reached out long, knobbly fingers to pat her hair.

Hilde's eyes blurred. She remembered making the same gesture with Peer—was it only yesterday? She remembered the touch of his hair, cool and thick and silky.

She shuffled along the floor, still picking things up— whatever Harald said, she wanted to save as much as possible—and came across the little bone box, splintered and crushed. The fly was gone. Whatever magic Astrid had made with it, for good or ill, she would never make it again.

"I did find him." It was Astrid's voice, drenched in tears. She was sitting up at last, her eyes red with crying. The bruise on her cheekbone was turning a shiny purple.

"I did find Peer. But I think he was dying. I'm sorry, Hilde, I'm so, so sorry. I'm sure by now it will be too late."

CHAPTER 19

Down the Dark River

Peer wakes . . .

. . . to the sharp sound of Loki barking. It's still night. His head pounds, and his arm throbs. Loki barks again, angry growling barks as if he's holding something at bay. There's a dreadful smell, sweet and rotten. And a strange noise, a twittering, giggling sort of noise. Peer lifts himself painfully to see.

He's lying in a steep, secret gully, roofed with trees as thick as thatch. To his left, a few feet away, the creek pours past. To his right is the dark side of the gully, riddled with even darker irregular holes, each with a spoil heap of earth at the mouth—some kind of animal lair.

But the noise from the holes doesn't sound like animals. It's a nasty shrill chattering that stings the senses. Deep within, small eyes gleam white, like tiny pearls.

Loki dashes recklessly forward, then cries and yips. Stones rattle into his face. He turns and bolts away, tail low. The next second Peer is hurled back. His head cracks on the rocks. He cries out. The things scramble all over him, snickering—scrawny things with puffed chests and nipped waists and cold scratching fingers. Their white eyes look sightless, like the eyes of a cooked fish. Pinching hands grip and roll him over. The stone grazes his face. Again he's rolled, this time onto damp earth covered in twigs and pine needles.

And they fasten him down, forcing twigs into the soft earth between every finger, stretching out his arms and legs, tugging back his hair. They ram a forked stick over his neck and use more to pin down his wrists and ankles. Peer struggles, but he's weak and dizzy, and there are so many of them, clinging to him, crawling over him. Soon he can't lift a finger. He rolls his eyes and shouts, and one of them slips a sharp piece of wood into his mouth and twists it, propping his mouth wide open.

Peer gurgles and retches. Blood trickles down his throat. He prods his tongue at the wooden gag, but it's too tightly jammed to shift. His jaw aches already.

He waits in flinching horror. What will happen now? But the things, whatever they were, seem to have finished. One moment they're swarming over him, the next, they scuffle to get in through the entrance to the nearest hole. A sprinkle of earth is kicked out over him. And they've gone.

That's it? But they can't leave me like this!

Peer jerks and twitches at his bonds, but nothing gives. He tries to cry out, but can only manage a muffled "Angh—ah!"

And who's going to hear?

He struggles again, then lies limp. Threads of saliva trickle from the corners of his mouth. Tears fill his eyes.

I don't want to die this way. Not like this. I should have let Harald kill me. Died fighting. I bet Thorolf didn't run.

His hurt arm throbs. Chilled, exhausted, he slides away into a world of dreams. He's with Hilde on the beach, and she says, "I love you, too," her eyes shining in the starlight. He's back in the house, and he's just run Harald through with Gunnar's sword. Everyone cheers, everyone thinks he's a hero. He's sailing *Water Snake* into Trollsvik. Bjorn's there on the jetty, smiling his old smile. "Well done, Peer. I knew you could do it."

Lies.

Day comes. He wakes slowly, staring up at a brown tangle of interlaced branches tipped with fringes of dark green. The sun shines through it in white blinks. The holes in the bank are just holes, crumbling at the edges. Surely it was all a bad dream?

But his mouth gapes open, wide, dry. Even his throat is dry. He lies on the cold bank, pegged down, unable to move. The water bounds past, chuckling and burbling, but he can't reach it or see it. The forest is peaceful. From time to time a striped squirrel scampers down a tree, or a dove coos, or a crow calls harshly. Somewhere close a lot of flies whirl and hum over the source of the bad smell. Peer doesn't want to think what it is.

Sometimes, disturbed, they rise in a buzzing cloud. One big one finds Peer and explores his face curiously, walking with tickling feet over his eyes, nose, and mouth. Its body glints like green armor. He squints at it, helpless, unable even to puff it away.

Paws pad around his fallen body; a nose pushes into his face with a worried sigh that scares the fly off. Loki. *Poor Loki, that's all you can do. If only the Nis could come and set me free.*

It's cold in the gully. But Loki settles against Peer's side, and a little warmth creeps through. Slow sunspots trace their way over Peer. He drifts in and out of consciousness, woken sometimes by gripping cramps. Once he hears an ax chopping, or perhaps it's only a woodpecker. Once when he wakes, Loki is not there, and he hears him drinking. And the long, slow, agonizing day passes, and the pine trees huddle together overhead, and darkness returns.

Peer falls into a dream deeper than any he's had yet. He seems to be awake, sitting up, free of his bonds. The pain is gone. He hears a splashing from the creek, looks around, and sees without surprise the tall black dragonhead from the *Long Serpent*—alive, long bodied, writhing its way upstream with head raised, horns twitching, fiery eyes turned on him.

You're alive! Peer cries. *They didn't kill you after all.*

The dragon's jaws open in a long hiss. Then it speaks, using his father's voice: *Alive for you. Alive whenever you think of me.*

Peer is filled with joy. *Father! Where have you been all this time?*

In the land of the remembered dead, says the dragon gently.

It's wonderful not to be alone anymore. There's so much to say, so much to tell, Peer doesn't know where to start. *Have you been watching me? If only I'd known. I've kept trying, Father, really I have. But it's been so hard.*

I know only what you tell me, says the dragon, but Peer isn't listening.

He pours it all out: *I came to find Thorolf, but Thorolf's dead. I fought Harald, but I ran away. I wasn't brave enough—I can't use a sword. And I've left Hilde behind, though I promised Ralf to look after her. And ...*

Hush! The dragon shoots its long neck forward and twines around him. Its wet, rough skin sizzles with life. Wherever it brushes against him, he feels a tingling shock. *What more could you do?* it demands.

I don't know.

The dragon snorts. *What did you leave undone?*

Nothing, says Peer slowly.

It touches him with a serpent's tongue, cold vivid kisses. *Then you did well.* It rears over him, fierce and glad, as it did on the prow of the longship. *You did all you could, Peer, Ulf's son. You faced your fear and kept faith with your friends.*

Peer is silent. At last he asks, *What happens now?*

Come with me.

The dragon loops, gliding down the bank and into the water. *Come!*

Peer rises. Loki is nowhere to be seen, and for a moment that worries him, and reality, if this is reality, quivers like hot air over a fire. Impatiently the dragon shakes its fringed mane, and Peer hurries, wading into the creek. He puts his arm over the dragon's strong sinuous neck, and a moment later they are streaking downstream together. The banks whirl past. Peer has never known anything so powerful. The dragon's body lashes against him like a snake's, tugging him through the water, whipping around rocks, surging over little cascades where the spray flashes like ice. Enormous trees tower overhead. Their black branches reach into the sky like arms trying to tear down the stars. Their thick roots plunge deep into the river as if exploring to the bottom of the world.

And now the banks are becoming cliffs that lean over the water, reaching toward each other till they touch overhead, and all light vanishes. The noise of the river grows louder and louder, growling and rumbling. Fear touches Peer like a drift of spray, like a cold caress. *Where are we going?*

Away, says the dragon dreamily. *Away together, far from pain. Down the dark river.*

No! Peer frees his arm from the serpent's neck. Instantly the black water plucks him away. He fights the pull of the current, kicking fiercely. *I can't follow you, Father. Not yet. You're dead. I want to live. I want to live. . . .*

And the tilt of the river steepens, and he's falling, falling over the waterfall, a long, slow tumble forever and ever.

He wakes with a jolt, spread-eagled on his back. *Still here.* Every muscle in his body seems to be tearing itself away from the others. Each breath is shallow torture. He can't even groan. How long can this go on?

Help me. Father. Somebody. Anybody, please, help me.

Loki growls low, vibrating against him. Panic flares through Peer's veins. *Are those creatures coming back?*

But something splashes, disturbing the rhythm of the creek. He turns his eyes painfully toward the sound.

Movement. A stone plops. Black against the faint sheen of the water, shadows stoop and straighten, flitting toward him. A voice calls, cool and curious as a bird. Loki growls again, then whines and trembles.

An extraordinary face appears hanging over him, as thin as the blade of an ax. The eyes gleam, so closely set they look like a single green stone sticking through the narrow forehead. The face is almost all nose, bulbous and huge. A sharp, down-turned mouth looks comically disapproving. It warbles a rapid string of sounds that may be a question.

Peer tries to speak. Croaks. Hot and cold waves are washing up and down his body, and he seems to be shrinking, but at different rates. He feels at once very heavy, and very small. Yet his feet are miles away. His hands are useless cramped claws far off at the ends of his arms.

More of the thin faces peer down at him. Cold, gentle fingers prod and probe into his sore, cracked mouth. With an agonizing twitch the wooden gag is pulled out, and tears of relief spring to his eyes as he tries to close his jaws over his swollen tongue. The Thin Faces uproot the forked sticks and stakes pinning him down, and toss them away.

An angry chittering comes from the holes in the side of the gully, and sticks and stones fly, but nothing else emerges. Peer struggles to move. His rescuers drag him up, but he falls over. Loki circles anxiously.

The Thin Faces whistle quietly together. They arrange themselves on each side of him and pick him up. Their hands are cold and damp, but strong. They're not tall—only child-sized—and he finds himself bumping along close to the ground. A low singing starts up, "Hoi . . . hoi . . . hoi . . ." They stamp their feet in time, dancing down to the creek, where they lower him into the water. The shock is delicious. He rolls over and buries his sore face in the swift coldness, sucking and lapping and gasping.

"Hoi . . . hoi . . . hoi . . ." Before he's had half enough, the Thin Faces catch his arms and pull him up the opposite bank. Low fir branches shower needles into his hair, and his heels drag on the soft loose surface. They swing him up, running at a steady jog-trot. Peer hangs jolting between them, upside down, staring into the crooked sky above the trail. It streams past, pale with predawn light, brushed with branches of black yew, spruce, and pine. Loki bounds along, keeping up with him, sometimes on one side, sometimes on the other.

Tiny clouds appear overhead like pink feathers. Birds call. Sixty feet up, the tips of the pines are touched with gold. The Thin Faces glance uneasily at one another and warble. Their profiles are strong against the brightening sky. Their skin is brown with a greenish bloom, like bronze, and their long lank hair is looped up in identical topknots.

They stop and lower Peer to the earth. Heads hanging, they melt shyly away into the forest almost before he can get a good look at them. The last one hesitates. It raises a slender arm and points up the trail. And then it's gone.

Returning blood jabs a million needles into Peer's hands and feet. His wounded arm throbs. He rolls over, pushes himself into a crawling position, sits up. Loki watches intently, wagging his tail.

"Loki," Peer says with his sore tongue, and it feels like the first word he's ever uttered. "Loki, boy."

He can't begin to cope with what's happened. The dragon—the black river—he tucks it away inside himself to look at later.

He struggles to his feet, pulling himself up against a tree. "Well, they left us on a path," he says painfully. "It must go somewhere. Let's find out."

The path slants along the side of a steep valley with a creek at the bottom. Peer can hear it below him, hidden by trees. He hobbles along, seized by unexpected crippling cramps. It may get warmer later, but it's cold down here in the shadows.

After an hour or so the trail steepens, curving away from the creek. The noise of the water fades. Peer climbs doggedly on. The trees thin, and a breeze picks up. He comes out onto a ridge and the sun burns the back of his neck. There's a view of more hills, covered with forest in which the endless green is already interrupted by autumn reds and golds. His heart sinks at the sight. Where in all this wilderness can he go?

The path fades, threading downhill over dry ground to vanish under a litter of dead branches and undergrowth. Wherever he sets his foot, brown grasshoppers scramble and jump, and their *tick, tick, zizz* fills the air. He battles on, clambering over fallen trees, stumbling through ankle-deep moss. When he finds the trail again, he doesn't know if it's the same one. Or if it matters.

It dips into a small ravine with a trickle of water at the bottom. The trickle becomes a brook, swirling over a series of waterfalls like deep steps. Peer stumbles on, not sure why, except that to stop moving is to give up hope entirely. But he has to rest more and more often, and each time it's harder to get up. Small goals become important. *I'll get to that bend in the stream before I stop. As far as that tree with the silver bark. As far as that overhanging rock.* At last he's not sure for how long he's been wandering, or how many nights he's spent in the forest.

Once he almost steps on a little snake, lying in a patch of sun like a finely braided green leather whip. It pokes out a scarlet tongue and shoots into the undergrowth. Once he finds a tangle of fruiting blackberries, and shoves the sweet berries into his bruised mouth till his fingers drip.

The path brings him to the top of a steep bank, thick with birches and aspens. The brook plunges over in a long horse tail, splashing off little ledges on the way down. At the bottom, between layers of golden leaves, is the silver glare of water. Echoing up from the water is childish laughter and splashing.

Children?

How? Whose? But it doesn't matter: There are people down there. He slithers downhill, Loki at his heels, skidding, sliding, catching hold of branches to check his descent. He tumbles out of the trees.

A stretch of open water spreads away, level and bright. Along the water's edge, against the fringe of the forest, is a village of conical huts or tents, constructed of tall poles propped together and wrapped in sheets of white and golden birchbark. There are fifteen, twenty of them. It's a big place, bigger than Trollsvik. White smoke rises from cooking fires. Slender white boats lie drawn up on the shore, and a band of bare little black-haired children are chasing one another through the shallows.

Skraelings?

The word doesn't seem to fit the happy children and the white and golden village.

Then the children see him. Eyes and mouths widen. They take one look at this pale, shambling, bloody creature and scatter screaming, as though some kind of demon has dropped out of the forest. Peer doesn't blame them. The village erupts. Dogs howl. Mothers run out to snatch up their babies. Fathers scramble from their doorways and run yelling at Peer, shaking light axes and brandishing spears.

Peer sits down. In truth his legs have simply given way. But it seems sensible; no one can think he's dangerous if he's sitting on the ground. And if they want to kill him, they'll do it anyway. And he's too tired to care. He grips Loki's collar and waits for them to come.

It works. A crowd of men and boys surrounds him, arguing loudly, threatening him with their spears but not touching him. Their dogs skulk around snarling, foxy-faced, with curling bushy tails. Peer looks up, beyond fear, smiling stupidly, just thankful to be with people again. Dark eyes glitter down at him, suspicious, doubtful. He sees details—a cluster of red feathers swinging from a brown earlobe, a long necklace of white beads, a checkerwork armband in black and blue and white.

And then . . .

Can there be fair-haired Skraelings? A young boy scrabbles his way to the front of the crowd. His chest is bare. He wears a breechcloth of soft leather. His shoulder-length, white-gold hair is braided at the front and tied with discs of white shell and bunches of little blue feathers. His round face, pale under the tan, is marked with paint—a black line drawn from his forehead down over his nose, and white diagonal streaks across each cheek. His blue eyes blaze at Peer, furious, incredulous, and more than a little scared.

"Who are you?" he demands in clear, aggressive Norse. "Where have you come from?" The paint on his face wrinkles as he scowls. "Did Harald Silkenhair send you?"

CHAPTER 20

Thorolf the Seafarer

Hilde dreamed. She thought she was running through the woods, trying to catch Peer, who was running ahead of her and who wouldn't stop, although she called and called. He vanished into dark trees, leaving her alone and lost.

She woke, and the waking was as bad as the dream. She lay in the gloomy flicker of the fire hall, knowing that Peer was gone. Nothing good would ever happen again. Astrid lay asleep beside her, her arm over her face.

Gunnar had shut his door against Astrid, leaving the girls no choice but to sleep in the fire hall with the men. Hilde didn't know why it should be different from everyone sleeping together as they had on the ship. But it was, and the men thought so too. There was a wide gap between herself and Tjorvi, the nearest sleeper.

Miserably she went over what Astrid had told her about Peer. He had fallen into some sort of trap; that was all she would say. When Hilde had pushed for details, Astrid got angry. She'd said, "It wouldn't help to tell you. And anyway, it's hard to explain. It's like looking through a tiny window, a peephole, at something bright and small. You can't see everything. In fact, you can't see much of anything."

"But you've found him," Hilde burst out. "Then let's go and rescue him."

"But I don't know how to get there," Astrid said. "Oh, Hilde, think about it. Think how a fly flies! I'd never find the way."

Hilde thought of it, the random career of a fly whirling through the woods, past tree after tree after tree . . .

"You said he was trapped," she'd said at last, dreading the answer. "What sort of trap?"

Astrid wouldn't tell her for ages. And when she did, it was worse than Hilde could possibly have imagined. "He couldn't move. I think he was pegged down."

Pegged down!

In agony she racked her brain to think of something— anything—that could be done. But there was nothing. Tjorvi and Arnë would look for Peer again tomorrow. She would go with them. But it would be no good searching and calling, because when Astrid's *sending* had found Peer, he had seemed to be dying, so by now he was probably dead. Perhaps there were things in the woods that weren't harmless like the little *wiklatmu'jk*. Perhaps the elusive Skraelings had killed him.

Her mind was running in hopeless circles when she was startled by an unexpected sound. A single muffled thump on the door.

Peer!

Her heart jumped into her throat.

It's him; it's got to be.

She sat up instantly, casting a look around the room at the assembled bodies. All sleeping like the dead. No one else had heard. Her bare feet touched the damp earth floor. Taking fast, shallow breaths, she tiptoed past the fire. *Peer's come back. He's waiting outside. Who else would be out there? It's him; he's safe.*

The relief, oh, the relief! Her terrors faded. The childhood reassurance was coming true: *It was just a bad dream. Everything will be all right.* Happiness was possible. Life was worth living. *A second chance; we've got a second chance.*

There was another thud against the door, followed by a strange scratching sound, like claws. Loki. Of course Loki would be with Peer; he never left him.

I'm coming, I'm coming . . .

He was so clear in her imagination, standing wearily on the other side of the door, perhaps leaning against it, holding himself up. In a moment she would see him, speak to him, touch him. She seized the wooden bar that fastened the door at night. It was heavy, but she managed to lift it from its sockets without a sound and lay it quietly on the floor. Trembling with cold and excitement, she raised the latch and eased the door back.

A freezing wind whirled into her face, smelling of salt and seaweed. It blew her hair into her eyes. "Peer?"

The night was dark, cloudy, but surely there was someone on the threshold. Taller than Peer. A figure—or figures. . . . She wiped her hair away and craned into the night with a cry of disappointment. Peer was not there.

The wind pushed into the house. It rushed up the room, sweeping the fire low. Along the darkening walls, men raised sleepy heads, lifting themselves on their elbow. Hilde turned.

A wet trail crossed the floor, as though someone had run through the room with an armful of soaking washing. A person was disappearing through the door to the inner room—a big man, his clothes black and dripping. The door slapped shut.

There was a strangled wail from Floki. "Oh, gods!"

His voice was drowned by Gunnar's waking yell of terror.

Hilde stumbled. Something squirmed between her feet. She looked down. The dragonhead lay there, inert, its blind eye staring at her, its mouth curled in a sardonic grin. She backed away from it, knuckles against her teeth.

It didn't move; it couldn't have moved.

But there it was. And how had it got there?

Frantic men scrambled from the blankets, grabbing axes, drawing knives. The dim end of the room filled with shadows as they threw themselves at the door of Gunnar's bedchamber. What a crowd they made. *There's too many people. Who are they all?* Breathless, she counted faces. That was

Tjorvi, all right, pressing against the door with Arnë—but who was that hollow-cheeked fellow beside him, who ducked away as she looked? Between Floki and Magnus was someone whose head gleamed unpleasantly, like bald bone. And who was that, grinning most inappropriately over Halfdan's shoulder?

From beyond the door came a series of half-throttled screams.

"It's stuck!" Tjorvi gasped, sweat pouring down his face. "It won't shift. Someone's barred it—on the inside!"

"Then break it down." Teeth bared, Harald swung around, his gold hair flying. "We need a log, quick. That one!"

"Not that one!" Hilde screeched. It was the dragonhead he was pointing at, and it was now much farther up the room. "Don't touch it!"

Harald bent, stared, cursed. He grabbed an ax from the feeble hands of Floki and began attacking the door with huge hacking swipes.

Someone touched Hilde's elbow and she almost jumped out of her skin.

"What did you stop him for?" said Astrid viciously. She was very pale. The bruise on her face stood out. Her lips were parted and her breath came quickly.

"Nobody ought to touch that thing—not even Harald," said Hilde vehemently. She didn't know why. Then she did. *When the dead fight the living, I'm on the side of the living.* It was as simple as that.

Astrid pointed at the ruined dragonhead. "But you did. You

took it away. Where did you hide it?"

"In Thorolf's house."

"*Thorolf's house?*" Astrid began to laugh. "No wonder we have visitors. Can you see them, too? Poor fellows, they're not in very good shape anymore—not after sword and fire and seawater . . ."

Tjorvi had an ax now, and he and Harald were taking turns at the door, which shuddered and jumped. Splinters flew. They opened a long gash in the planks. Harald tossed the ax aside and called, "Father? Father!"

The screaming had stopped. Harald ran desperate hands through his hair. He looked wildly around. "Astrid! Help him!"

"How?" said Astrid calmly.

Harald seized her arm. "You're a troll, you've got troll powers, haven't you? Do something!"

Astrid showed her teeth. "And if I'm a troll, why should I help you or him? Maybe I did this! Maybe I let them in."

Harald grabbed a fistful of her bright hair. He jerked her head back and pressed his knife against her throat.

"No! Harald, she didn't." Hilde caught her friend's arm. "Astrid, everyone knows you're not a troll. Please help us. Please!"

Astrid's face twisted stubbornly. She looked at Harald out of the corners of her eyes and gasped, "Threaten away, Harald Silkenhair. I can't help Gunnar anymore. You saw to that."

"What do you mean?" Harald yanked her hair. Astrid started to laugh again, a high-pitched sound not far from weeping. "The soul has wings, Harald, did you know that? Even Gunnar's soul. So I hid it for him in an egg, a little bird's egg. And it was quite safe with me—till you stamped it into pieces this afternoon."

She lifted her voice and screamed, "Hear me, Gunnar, if you can! You should have trusted me, not Harald. And now I wouldn't help you if you came crawling to me along the high-way. *A cold wife and a cold bed. A cold life and a cold death to you, Gunnar Ingolfsson!*"

Harald flung her away. He hurled himself at the weakened door, and Tjorvi and Magnus joined him, throwing their shoulders against it.

It gave way, pitching them into the darkness beyond. They fell through on hands and knees. Hilde saw Harald scrambling up. "Bring torches!"

She ran to the fire and plucked a burning stick from the embers—ran to the broken door. All the men were pushing their way in. Floki hung back, his mouth trembling—afraid to go in, afraid to stay in the fire hall by himself. Hilde held out her hand, and he gripped it tightly. Like children they tiptoed into the room together.

Gunnar lay uncovered on the bed, his arms outspread. There were deep black marks on his bare throat. His skin ran with water; his hair was soaked. The air in the room smelled chill and shocked, as though a wave had burst through it. The bed linen dripped quietly onto the floor.

Floki's hand shook in Hilde's.

With a cry, Harald cast himself on the bed. He got an arm behind Gunnar's shoulders and heaved him up, cradling him. Gunnar's arms hung down and his eyes stared at nothing.

Thorolf the Seafarer had been—and gone.

They built up the fire till it blazed, and huddled around it, listening to Harald weeping behind the broken door.

"Harald's brave enough," Halfdan muttered once. "Sitting up with *that*."

The men nodded. After a while, and almost as though he couldn't help it, Magnus said, "What if *Gunnar* won't lie quiet?"

That made everyone draw closer together—except Astrid, who sat alone and silent near the door.

But the night passed without further disturbance. When a little gray light crept through the smoke hole, Hilde began stiffly to set about stirring up some warm groute. She didn't ask Astrid to help: Astrid looked as though she might never move or speak again. Hilde set a small bowl aside for the Nis. She knew it was frightened of ghosts. She hoped it was all right.

Harald came out of his father's room. The men jumped nervously as if expecting a monster. He paused in the doorway. "A funeral," he said coldly. "Build a pyre. We'll burn his body and raise a mound to cover his bones. Pull down the other house to make material for it. I don't want a turf or a hearthstone left in place. And from now on this bay will be called Gunnar's Grave. Where is the dragonhead? Has it been burned yet?"

"No," said Halfdan nervously. No one had liked to touch it. They all looked where it lay, halfway up the room.

"Put it on the pyre," said Harald. "Put it at his feet."

They built the pyre on the beach and carried Gunnar out on a board, wrapped in his cloak. The weather had changed. Spatters of rain drove in from the sea. Out in the river, *Water Snake* tossed at her mooring. Hilde looked at her sadly. *All that long journey—for this?* They stood in the cold wind, watching the flames roar up. Astrid waited at a distance while the funeral pyre burned, her cloak and dress fluttering in the wind. She looked like a sort of ghost herself, Hilde thought. She had been "the skipper's wife." Then she had been "the troll girl." What was she now? Widow or faithless wife? Hilde was afraid for her—afraid of what Harald might do.

Back at the house, after the funeral, Harald sat on a low stool by the fire, empty-handed and silent, staring into the flames. At last he raised his head and called across the fire. "Astrid!"

Hilde drew a sharp breath. But Astrid came around the fire and stood in front of Harald. He said slowly, "My hair needs combing. Comb it for me, Astrid."

Blank-faced, Astrid sat on the bench behind him, lifted a long strand of his hair and began to run her comb through it.

After a while Harald slid to the floor and leaned against her knees. He tilted his head into her lap and closed his eyes.

Astrid combed mechanically, spreading out the shining strands till her knees were covered in a silken cloak.

They went to the beach the next day to recover the bones. The rain had beaten into the embers, and the fire was out. Raking through the debris, Floki gave a yelp of horror. The dragon-head thrust its snout out of the ashes, a long, black, staring, crooked thing, no more scorched than it had been before. Magnus turned it over with a flinching foot.

"Of course it won't burn," said Tjorvi angrily. "It's lain in the sea too long. Soaked in salt water—damp right through." Everyone nodded. No one believed it. They kicked it down to the tide line, where some winter storm might wash it away.

CHAPTER 21

War Dance

Along the lake edge the ice was a thin pavement that crackled and broke under their feet. Peer's breath smoked as he followed Kwimu and Ottar back toward the wigwams. They'd been checking the traps around the beaver dam, and found two fine fat beavers, which had rashly triggered the deadfalls.

How quickly summer vanished! In a few brief weeks, since he'd been here, the trees had burned themselves up in a bonfire of color—red, purple, gold. Now all that was left was bare black branches and dark green firs and bluish spruce. A powdering of snow had fallen, and Peer was glad of the warm moose-hide wrap, as big as a blanket, which Nukumij had given him.

The still water above the beaver dam was already half

frozen—thin shelves of ice spreading out from the edges. As they walked away, Kwimu said something that made Ottar laugh. "Kwimu says the beavers are like the People. They build lodges and live together in families. He says if they were just a tiny bit cleverer, they'd stick out their heads and talk to us. Then we'd have to stop hunting them."

Kwimu waited till Ottar had finished translating, then he grinned at Peer. Peer grinned back. It had been a long time since he'd had a friend his own age, and you couldn't help liking Kwimu. With his long black hair and strong, regular features, he was as handsome in his way as Harald Silkenhair, but there the comparison ended. Kwimu always had a smile ready, or a helping hand. Ottar adored him.

Peer was glad to be of use at last. The day he'd staggered out of the woods, he'd just managed to explain to Ottar that he wasn't an enemy, that Harald Silkenhair had driven him out. Then he'd collapsed, and lain ill for days. He remembered fleeting snatches: waking from dark dreams to see the fire flicker, smelling the strong green smell of broken fir branches. Crying out, struggling against the grip of hands before realizing dimly that they meant only to poultice his arm, or tilt him up to pour odd-tasting drinks down his throat. Lying with eyes shut, listening to human voices flowing over him like water. Then one night he'd woken to the sound of a light, shifting rattle, followed by the thud of a stick on a bark drum. Close by, someone began singing—an intricate, flowing song that died away at the end of each breath and began again with renewed strength: *"Yah weh ah hah yay oh. Ah hah yay ah hay oh . . ."*

It was Grandmother, Nukumij, singing a medicine song to cure him. Its lilting, ever-changing rhythm seemed to bring back his spirit from wherever it was wandering. From that moment he got better. Soon he was sitting up and learning about the people who had helped him.

There was Grandmother, of course—so tiny she seemed almost lost in her voluminous beaver-fur robes, but whose skillful hands were always busy and whose bright eyes saw everything. There was Kwimu's father, Sinumkw, so stern and stately that Peer was a little nervous of him—until he smiled, when he looked just like Kwimu. There was Kwimu's quiet mother, and Plawej, a sweet-faced young woman with a plump, black-eyed baby, whose husband was away on a hunting trip. And Kwimu's little sister, Jipjawej—too shy even to look at Peer till, remembering a trick that charmed the children at home, he cunningly carved her a small wooden whistle. The first time he blew on it, she jumped. Then she took it with a quick, delighted smile.

Ottar watched her tooting on it as though he rather wanted one himself. "I'll show you how to make them," said Peer. "So if Jipjawej loses hers, you can make her another."

Ottar was no older than Sigurd. Cutting away at the whistle, he told Peer how he'd seen his father killed—how he'd climbed on the roof and hidden from the murderers . . . and watched them sail away, leaving him to die.

"And for nothing," he said bitterly. "For an argument about some furs. Pa set the traps and did the work, and then Harald came along and claimed half of them. He said Pa and Gunnar had agreed to go halves on everything." His voice rose: "But that was a lie. Pa said they'd only agreed to share the expenses of setting out, and what we brought back was up to each of us. 'Then you won't give me the furs?' Harald said.

"He sounded really nasty. Up till then I'd liked Harald. He looks like such a hero, and he used to say funny things that made me laugh." Ottar scowled and shivered. "Well, next morning, while we were still getting up, we heard a dreadful yell from outside. I was eating breakfast and I nearly dropped the bowl. I didn't know if it was a man or a wolf. Pa said, 'What in thunder is that?' And the door burst open. They all had swords and axes." Ottar looked up with a tortured face. "How could they do it, Peer? They were supposed to be our friends."

All too easily, Peer thought. Prime fox and beaver skins sold at home for several silver pennies apiece. No wonder Gunnar could afford to buy Harald that expensive sword.

"And now he's back," Ottar stated. He swallowed. "Do you think I ought to try and kill him?"

"No," said Peer firmly.

"But it's my duty, isn't it? To avenge my father?"

"Do you really think your father would want you to fight Harald?" Peer asked. And Ottar thought about it. "No," he admitted finally, looking relieved.

With Ottar's help, Peer told the family about his ordeal in

the woods. The creatures who'd fastened him down were known as the Spreaders, and Ottar said that they ate rotten flesh. Peer remembered the sweet, fly-ridden stink of the gully, and shuddered quietly. On the other hand, the Thin Faces were known to help lost travelers. "And Grandmother says they don't help bad people," Ottar said with a grin. "So she thinks you must be all right."

But when, shyly, Peer told them a little about the dream of the dragonhead, Grandmother's eyes snapped with excitement. She plunged into a long speech, and Peer listened helplessly, wishing he could understand. Ottar did his best. Grandmother was trying to tell him that his father's spirit had taken on the form of a *jipijka'm*. Peer got Ottar to say it again, and Grandmother nodded, repeating the word several times. So far as Ottar could explain, it was a sort of horned dragon, magical and dangerous, with powers to change and heal. "She says . . ."—he stumbled—"the *jipijka'm* is your *tioml*. Your power, I think. Your strength."

Grandmother's whole face crinkled up into a smile, and she leaned forward and patted Peer's hand. She said something else, nodding again. "Jipijkame'ji'j," said Ottar. "That's what she'll call you. Young Dragon."

Young Dragon. A thrill of pride ran right through him. Then he thought of the Nis, and laughed a little. Nithing the Seafarer! Peer the Young Dragon! Peer Barelegs! What a difference a name could make.

❉   ❉   ❉

Dusk was coming early. The sky sagged over the world like a sleepy gray cat settling down into its basket. It was snowing again, tiny white grains that swept across the ground without sticking. Peer transferred the beaver from one cold hand to the other, wishing he had mittens like Kwimu's. Kwimu caught his eye and said something, lifting an eyebrow with a teasing smile.

"Kwimu's asking about these girls that came on the ship with you," Ottar reported, his face a mixture of embarrassment and disdain. "He says, 'Are they your wives?'"

"My—" Peer felt his jaw drop. "No, they're not!"

"He says, 'But you want them to be?'" Ottar mumbled.

"One of them." Peer bit his lip, grinned, and nodded. Kwimu's eyes danced.

"He says it's easy. First you ask her father. If he agrees, go to the girl and toss a stick into her lap. If she likes you, she tosses it back. If she doesn't, she throws it away."

"Er . . . tell him it's not quite as easy as that."

Kwimu shook his head with a rueful expression, and Ottar explained. "He says, 'It never is, and is she pretty?'"

"She's very pretty," said Peer quietly.

Ottar wriggled. "I'm going on ahead. I don't want to talk about girls anymore." He ran off with Loki, pretending to throw a stick for him, while Loki jumped and barked.

Peer's smile faded. For the millionth time, he thought about Hilde. And for the millionth time he wondered what to do. The year was on the edge of winter. The sailing season was over. Back at Serpent's Bay they'd be dragging *Water Snake* up onto the shore on rollers. They'd take down the mast and lash the sail over her, leaving everything trim and snug, ready for months of snow and ice. The men would go out trapping for those precious furs. Hilde would be stuck indoors.

When will I see her? How can I let her know I'm still alive?

Even if he could find his way back to the bay and speak to Hilde secretly, even if she agreed to come with him, even if Sinumkw could be persuaded to take in another foreigner—what would be the use? *We still have to get home, and there's only one ship that can take us.*

Sometimes he thought he should leave Hilde where she was. Gunnar and Harald weren't likely to harm a girl. That way she'd have a chance of sailing home again—about four years from now. *By then she'll probably have married Arnë. She'll think I'm dead.*

There has to be a way. . . .

The pale cones of the wigwams loomed against the trees, and the village smells blew on the wind: smoke and fish oil and all the salty litter of human living—wood chips and leather and roasting meat. If he shut his eyes it reminded him of Trollsvik.

Oh, to be home. To be walking up to the farm, past the brook where the water runs sleek over the little stones, knowing that Gudrun and Hilde and Sigrid are all safe inside waiting for me, with supper hot in the pot and old Alf thumping his tail in greeting—

Keen and close and shrill, a woman screamed.

Peer jumped, looking for danger in the early darkness and whipping wind. But the noise came from inside the thin birchbark walls. *"Akaia! Ah, ah, ah! Akaia!"*

Ottar shot into the wigwam like a rabbit into its hole. Kwimu and Peer ducked through the doorway after him.

"Akaia!"

Plawej knelt by the fire, doubled over, tearing at her hair and face. *"Ah, ah!"* she screamed, throwing herself backward and forward. The other women tried to restrain her. They were all crying, even Grandmother. Tears ran down her wrinkled face. *Someone's died,* Peer thought in horror. *Where's the baby?* He looked quickly around, and saw Jipjawej hugging it, stiffly wrapped in its elaborate cradleboard, but alive all right. *Not the baby, then. So who?*

A dozen young men clustered at the far side of the fire, talking to Sinumkw in angry, urgent voices. They saw Kwimu, grabbed him, and rattled off the same story. Whatever it was, it made Kwimu's face harden till he looked years older.

Ottar slid out of the throng, and Peer caught him. "What's happened?"

"It's Kiunik," Ottar looked white and shocked. "Kiunik, he's married to Plawej. He's Kwimu's uncle. He's been found dead with his friend Tia'm. Both killed. I can't believe it."

"Killed? You mean deliberately? But—"

Peer broke off. A voice rang out of the past, Tjorvi's voice, rough with anger. *Skraelings. Just a couple of young fellows, cooking over a campfire.*

Oh, no.

Ottar was still talking. "They'd been away for weeks; Plawej was getting anxious. Some of the young men went looking for them ..."

"Toward the sea?" Peer croaked. "To Serpent's Bay? Down the river?"

"Yes." Ottar's eyes narrowed. "Kiunik wouldn't stop hunting there. He said we shouldn't be driven out. He said he'd hunt where he liked."

"Did one of them"—Peer's mouth was dry—"did one of them have a big bear-claw necklace?"

"Kiunik did!" Ottar grabbed him. "Why? Do you know something about it?"

Peer looked at Plawej. She wasn't wailing now. She was crushing charcoal from the fire between her palms, and methodically, drearily, blackening her face.

Two men, murdered, and I haven't once thought about them since.

"I know what happened." Peer felt almost as guilty as if he'd done it himself. "Harald killed them."

Ottar's face scrunched up. He flung himself at Kwimu, tugging his arm and shouting. Everything quieted for a second. Even Plawej raised her blotched, blackened face in tearstained surprise. Sinumkw turned slowly.

Peer quailed. Sinumkw surveyed him as an eagle might, looking down on a man from some great height or icy moun-

tain. His strong, severe face was carved with lines of author-
ity, and, now, of sorrow and distrust. His black hair was
drawn back and knotted with painted strings; on his breast
his knife hung from a cord, and looped about his neck was
row after row of beads, strung with copper discs and pearl
shell. He looked more like a leader of men than Gunnar had
ever done. He spoke slowly, coldly, emphatically.

"He says, 'Why didn't you tell us this before?'" Ottar almost
spat the words.

Excuses whirled through Peer's head. *I heard about it, but I
didn't see it. I was shocked at the time, but so much else has happened since. I thought it was an awful thing, but it happened to
"Skraelings," and I hadn't met any then. It didn't seem quite real.
I've been ill.*

He met Sinumkw's fierce, dark eyes, and knew that not one
of these sly, shameful answers was possible. "I ought to have
told you," he said quietly. "I forgot. There's no excuse."

Sinumkw's face remained stern. He paused, and asked
something.

"He wants you to say what happened," Ottar said.

Peer explained what he knew, even to the theft of the bear-
claw necklace. Ottar translated. The young men murmured
angrily. Sinumkw held Peer's gaze, searching him for the
truth. Peer faced him, sweating but steady. An odd thought
went through his head: *He's like my father.* From different
worlds, different lives, they shared an inner dignity and stillness, demanding respect.

At last Sinumkw gave a slow, stiff nod. He began to speak, a few sentences at a time, waiting for Ottar to translate.

"He says you were ill, and didn't know Kiunik or Tia'm. He says you were not to blame for their deaths. He says he already guessed who killed them, because they were so close to the Place of Ghosts. He says he warned Kiunik not to go there, but Kiunik went because he was brave"—Ottar's voice wobbled and caught—"and proud, like a warrior. He says Kiunik was right."

Sinumkw stepped to the center of the wigwam, to the swept earth floor around the fire. He lifted his voice so that everyone could hear, and went on speaking, more rapidly this time.

"He says when he heard that the pale people had come back, he wasn't sure what to do," Ottar whispered. "He says he didn't want to fight them because there are not many of them, and they took the bay out of ignorance, not knowing it was ours. He says our lands are wide. If they wanted to live in the Place of Ghosts, he thought they could do so without troubling us, even though they are bad men who kill each other. But now, he says, two of our own young men have been killed. He says . . ." Ottar chewed his lip, nearly in tears. "He says they killed Kiunik and Tia'm and left their bodies lying to be eaten by animals. Muin and Kopit, who found them, could hardly recognize them. But they gathered up the bodies, and wrapped them in bark, and left them on a—a sort of platform, a scaffold in the woods, to keep them safe, and soon

286

we'll go and take them to the burying place. But before that, Sinumkw says, we have a—a duty to them. Their ghosts are waiting outside in the dark right now to see what we will do. He says they will be angry if we don't send them on their way with honor. They need revenge."

The warriors yelled—a crash of approval. "*Heh!*"

"'Let us give it to them.'"

"*Heh!*"

"'We will go to the Place of Ghosts.'"

"*Heh!*"

Ottar's face was sharp and glowing. "'We will pull down their houses and leave not one alive.'"

"*Heh!*"

"And he says—yes! He says we'll rip off the scalp of the boy with the long golden hair and dry it in the smoke, and Kiunik and Tia'm will take it with them on their journey! Hooray!"

"*Heh! Heh! Heh!*" the young men roared. Sinumkw gestured, and Kwimu stepped forward with a shallow birchbark bowl. Sinumkw dipped his fingers in and brought them out covered with thick red pigment. Deliberately, ceremoniously, he smeared the paint over his face.

"War!" Ottar whispered.

"*Heh!*" shouted Kwimu. He too dipped his hand into the pigment and dragged red fingers across his face.

"*Heh!*" shrieked Ottar.

Even Peer felt the surge of excitement. *This will teach Harald Silkenhair a lesson!* All the powerlessness he'd felt in the face of Harald's insults boiled up inside him. Harald, the bully with the sword—if he could see what was coming to him!

"*Hey! Hey!*" he yelled in unison with the other young men. Everyone was crowding to redden their faces. Peer found himself waiting in line. The *pat-pat-pat* of a drum started up—a stick knocking on a thick roll of birchbark. The men began a dance step, heads high, arms held out with clenched fists. They sang and stamped.

Peer came level with Kwimu. Kwimu's eyes were hot and bright; his face was taut under the disfiguring pigment. He held out the bowl to Peer. There wasn't much left, but Peer scooped some out and touched it to his face.

The young men swept him into the dance. It wasn't difficult—a step forward and a step back. Stamp, step, around and around. Stamp, step, around and around. Stamp—

What had Sinumkw said?

We will pull down their houses and leave not one alive?

The wigwam spun. He staggered out of the dance and crouched on the fir boughs that lined the floor, taking deep breaths. Ottar danced past, and Peer thrust out a foot to trip him.

"What's that for?" the boy cried angrily.

"Wait, Ottar—it's important." Peer grabbed his arm as Ottar tried to pull away. "What are we thinking? We can't do this. We can't attack the houses."

"Why not?" demanded Ottar. "Harald deserves to die!"

"But what about the others? The girls? My friend Hilde and her friend Astrid? And . . ." *And Tjorvi and Arnë,* he was about to say, *who didn't even sail with Gunnar before. And Magnus and Floki and Halfdan—I don't want any of them to die. . . .*

He looked into Ottar's indifferent face and realized that to him they would be only a string of names.

"I expect you can save the women," Ottar said. "We can ask Sinumkw if you like. About the others, I don't care. They didn't care about Kiunik, did they? Or Pa?"

"What if they surrender?" Peer demanded.

Ottar stared. "Harald and Gunnar won't surrender! And I don't want them to. They killed my Pa, and I want them to die!" He wrenched himself free and whirled off into the dance, singing.

Peer put his face in his hands. He rubbed his cheeks, wiping his red fingers on the fresh green fir branches, and looked at the dancing men with sudden loathing. What was all this singing about? Who were these people—these *Skraelings*—who danced and sang about going to war?

Someone touched his arm. It was Nukumij—Grandmother. She sat down beside him and pointed to his face and then at the dancers, smiling sadly. She shook her head, and made an eloquent gesture that took in the war dance, the fire, the sad figure of Plawej with her woeful, besmeared face.

Peer thought he understood. *Killing people,* she seemed to say, *is such a terrible thing that we have to work ourselves up to it.* Making a ceremony out of it—did that make it better?

Better than Harald's casual killings?

These weren't people who disregarded life. Those beavers he and Kwimu had trapped—every scrap would be used: the meat, the fur, even the chisel teeth. Then the bones would be placed respectfully in running water, so the dogs couldn't chew them. Far in the woods, Ottar told him, was the wigwam of the Man Who Brings Back Animals. He would sing his song of power to bring the bones to life, so there would always be beavers for the People to hunt.

That was what they believed.

Harald Silkenhair had killed two young men with no ceremony at all, and left their bodies lying.

Why should Sinumkw care about Magnus or Tjorvi or the others? Why should anybody care about someone else whom they'd never met?

But I care. I'm in the middle. I know them all. Probably Harald deserves it. But nobody else does. I can't let them die.

He groaned, and Grandmother reached out and took his hand. Her fingers were warm and dry, a bunch of slender bones covered in wrinkled brown skin. His own were pale in comparison, even after a summer out of doors, even stained with greasy red streaks. She squeezed gently, a gesture of compassion, and let go. They sat quietly together.

Ottar flung himself down beside them, flushed and panting. "Hear them singing?" he asked. "Want to know what it means?

"Death I make, singing.
"Heh! Hey!
"Bones I break, singing.
"Hey! Hey!
"Death I make, singing!"

CHAPTER 22

The Fight in the House

B y dusk the next day, the war party had covered half the distance to the shore. Sinumkw called a halt in an open glade, a tilted clearing on a hill shoulder, facing east toward the sea. A wind sharp as a skinning knife sliced between the trees, ruffling the black fur of pines and spruce, moaning through the skeletal arms of oaks, chestnuts, and maples.

Peer looked at the war band. Nearly fifty men had set out from the village for the two-day walk to the shore. All wore red on their faces. All were wrapped in thick clothes against the cold: double layers of beaver robes, long leggings, and hide boots. All moved quickly and easily over the snow on wide, flat snowshoes that they tied to their feet.

"There's no shelter here," he said in a low voice to Ottar. Ottar had insisted on coming. The young men treated him as a favored little brother with a right to be here.

"There soon will be," said Ottar confidently. "Like this!" He kicked off one of his snowshoes and started using it as a shovel to scoop out a hollow from the snow. Kwimu and Peer joined in, flinging out more and more snow to make a hole four feet deep and seven or eight feet across. All the men were digging shelters. They broke branches from the fir trees and threw them in to layer the bottoms of the holes with a springy crisscross. Larger boughs partly roofed the shelters. And soon small fires were spiraling upward.

The shelter had a cozy feel, like a snow nest. The wind sped by overhead but couldn't reach them. Peer leaned back on the branches, fed Loki a strip of dried meat, and, chewing on one himself, stretched out his feet to the fire.

While the other young men chatted, checking their bows, axes, and clubs, Peer worried about his role tomorrow. To try and get Hilde out before the fighting started, he'd volunteered to carry Sinumkw's declaration of war. Anything could happen in an attack. Sinumkw had agreed not to harm the girls, but Hilde would certainly defend herself, and then what? It gave him a chance to explain to her what was going on. But it meant walking openly into the house and talking to everyone.

Grimly he foresaw how his news would be received. *Even if Harald doesn't skewer me straight off, Gunnar won't let the girls leave. He won't trust me, and he certainly won't trust the "Skraelings," and he'll never give up Harald.*

They'd be killed in the end, of course—eight men against fifty. But with their steel-edged weapons, they'd do some damage first. He pictured Kwimu or Ottar falling, sliced down by Harald's sword. Blood spreading in the snow. Death and injuries and pain and misery. What was the point?

The stars looked like frost crystals in the black sky. In the light of the small fire, the young men's painted faces glowed a startling, fearsome red. But their expressions were thoughtful as they talked together quietly. He wished he could join in. These could be friends—if they weren't going to war against his other friends.

Ottar turned to Peer. "Do you believe in Valhalla, Peer? Where do you think we go to when we die? Kwimu says the People walk along the Ghost Road to the Land of Souls. Look, you can see it up there." Kwimu pointed upward. A glimmer above the trees was the line of the Milky Way, spangled and studded with stars. A royal road for the feet of the dead. Peer's breath caught.

"I don't know," he answered. "My father used to say we cross over a bridge."

"It looks like a bridge, doesn't it?" said Ottar, staring up. "I hope it's the same one. Wherever Kwimu goes, I want to go there, too."

Crossing a bridge . . . floating away down a dark river . . . Perhaps all the journeys ended at the same bourne. Peer thought of his father and was comforted.

Snow fluttered down again. Shadowy flakes whirled into

the fire like moths. Peer's breath smoked. The wind wailed. Or was it a wolf or some other animal, crying?

Kwimu cocked his head, listening. He took off the fox-skin pouch that usually dangled from his belt. It had the face and paws and tail all attached, and Peer had sometimes seen him playing with it, stroking it and pretending to make it pounce. Now Kwimu scrambled lithely out of the shelter and disappeared into the snow. He came back almost immediately, without the pouch, said something, and lay down. The others followed suit.

"What's that about?" Peer whispered.

Ottar yawned. "It's all right. He's leaving Fox on a tree branch not far away. To warn us of danger."

"Fox? You mean his *pouch*?"

Ottar scowled. "It's his *tioml*. His power. You don't notice much, Peer. Haven't you seen how it comes alive?"

"But . . ." Peer shut his mouth. He wasn't sure of anything, he decided. And, about midnight, they were woken by a shrill, yapping bark from close above. Loki stirred and grumbled. Peer sat up and saw Kwimu and the others, dark shapes against the snow, heaving up on their elbow.

The fire was out. On the cold wind came a distant howl, a lonely, hungry sound. It drew nearer. Beside him, Peer saw Ottar's eyes gleam wide.

Out of the woods, into the clearing, a moose came leaping in an arc of snow—running for its life. Peer rose to see it better. Without checking, it lifted over the shelter in a single bound, kicked a freezing dust of powder snow into Peer's hair, and galloped into the trees on the downhill side of the glade.

After it something came rushing through the trees, with crashing of undergrowth and explosive cracks of branches. It must be enormous to make such a noise. Wolf? Bear? Impossible. *Here it comes,* he thought in growing apprehension, *and it's big. It's very big—*

"Down! Get down!" Ottar grabbed his leg and jerked it. In disbelief Peer saw the tops of the pine trees shiver and sway apart. He sat down hard. *It's here!* It was overhead—a striding shadow against the stars, a yell that threw them to the ground, a double shock of mighty footsteps leaping over them.

It was gone. The woods swallowed it. An odd musky smell blew back on the wind.

And a small animal slunk light-footed over the edge of the snow shelter, dashed to Kwimu, and disappeared under his cloak.

A murmur of voices rose. In the eerie snow light men scrambled from the dugouts. Peer too clambered up into the cold. Ottar pulled him over to see a great shapeless tread mark stamped into the snow on the very edge of one of the other shelters. They all grouped around it, excited and afraid.

"*Jenu,*" Peer heard. "*Jenu . . .*" He turned to see Kwimu standing somberly, staring into the trees. The fox pouch hung limply from his belt, dark-eyed and grinning.

"What was it?" Peer asked quietly.

"A sort of—ice giant." Ottar's teeth rattled. "That's the

s-second time I've seen one. I'll t-tell you about it—but not out here."

Again and again that night, huddled in the snow shelters, they smelled the strange musky smell on the wind and heard the *jenu's* distant scream as it quartered the woods in search of game, but it never came so close as that first time.

"Doesn't it ever rest?" Peer whispered.

Ottar whispered back, "Kwimu says never."

With the dawn, they clambered out of their snow holes, stiff and shaken. It wasn't a good omen for the day ahead, Peer thought, hoping they might give up and go back to the village. But his companions were strapping on their snowshoes and setting off, and with a heavy heart he knelt to do the same. As Kwimu bent beside him, Peer got a good look at the fox pouch. Whatever it had done in the night, it was definitely not alive now. The eyes were made of little black shells.

And the day passed in trudging along slanting hillsides, under the lee of rocky ridges and over open tracts where fire had swept through the woods and tree stumps poked through the snow like black teeth. Peer couldn't recognize anything from his autumn journey. Apart from their own passing—the creak of the snowshoes, and the swish of robes—the woods were abnormally silent. White spines of snow lay along every branch and twig. Snow spread endlessly under the trees till the woods looked like a white cavern held up by dark pillars. His eyes ached from the whiteness, and his ears ached from the lack of sound.

At last, in the blue dusk, they descended one last slope. At the bottom, snow curled over the banks of a river, frozen over except for black cores and sinkholes out in the middle, where the ice was still treacherous. Following the bank, they came out to frozen marshlands where the snow was thinner, swept by a wind that drove it like dust before a broom. Beyond the marshlands, Peer could hear the pounding of the sea.

Serpent's Bay! It looked different under the snow. Ottar pushed alongside, staring. "What have they done?" he said hoarsely. "They've pulled down our old house."

Only Gunnar's house was left. Peer stared hungrily at it. Hilde was there. *So close!*

The sky was dark over the sea, shading to a lingering paleness over the forest in the southwest. A fingernail moon clung there, setting into the trees. Sinumkw led the war party silently along the edge of the woods, the frozen flats on their left, till they came to the spot where in summer the brook rushed down the slope. Now it was a white cascade of leaping ice—intricate and silent. With Thorolf's house no longer in the way, there was a clear view to the doorway of Gunnar's. Sinumkw signed to his men to stop. It was a good position, a little uphill from the house, and camouflaged against the dark trees.

Ottar shivered—with old memories, Peer thought, not with cold. Kwimu put an arm around his shoulders. Sinumkw turned to Peer. Peer couldn't read his face under the dark war paint, but his eyes gleamed. Ottar translated. "Sinumkw says,

'Now do what you came for. Carry our challenge. Tell them who they killed and why we have come.' And he says if you can get the girls out, do it before the moon sets. That's when we'll attack."

"It's mighty cold tonight," said Arnë to Hilde. He wiped the last of the broth from his bowl with a lump of bread. "It will be a long winter."

"I know," said Hilde, rousing herself with an effort.

She looked around. Astrid sat on the floor close to the hearth, mending clothes in the firelight. At the far end of the fire Harald sprawled moodily in his father's chair, a low trestle table in front of him. He ignored his food, playing with his knife, twiddling it on its point and catching it before it fell over. The rest of the men were eating silently, heads down. Sometimes one of them coughed, or nudged his neighbor to pass the bread. Floki had a bad cold, and sniffed steadily— juicy, bubbling sniffs. "Can't you stop doing that?" Magnus grumbled. No one else spoke. Nobody had much to say these days.

Somewhere in the rafters, Hilde supposed, the Nis perched, swinging a leg and watching them. If it wasn't dying of boredom. *There'll be months of this.* Months of monotonous, dark indoor life. She wondered how she could bear it.

Arnë watched her. He cleared his throat. "It would be easier, maybe, if we two could help each other."

She turned drearily. "What do you mean?"

"Peer's not coming back, Hilde," Arnë said quietly. "You know that. Not after all this time. I know you were fond of him—but aren't you fond of me, too? You've known me for a long time. If you'll marry me, I'll take care of you. I won't let you worry about anything."

Hilde felt a twisting sensation inside her chest, as though he had taken her heart in both his hands and wrung it out. She met his clear blue eyes and remembered Astrid's words: *Arnë's quite ordinary*. It was true. Nice, yes, but ordinary. She wondered why it had taken her so long to notice.

"Of course I like you, Arnë, but you can't 'take care' of me."

"I'd like to try."

"You don't understand." She closed her eyes and saw, as if by lightning flashes, picture after picture against the darkness. Peer gripping her arm on the ship and dashing off to deal with the Nis. Peer telling Harald the lie about the seagull. Peer facing Harald down not once, but many times, armed only with his bare wits, and, finally, with a burned dragonhead. She opened her eyes. Dammed-up tears spilled out. "Peer never tried to take care of me. He just took it for granted we'd do things together. You say you'd look after me. But in all this time, the only person who's stood up to Harald—the only person brave enough—has been Peer. And I miss him—so much."

Arnë rubbed his eyes. On the back of his wrist Hilde saw the scar where he'd turned aside Harald's harpoon. *Arnë's a good friend. What's wrong with me? Why can't I be nice to him?*

"I'm sorry," she muttered, ashamed. "But it's no good, Arnë. Don't ask me."

"I see it's no good asking you now," said Arnë. "I spoke too soon. Don't worry, I'll wait."

Though he looked sorry for her, she sensed he was confident that she'd change her mind. She began to protest, and fell silent. What was the use? Maybe he was right. Maybe Astrid was right. If the person you wanted died, you just had to accept it and move on. Didn't you?

No, she thought passionately. *No!*

"Floki," said Harald in a cutting voice. "Will you stop that revolting sniffing? You sound like a pig."

A slight ripple went down the room—men lifting their heads and then deciding not to look. Floki flushed and smeared his nose with the back of his hand. "Sorry," he muttered, and sniffed again almost at once.

"Gods!" Harald stared at him in disgust. "You're like a human water clock. We ought to stand you in a corner and keep time by the drips."

Now that, thought Hilde, *is the sort of remark that used to make Floki giggle. See how he likes it when it happens to him.*

This time there were no smothered chuckles. Most of the men ate on steadily, pretending not to notice. There'd been a lot of this lately: everyone tiptoeing around, afraid of setting Harald off. Since Gunnar died his moods had become dangerously unpredictable and his mocking tongue was sharper than ever. Every morning he called Astrid over to comb his hair, and Hilde could not watch without a shiver. She didn't know why it frightened her, but it did. It was like watching a cat playing with a mouse, knowing that sometime the claws would come out. But Harald seemed to enjoy it, and if Astrid found it humiliating, she didn't say so. She never referred to it. The baby was showing more by now, but she never spoke of that, either.

She doesn't talk about anything. She never smiles.

Floki, who had been glancing covertly at Harald and struggling not to sniff, gave up the battle. *"Sssnnnfff!"*

Everyone jumped. Harald heaved a cold sigh. "Someone should make a poem about you, Floki. Though I wonder if anyone could do you justice. Let's see . . . 'Indoors, Floki's nose drips into the pot. Outside, it sprouts an icicle of snot.'" He showed his teeth. "How's that? Not bad, I feel, on the spur of the moment."

"I've got a cold," Floki muttered. "I can't help it."

"I know that, Floki," Harald said soothingly. "I know you can't help it." Floki's worried forehead cleared, but Harald wasn't finished. "But tell me something. Is there anything you can help?"

Floki looked this way and that.

"Answer the question," said Harald pleasantly. "You look like a pig, you sound like a pig. Granted. But do you have to be as stupid as one? Do you have to be a bandy-legged, red-faced, useless idiot?"

Floki twisted his shoulders miserably. He tried to grin, but there were tears in his eyes.

Magnus growled, "Come on, Harald, stop picking on the lad. Like he told you, he can't help having a cold."

"Ah!" Harald's blue eyes flicked to Magnus. "Magnus, rushing in to look after Floki, as usual." He spun his knife and caught it. "You should be in petticoats. You fuss over him like an old woman, don't you? Why is that, Magnus?"

Magnus flushed a slow, angry red.

With widening eyes, Floki plastered his fingers to his face and exploded into a huge, wet sneeze. *"Aaaarcchoooo!"*

Harald grabbed his cup. "Get out of my sight, you fool!" he yelled, and threw it. It bounced off Floki's head, splashing Magnus with weak ale. Floki squealed in pain. Magnus jumped up.

"Right! I'm sick of your sneering ways, Harald. I stood by while you drove one young lad to his death, and I'll not stand by while you start on Floki. Who gave you the right to push us all around?" He glared at Harald. "Your dad was all right, but I can't stand the sight of you. If you was old enough, I'd pick you up and break you in half."

"Shut up!" Harald's voice slashed like a whip. "Tuck Floki into bed and kiss him good night. That's what you're good at, isn't it?"

With an incoherent roar, Magnus launched himself at Harald's throat. Harald stood. The trestle table collapsed between them. Harald put his chin over Magnus's shoulder, hugging him close. His right arm jerked, once, twice. He stepped back. His knife was covered in wet blood. Magnus slid to the ground.

It happened too fast for anyone else to move. Hilde stopped breathing. All around the table were open mouths and horrified eyes.

"Oh, gods. Magnus!" A wail from Floki broke the silence. He scurried around the table and dropped to his knees, grabbing Magnus's arm, rolling him over. "Oh, gods!" He patted Magnus desperately. "Wake up, wake up! Oh, gods, Magnus!"

Hilde stared at Magnus. There was a bloodstained slit in his shirt. His mouth hung slack, showing his missing teeth, and his eyes were setting in his head.

Floki looked up, fingers curling and uncurling. "Tjorvi!" He threw himself at Tjorvi, grabbing fistfuls of his clothes with trembling urgency. "The life-stone, Tjorvi, give it to me, quick!"

Big Tjorvi gaped. "What?"

"That life-stone," Floki shrieked. "The one you told us about. The one your friend got from the eagle. You can have it back later. We need it for Magnus. Quickly, he's dying!"

Tjorvi's face twisted in shocked understanding. "There isn't any life-stone, Floki. It was just a story."

Floki stared at him, panting. "But—we need it."

"There isn't any life-stone," Tjorvi repeated.

Floki dragged his hands down his face, staring at Tjorvi with wild eyes. He fell down beside Magnus again, shaking him. "Magnus—Magnus . . ."

"He's dead," said Harald drily. He still held the knife in his hand.

"Oh, gods." Tears poured down Floki's face. His nose ran. "You killed him. You killed Magnus."

He got up, arms and legs scrabbling as though he could hardly control them. "Then I'll kill you! I'll kill you," he screamed, and snatched a knife from the table. His hands were shaking so hard that he fumbled and dropped it. Harald laughed, but the others were coming out of their shock.

"That was murder," Arnë yelled.

"Aye!" Tjorvi growled, and there was a chorus of agreement.

Harald flicked the knife into his left hand and drew his sword with a scrape of steel. "Come and tell me so," he taunted. "Come on!" He threw back his head to make his hair shake. "Who's first? Who wants to meet Bone-biter? Come and kill me, Floki!"

Sobbing, Floki tried to fling himself forward, but Tjorvi grappled him back. Harald laughed again, shrill and loud. He stepped across Magnus's body and began to chant, beating time on his chest with the fist that held the dagger.

"My name is Harald Silkenhair!
I am the son of Gunnar One-Hand.
He gave me my blade, Bone-biter.
Ha!
I was bred for battle.

305

My mother fed me on wolf meat.
She gave me knives to play with,
To teach me the sharpness of swords.
Ha!
I will dance between the spear-points.
I will split skulls.
Who dares to meet me?"

The men hung back. To get to Harald they had to get past three feet of pointed steel.

Under Harald's feet, poor Magnus lay sprawled in all the indignity of death. Floki was weeping in awful, shrill whimpers. A haze of shame and defeat floated in the room.

Astrid backed up close to Hilde and spoke between her teeth. "You threw a bucket of water over him once. Could we try it again?"

"He didn't have his sword then," Hilde murmured. But Astrid was right: They had to think of something, fast. She could see Arnë creeping forward, and Tjorvi shifting his balance. Harald was watching with pinprick eyes, laughing silently, his sword braced.

What would Peer do? Distract him somehow. There was a chirrup from overhead. The Nis! Her gaze flew upward. Could the Nis distract Harald? The Nis was beside itself with excitement. It teetered on the edge of the rafter, eyes popping, pursing its lips in an exaggerated *Sshh!* Sure of their attention, it jumped from beam to beam till it crouched directly over the clothes Astrid had been mending by the fire, and jabbed a long forefinger downward.

Hilde stared. *What? A cloak, a couple of tunics, some leggings?* And now the Nis was pointing excitedly at Harald....

Astrid's face came alive. She clutched Hilde's arm, sprang forward, snatched up an armful of clothes, and threw them over Harald's sword and sword arm. The blade sagged, muffled in fabric. Harald jumped back, swearing, trying to shake off the clothes, but Hilde tore a blanket from the sleeping bench and sent it sailing at him.

The girls went crazy. They grabbed everything they could off the benches and sent cloaks, jerkins, blankets, socks—a perfect snowstorm of clothes—whirling at Harald. Up in the roof the Nis squeaked deliriously and hurled Harald's own boots at his head.

Harald staggered. A pair of Floki's trousers hung drunkenly over one eye. His sword was tangled in the folds of Tjorvi's heaviest cloak. Arnë leaped on him, bearing him to the ground. Tjorvi followed. They pinned him down, and wrenched the sword out of his hand.

Astrid and Hilde leaned on each other, laughing and crying. The men dragged Harald to his feet. The floor at that end of the fire was a mess of clothes. Magnus's feet stuck out from under it. Hilde sobered abruptly. Rough, cheerful Magnus was dead, and their little victory couldn't change that. Floki, weeping like a rainstorm, went on his knees to clear the clothes from Magnus's face.

Tjorvi looked down at him, and then at Harald, whose face was ugly with rage. "What shall we do with you?" he asked heavily.

"Take your hands off me," Harald spat. Then his eyes went black with shock, and he stared down the room at something behind them—something that could not be happening.

The house door scraped slowly open, revealing a wedge of black night and white snow. Someone walked stiffly in. Someone—or something. The clothes were strange, and covered in painted symbols. The face was stained with blood, but it looked familiar.

Hilde went cold. It was Peer's face.

It was Peer's ghost.

CHAPTER 23

Death in the Snow

Peer blinked. He'd expected surprise, but not this. Every person in the room stood in stiff, arrested positions, gaping in terror. He stepped forward, and they all stepped back. Tjorvi let go of Harald. With a strangled yell, Floki jumped to his feet. "It wasn't us," he babbled. "You can't blame us, it wasn't us. It was him! Take Harald, not us, it wasn't us . . ."

Peer looked at Hilde. Her hand had flown to her mouth and she was gazing at him in apparent horror, her eyes huge. He swallowed. "Hilde. It's me. I'm back."

Astrid gripped Hilde's arm, steadying her. Hilde clutched her, swaying. Then she stepped slowly forward. *"Peer?"* It was a breath of a word, her lips barely moving. "Peer?"

Just then Loki nosed his way around the door. He saw Hilde, flattened his ears, and threw himself at her with a yelp

309

of joy, tail wagging. Hilde shrieked. "It *is* you! It's Loki! Oh, *Peer*!"

She fell on her knees and gathered Loki into her arms, pressing her face against his fur. He wriggled ecstatically, licked her face, tore himself away to dash around the room, greeting people, and returned to Hilde again. But by this time, Hilde was on her feet, locked into Peer's arms, her face buried in his shoulder.

Peer thought he could stand there forever, happiness blazing through him like a pillar of fire.

She looked up. "What's on your face? Blood? Are you hurt?"

He'd forgotten how he must look. No wonder they'd been staring. "Paint," he answered, rubbing at it. "I'll explain later." He looked around, realizing for the first time that something was going on. Why was Floki crying? "Where's Gunnar? I've got a message for you all."

Hilde drew a deep, deep breath and collected herself. "Gunnar's dead." By now the rest of the room was coming to life. No one could think Loki was a ghost. The men looked at Peer with a mixture of delight and disbelief. Tjorvi was beaming, Arnë shaking his head.

"Gunnar's dead?" Peer exclaimed.

"*Magnus is dead, too-oo-oo.*" It was a doglike howl of misery from Floki.

Peer's scalp crawled. The men began yelling, "That's right!"

"Harald killed him! Stabbed him to death in front of us . . ."

"Just now, before you came in. Look, he's there on the floor."

Shock punched through Peer. Magnus was sprawled on his back at the other end of the hearth, staring at nothing. His hands curled half open. His big toe stuck out through a hole in one of his socks.

"What message, Barelegs?"

Peer swung around.

Harald had picked up his sword. He was standing on the other side of the hearth, staring across the flames at Peer. Harald's head jerked, and for a second Peer thought he was motioning him aside. But the jerking continued, and his mouth twitched. The fire danced in his eyes.

"Why did you let him go?" Halfdan yelled at Tjorvi.

"Why didn't you get rid of his sword?" Tjorvi shouted. Peer ignored them. He knew better than to take his eyes off Harald.

He spoke loudly. "This is what I came to say. I've been living with the Skraelings. They sheltered me, took me in. But you killed two of them, Harald. Kiunik and Tia'm, their names were. Their people have found out, and they want your blood."

He raised his voice over the growing murmur. "They'll not hurt the girls. I came to take the girls away. The rest of you could try to surrender. There's a war band out there, fifty of them, with bows and spears and axes. If you surrender, I'll do what I can to help you. But they're angry. They've got a right

311

to be: Their kinsmen were murdered. . . ."

Harald's voice lifted over the hubbub. "Traitor! You led them here!"

In spite of the seriousness of the situation, Peer laughed out loud. "Led them? I couldn't have found my way here without them. They know these woods, Harald—we're the strangers."

"Skraelings?" Harald threw his head back. "*Hooo-ooo!* Skraelings! Hear him, lads? Are we a match for them? Are we men?"

"Peer," Tjorvi bellowed, "if we surrender, will they harm us?"

"I don't know." He had to be honest. "They don't like cowards. But there's so many—if you fight you'll die anyway. . . ."

"They don't like cowards?" Tjorvi said bleakly. "Who does? All right, if we've got to die, let's take a few of them with us."

"No!" Peer yelled. But the others were nodding. "Aye!" "Die like men!" "Like heroes!"

"I don't want to die," sobbed Floki.

Harald kicked him. "Get up, Floki, you son of a pig. Find yourself a weapon and act like a Norseman." He faced the men, sword uplifted. "Who's your leader?"

There was a confused murmur:

"Harald?"

"No, no . . ."

"Yes—we really do need Harald now. . . ."

"Who's with me?" Harald shouted.

"We are! We all are!"

"*I DON'T BELIEVE IT!*" screamed Hilde. She jumped forward, fists clenched. "Harald just *killed* Magnus, and now you want him to lead you?"

"Who else can do it?" Halfdan snarled. "We need a leader—a war leader. We can sort out the stuff about Magnus later."

"There won't be any later!" Peer shouted.

"Not for you," said Harald, and he sprang at Peer over the fire.

For an endless second Peer saw him coming, his golden hair floating out, underlit by the firelight, his mouth opening in a war cry, his eyes reflecting the flames.

"Run!" Astrid screamed.

Peer ducked under Harald's sword stroke and bolted for the door. *Here I go again,* he had time to think ironically. *Would it always, always come down to this—he's got a sword, and I haven't?*

The cold wind bit his face. Loose snow smoked along the ground. The thin moon was touching the crest of the hill. He ran for the trees and the safety of Sinumkw's men. It was farther than it looked. . . . His foot plunged into a hole under the snow and he pitched forward, hitting the rock-hard ground with an impact that drove the breath from his lungs.

He writhed onto his back, pulling up his knees, trying to suck in air while tingling stars popped and blistered in front of his eyes. A foot crunched into the snow beside his head. It was bare. Harald had run out into the snow after him without boots. Unable to breathe or speak, Peer twisted to see a sword point inches from his nose. It looked enormous, dwindling upward to Harald's fist, and finally his far-off face, dark against the sky.

"If you've never killed anyone, Barelegs . . ."

Peer wheezed. A thread of air wound into his lungs. Nothing like enough. He doubled up. If he could get one breath, one, before Harald killed him.

". . . you won't know . . ." Harald paused. "You won't know how good life truly tastes. You can't know at all."

The sword point pulled back from his face. "And now for a good death," whispered Harald. He sounded happy. Peer set his teeth and waited for the blow.

With a strange rushing whirr and a thump, something struck Harald. He staggered, clawing at his right shoulder, where a slim shaft stuck. He ripped it loose. Blood ran down his arm and dripped dark into the snow. Harald threw back his head, opened his mouth, and howled at the stars. *"Ahooooooooooooooh!"*

It echoed into the sky, a cry to melt your bones—wild, fluid, splitting into a double shriek that rose and fell and trailed off into unending loneliness. Peer cringed into the snow, while all the hairs on his neck rose. Still the expected blow did not fall. Harald stepped away.

Icy air rushed into Peer's lungs. He pushed himself up, coughing.

Another arrow hissed past his shoulder, burying itself in

the snow. A string of dark figures detached from the edge of the woods and rushed out over the white flats, whooping. In the pale snow light, Peer couldn't see faces, but he knew that Kwimu and Sinumkw were leading them. Harald was racing barefoot to meet them, his pale hair streaming, throwing his sword into the air and catching it. He howled again, and the hillside echoed: *"Ahoooooooooooooh! Hoo, hoo, hoo!"*

"Come on, lads!" Tjorvi, Arnë, and Halfdan pounded out of the house, waving axes.

"Arnë! Halfdan!" Peer shouted in despair.

"Peer!" With a rush of skirts, Hilde threw herself down in the snow alongside him, panting and actually laughing.

He turned on her in fury. "What are you doing out here? You could get killed. They're shooting!"

"I don't care." Her eyes were bright. "I'm not losing you twice."

He flung an arm over her shoulders and kissed her. She kissed him back. Her mouth was cold, then warm. The wind hurled stinging snow into their faces, as fine as salt. They clung to each other.

Harald began a series of sharp yipping barks, climbing to another fearsome howl. Peer half rose. Hilde dragged him down. "Stay with me!"

They heard the echo from the woods. How could the hillside twist and wring the sound like that, to fling it back clearer, longer, louder?

That's not an echo. It's an answer.

315

He jumped up, heedless of flying arrows. "Sinumkw!" he yelled. "Kwimu! Up there on the ridge! Look behind you!"

It didn't matter that he was using his own language. His urgent voice and pointing arm did it all. Black on the crest of the ridge, something impossibly tall stalked long-legged against the moon glow, a flickering shape behind the trees, now visible, now gone. It raised long, angular arms above its head and screamed, a scream to shred your nerves and tear off the top of your head and rip open your brain. Then it jumped below the skyline. The trees shook as it crashed downhill.

The war party turned, scattering and re-forming to face the woods.

"Tjorvi! Arnë!" Peer bellowed between his hands. "Look out!"

The Norsemen flung themselves down. From the edge of the woods the *jenu* burst in an avalanche of snow, frozen clods, and broken branches. It stopped at the base of the slope, one arm hooked around the top of a bending pine, and leaned out slowly, swiveling this way and that as if searching for someone.

"What *is* it?" Hilde hissed hysterically.

"Get back to the house—" Peer stopped. It was all open ground between here and the house. If Hilde ran, the *jenu* could catch her in a few strides, and he was sure it would chase anything that ran away.

"Keep down." He grabbed her arm and towed her toward the war band.

She struggled. "They're Skraelings!"

"No, they're friends." It sounded stupid: Friends didn't attack with arrows. He added firmly, "Safety in numbers."

He hoped it was true. The war party crouched in a ragged arc, bows and spears at the ready. Bending low, Peer and Hilde scurried into the band of warriors. Friends . . . it was true. Muin and Kopit and Ki'kwaju—he knew all their names. Kwimu, kneeling with bent bow, flicked Peer a single glance of welcome and turned back to concentrate on the foe.

They were nearer now. Peer could see more. The thing had the horrifying proportions of a stick man: long exaggerated arms and legs, with swollen joints and splayed fingers. The naked, grayish body reflected the snow light as it stared about with huge, rolling, almost fishlike eyes. It opened a lipless gash of a mouth, lined with thin, pointed teeth, and howled like the north wind.

"*Owoooooooooooohhh!*"

Harald Silkenhair screamed in answer.

Hilde gripped Peer's arm. "It'll see him! Is he mad?"

Harald had been standing in the snow, transfixed. Now he was running toward the *jenu*, his pale hair floating. With a yell of defiance he whirled his sword, and threw himself at the monster.

Peer saw the sword carve a dark slash in the creature's thin thigh. The *jenu* bellowed. Its raking fingers came down and plucked Harald from the ground. Struggling, Harald swung the sword again, stabbing at the creature's face. The *jenu* tore the sword from his hand and threw it away. It brought up a bony knee and snapped him over it like a stick of firewood.

Hilde clapped her hands over her face. Sinumkw shouted. The warriors loosed their bows. Arrows rushed through the air, and some of them stuck in the *jenu*'s side. It brushed at them clumsily, as if they were thorns.

Tjorvi crawled up through the snow, worming along on his elbow. He reached Peer and gripped his arm with steely fingers. "What can we do?"

Peer shook his head.

The *jenu* began to cough. It threw Harald into the snow, where he lay like a broken doll. It retched and jerked, and finally gobbed something out into its hands, something pale and slippery, the size of a newborn baby shaped out of ice. The *jenu* stared for a moment. Then it pushed its heart back into its mouth and gulped. It grabbed Harald jealously and crouched down. Peer heard growling, a breathy, throaty sound. *It's going to eat him,* he thought, sickened. *And when it's finished, it will start on us.*

There was a shrill yell from the direction of the houses. Splashes of bright fire like living gold came jerking and weaving over the gray frozen ground. Two figures bounded through the snow, waving fiery torches. Loki raced ahead of them, barking.

The *jenu* sprang upright, snarling, clutching Harald's broken body to its chest.

Kwimu yelled. Tjorvi and Arnë shouted. Ottar screamed.

318

Floki came panting up, waving a blazing torch in each hand. Fire dripped to the ground, sizzling in the snow. He held one of the torches out, and Kwimu snatched it. Astrid ran up, her wild hair the same color as the flames. She flinched as Sinumkw leaped at her, seized both her torches, and ran at the *jenu*, whooping wildly. His warriors streamed after him. Peer grabbed Hilde's hand. Madly, together, everyone charged with Sinumkw, yelling, hurling spears and waving torches.

For a second, Peer thought the *jenu* would fight. It bent over them, hissing, and he choked on its powerful, musky stench, sweet and stale. Its eyes gleamed. Cradled in its sinewy arms, Harald lolled lifeless, his long hair trailing.

Then, like a dog protecting its bone, the *jenu* turned. They saw the nicked ridge of its spine, its thin buttocks and long bony legs scissoring away in ground-swallowing strides, heading for the river. It faded rapidly in the gray light. It leaped across the river and disappeared into the far woods. They heard one last distant shriek of rage and loneliness. And it was gone.

Ottar ran up, dragging something heavy along with him. "It's his sword," he sobbed. "I've got Harald's sword." He stared over the dim marshes toward the river and the black, watching woods, and let the sword drop into the snow. He looked up at Peer and tears ran down his cheeks. "I hated him. I hated him. But he was brave, wasn't he, Peer? He *was* brave."

"Yes, he was brave," said Peer slowly. "But I'm afraid that's all he was."

CHAPTER 24
Peace Pipe

How did you guess the thing could be driven away by fire?" asked Tjorvi in admiration.

Astrid and Floki looked at each other. "We didn't," said Astrid.

Floki shook his head. "Nah. We just thought—what's worse? Coming out there with the rest of you, or hiding in the house waiting for it to get us?"

"And there weren't any weapons left," Astrid added. "So the Nis said—"

"Aha, the Nis!" Tjorvi interrupted, glancing up. There were no secrets left. The Nis was sitting openly on a beam overhead, noisily guzzling a bowlful of hot groute garnished with the last of the butter. "That was the Nis's idea, was it? I wish I'd known we had a Nis with us all this time."

"Wait a minute," Ottar interrupted. "Let me tell the others all that." He turned and began to translate.

Peer drew Hilde against him. She whispered, "It's a full house."

It was. Sinumkw's warriors sat cross-legged on the floor by the fire, or sprawled on the sleeping benches. The firelight shone on their oiled black hair and brown faces, still smudged with war paint, and on their finely worked clothes. Peer smiled as he looked around. Trades and swaps were happening already. Halfdan had a tuft of blue feathers in his hair. Tjorvi was sporting Kopit's bear-tooth necklace, and Kopit had slung Tjorvi's steel-edged knife around his neck. Both looked very happy with their bargains, and they hadn't needed Ottar to translate for them, either.

"So the Nis suggested the torches?" Peer tipped his head back. "Well done, Nithing!"

The Nis squeaked cheerfully. It was licking its messy fingers, and a splash of groute dripped into Peer's hair. "I has lots of good ideas," it boasted. "Has you heard how we threw the clothes at Harald?"

"Hilde told me." Peer wished he could have seen Harald struggling to fight a rain of socks and trousers. *No wonder he ran berserk. . . .*

Then he felt sorry. After all, Harald was dead. *But he brought it on himself. He deserved it a million times. . . .*

"What name suits me best, Peer Ulfsson?" the Nis inquired. It upended the basin and stuck its entire face inside to

321

lick out the bottom. "Nithing the Seafarer or Nithing the Warrior?"

"Oh, well—um . . ."

"It was brave of you and Floki to come out," Hilde said to Astrid. "Weren't you afraid of hurting the baby, running like that?"

"It was time I did something to help." Astrid pressed a hand to her stomach. "He's fine. I can feel him kicking."

Sinumkw spoke to her across the fire, his dark eyes gleaming. Astrid raised her brows and turned to Ottar. "What does he say?"

"He says a brave mother makes a brave son," said Ottar.

Astrid's eyes filled.

"Don't cry," Hilde said softly.

"I'm not," Astrid muttered, dashing a hand across her face. "Well, yes I am. I'm thinking of Gunnar. He'll never see his son now. If it is a boy, I mean." She shivered. "And I promised I'd save him, and I didn't. I harmed him instead."

"You didn't harm him," Hilde protested.

"Yes I did. I was so angry when he slapped me. I wanted revenge. I wanted the *seidr* all undone. I could have warned Harald not to crush the egg, but I didn't. I'm not a nice person like you. It's true about troll blood, you see. It always comes out in the end. And my son will inherit it from me. He'll be the same."

"How can you know that?" Hilde began. But there was an

outburst of excitement in the roof. The Nis knocked its empty bowl off the beam, just missing Peer's head, and scrabbled in an angle of the rafters, scattering bits of straw and dust.

"See, see?" It opened spidery fingers and tossed something light into Astrid's lap. A tiny hollow egg.

"I finds it on the floor when I is tidying up," the Nis chirped, full of self-importance. "When Harald Silkenhair makes all that mess and leaves it for the Nis to clear away. And I thinks, *a thrush egg*! I keeps it—I puts it in my den to look pretty, in my nice nest up in the roof." It looked down at Astrid with sharp eyes. "It's empty," it added.

Astrid's hand closed around it. "Harald didn't smash it after all," she breathed. "Then—it didn't matter. . . ."

"Oh, Astrid," said Hilde impatiently. "Gunnar died because of what *he* did—not because of what you did. Do stop going on about your troll blood. Take my advice: Don't tell your baby anything about it, and he'll grow up fine."

Astrid looked at her with slowly dawning relief. "Do you think—if I'd never known . . . ?" She took a deep breath. "I could forget about it. I could be just like anyone else. . . ."

The Nis cracked its knuckles gleefully. "Always, always the Nis finds the answer. Maybe I should be Nithing the Clever. . . ."

Troll blood, Peer thought. *What does it mean to have troll blood?* He remembered how, years ago, his two bullying uncles had turned into trolls after drinking troll beer. He suspected they'd been trolls on the inside all along. Perhaps being a troll was more to do with the way you behaved than the blood you inherited. If you howled to the *jenu*, the *jenu* would howl back.

And tomorrow, thought Peer, *we'll give Harald's sword to Sinumkw. Kiunik and Tia'm can take it with them on the Ghost Road, on their long journey to the Land of Souls.*

He looked at Floki, who sat silently with lowered head. "Hey, Floki." Floki looked up out of red-rimmed eyes. Peer leaned across. "It was great, the way you ran out with the torches. Magnus would be so proud."

Floki didn't speak. But his rough, freckled hand came out to grip Peer's. He sniffed.

There was a short, shrill yap, a screech, and a roar of laughter. Peer looked up sharply. The Nis was shooting into the rafters, chittering hysterically.

"Did you see that?" Hilde stifled giggles. "The Nis got up the nerve to creep behind Kwimu. I don't know what it did— but it got too near that pet fox of his." She looked more closely. "It's not a fox, is it? What on earth . . . ?"

Kwimu smiled across at them. For a second, Peer was sure the fox winked. But a moment later Kwimu lifted it, and it was just a fur pouch, with the mask and paws and tail of a fox attached. He plunged his hand into it and pulled out a pipe. He lit it and handed it to his father.

The noise and chatter died. The Norsemen watched curiously: "He's swallowing fire!" "They'll never believe this at home."

"It's a sign of friendship," said Peer. "Isn't it, Ottar? If he gives the pipe to you, make sure you take it."

Sinumkw blew out a thin flutter of smoke. He rose ceremoniously and passed the pipe to Peer. Peer drew down a mouthful of sweet smoke.

"Arnë . . ." He held out the pipe. Arnë looked at it without moving. Then he scratched his head. "A sign of friendship, eh? All right, I'll give it a go." He took the pipe, sucked on it, and coughed. "Not bad!" he said with watering eyes, handing it on to Tjorvi. He added gruffly, "I'm glad you're not dead."

"Thanks," said Peer. They looked at each other with uncertain smiles.

With jokes and backslapping, the pipe passed around the room. Up in the rafters the Nis coughed and spluttered, pretending to be annoyed by the smoke. Considering it spent most of its time in the haze of wood smoke floating about the rafters, that was rich, Peer thought.

He stood on tiptoe and whispered, "Here's a good name. How about Nithing the Wise Warrior?" The Nis purred.

"What are you thinking?" Hilde asked Peer as he sat down.

He stretched. "Oh, lots of things. What to do next. How to spend the winter. When to go home. Whether Ottar will come with us. And who's going to decide it all? Now Gunnar's gone, who's going to lead us?"

"You, I should think," said Hilde.

"Me?" He stared at her.

"Yes, you." Hilde grinned at him. "Who else will do all the

thinking?" She leaned against him and whispered into his ear, "So go on. What's going to happen to us?"

Peer dropped his arm around her shoulders. He thought of the months of cold ahead: the blizzards, the creatures like the *jenu* lurking in the woods. He thought of trying to cross the immense ocean dividing them from home, with no Gunnar to guide them, and only five men to sail the ship. He remembered the storms and icebergs of the voyage out. He looked down at Hilde, and saw his own fears in her eyes.

"The winter will pass," he whispered back. "Perhaps we'll stay here in the house for the whole of it. Or, if they'll let us, we'll go back to the village with Kwimu and the People, and go hunting and trapping with them. Astrid's baby will be born there, and she'll have lots of women to help her, not just you by yourself. And then the spring will come. The ice will melt, and the buds will thicken on the trees. We'll take *Water Snake* out of her winter quarters and push her down into the sea. And we'll sail away.

"It'll take us a long time, weeks and weeks, but we'll sight Greenland and the Islands of Sheep. We'll follow the whales home. And then, one day, we'll see our own mountain again. Troll Fell.

"I wonder if it will be sunrise. Or sunset, or raining, or foggy even. Maybe we'll meet Bjorn in his faering, coming out to the fishing grounds. But anyway, we'll sail into the jetty and walk up through Trollsvik. And we'll see the farmhouse, with the smoke rising from the roof. And Gudrun will dash out to meet us, and Ralf will come running from the field . . ."

Hilde was smiling, though her eyes were full of tears.

"And I'll say, 'Here we are. We're back. And we want to get married.'"

"That will be such a happy ending," Hilde sighed.

"There's never any ending," said Peer softly. "Life goes on."

Over a thousand years ago—five hundred years before
Columbus—the Vikings reached North America. Leif
Eiriksson of Greenland sailed across what is now called the
Davis Strait, and named three lands on his way south:
Helluland (which means "Slab Land," a country full of
stones), Markland ("Forest Land"), and finally a grassy,
wooded peninsula where he and his men built houses and
spent the winter, naming the place Vinland for the grapes
they said they found there.

No one doubts now that Helluland, Markland, and
Vinland were parts of the northeastern coast of America. The
most likely candidates are Baffin Island, Labrador, and
Newfoundland, respectively. An excavated Viking settlement
at L'Anse aux Meadows in Newfoundland may be the actual
site where Leif built his houses.

Two sagas, *The Greenland Saga* and *Eirik the Red's Saga*,
tell how Leif and his men met "Skraelings," a scornful term
used by the Norsemen for all the Native Americans they met,

including the northern Inuit. Both sagas tell of battles between Vikings and Skraelings. When Leif's brother Thorvald found nine Skraelings asleep under their canoes, he and his men promptly killed eight of them. He paid the price for his aggressive behavior. The ninth Skraeling escaped to raise the alarm. A fleet of canoes attacked, and Thorvald died from an arrow wound.

So who were these "Skraelings"? The Native American people of Newfoundland were named the Beothuk. They saw off the Vikings. But European diseases and guns in later centuries drove them to extinction. The last of the Beothuk, a woman named Shaw-na-dith-it, died of tuberculosis in 1829. And with her died the last chance of learning the Beothuk's language, beliefs, and customs. Only a few scraps of information remain—not enough clues to build a story on.

So, since the Norsemen surely explored beyond Newfoundland, I have based Kwimu and his People on the Mi'kmaq people of New Brunswick—only a step farther south—who still live in the land of their ancestors, and many of whose beliefs, customs, and stories have survived to be a matter of living and proud tradition.

I didn't invent any of the magical creatures in *Troll Blood*. From the Nis to the *jenu*, they are my interpretations of creatures which have all been believed in by real people in the past. I wanted to write about the world in which such beliefs were possible—a world in which ordinary men and women coexisted with spirits and ghosts both helpful and harmful. I tried to imagine how the Norsemen and Kwimu's People lived and thought. I even had the fun of sailing a reconstruction of a real Viking ship on a Danish fjord. But, at the end of the day, *Troll Blood* is fantasy, not history.

Six hundred years ago, the London printer William Caxton published Sir Thomas Malory's story of King Arthur, *Le Morte d'Arthur*. I feel I can't do better than to pass on Caxton's warning to readers: "And for to pass the time, this book shall be pleasant to read in. But for to give faith and believe that all is true that is contained herein, ye be at your liberty. . . ."

GLOSSARY

All the Native American words in the book are from the Mi'kmaq language. Here is a rough guide to pronunciation. As a rule of thumb, *k* is pronounced as a hard *g*, and *t* as a light *d*.

eula'qmeujit	*(ay-oo-LAHK-may-oo-jeet)*	starvation
jenu	*(JEN-oo)*	ice giant, once a human being
ji'j	*(JEEJ)*	small (a suffix)
jipijka'm	*(jee-PEEJ-gahm)*	horned serpent; plural jipijka'maq
jipjawej	*(JEEP-ja-wedge)*	robin
kewasu'nukwej	*(gee-wa-SOO-nook-wedge)*	invisible spirit who chops trees
kiunik	*(gee-OON-ig)*	otter
kopit	*(GO-peed)*	beaver

kwimu	*(GWEE-moo)*	loon, diving water bird
kwetejk	*(gwed-EDGE-ig)*	St. Lawrence Iroquois people
muin	*(moo-EEN)*	bear
n'kwis	*(en-GWEES)*	my son
nukumij	*(noo-GOO-meej)*	my grandmother
nuji'j	*(noo-jeej)*	my grandchild
nujj	*(en-OODGE)*	my father
plawej	*(pl-OW-wedge)*	partridge
sinumkw	*(seh-NUM-k)*	wild goose
skite'kmuj	*(es-kuh-DEG-uh-mooj)*	ghost
skus	*(es-KOOS)*	weasel
sqoljk	*(es-HOLCH-ig)*	frogs
tia'm	*(dee-AHM)*	moose
tioml	*(DEE-oh-mull)*	powerful animal totem
wiklatmu'jk	*(week-laht-MOO-ig)*	race of tiny Persons who inhabit the shore

SOURCES FOR VIKING
LIFE AND CUSTOMS

To Visit
The Jorvik Viking Centre in York, UK
   The Viking Ship Museum, Roskilde, Denmark

Online
Have a look at www.vikinganswerlady.com. It's a terrific website that will tell you more than you ever dreamed was known about the Vikings.

Books
There are loads of good books about the Vikings. Here are some I have found extremely helpful.

Almgren, Bertil. *The Viking.* Gothenburg, Sweden: Nordbok, 1975.

Binns, Alan. *Viking Voyagers.* London: Heinemann, 1980.

Davidson, Hilda Ellis. *Gods and Myths of Northern Europe.* Baltimore: Penguin, 1964.

Fitzhugh, William W., and Elisabeth I. Ward, eds. *Vikings: The North Atlantic Saga*. Washington: Smithsonian Institution Press, 2000.

Ingstad, Helge. *Westward to Vinland*. London: Cape, 1969.

Jesch, Judith. *Women in the Viking Age*. Suffolk, UK: Boydell Press, 1991.

Jones, Gwyn. *A History of the Vikings*. Oxford, UK: Oxford University Press, 1984.

Magnusson, Magnus. *The Vikings*. Stroud, Gloucestershire, UK: Tempus, 2003.

Wahlgren, Erik. *The Vikings and America*. London: Thames and Hudson, 2000.

Primary Sources

You can't do better than to read some of the original sagas and stories for yourself. There are lots of different editions available.

The Greenland Saga
Eirik the Red's Saga
Grettir's Saga
Egil's Saga
The Prose Edda
The Elder Edda

SOURCES FOR
SCANDINAVIAN FOLKLORE

Árnason, Jón. *Icelandic Folk and Fairy Tales*. Hallmundson, May and Hallberg, transl. Reykjavik, Iceland: Iceland Review, 1987.

Asbjørnsen, Peter Christen. *East of the Sun and West of the Moon*. Garden City, NY: Doubleday, 1977.

Craigie, William. *Scandinavian Folk-lore*. London: Alexander Gardner, 1896.

Jones, Gwyn. *Scandinavian Legends and Folk-tales*. Oxford, UK: Oxford University Press, 1956.

Keightley, Thomas. *The Fairy Mythology*. London: H. G. Bohn, 1860.

Lang, Andrew. *The Book of Dreams and Ghosts*. New York: Longmans, Green & Co., 1899.

Lie. Jonas. *Weird Tales from Northern Seas*. Iowa City, Ia.: Penfield Press, 2007.

Online

You can learn some Mi'kmaq words and hear them spoken at www.firstnationhelp.com/ali/posters.

Another great online source with lots of information is www.native-languages.org/mikmaq.htm.

Articles

Hager, Stansbury. "Micmac Customs and Traditions." In *American Anthropologist*, Vol. 8, No. 1, January 1895.

Reade, John. "Some Wabanaki Songs." In *Transactions of the Royal Society of Canada*, May 25, 1887.

Books

Le Clerq, Chrestien. *New Relation of Gaspesia*. William F. Ganong, transl. and ed. Toronto: The Champlain Society, 1910.

Lescarbot, Marc. *History of New France*. W. L. Grant, transl.

and ed. Toronto: Champlain Society, 1907–14.

Maillard, Antoine Simon. *An Account of the Customs and Manners of the Micmakis and Maricheets* . . . London: S. Hooper and A. Morley, 1758.

McCurdy, Michael. *An Algonquian Year.* Boston: Houghton Mifflin, 2000.

Sagard, Gabriel. *The Long Journey to the Country of the Hurons.* George Wrong, ed. Toronto: The Champlain Society, 1939.

Whitehead, Ruth Holmes. *Elitekey: Micmac Material Culture from 1600 A.D. to the Present.* Halifax, N.S.: Nova Scotia Museum, 1980.

———— and Harold McGee. *The Micmac: How their Ancestors Lived Five Hundred Years Ago.* Halifax, N.S.: Nimbus, 1983.

SOURCES FOR NATIVE
AMERICAN FOLKLORE
AND LEGEND

"The Grabber-from-Beneath"
Bruchac, Joseph and James. *When the Chenoo Howls.* New
    York: Walker, 1998.
The Ndakinna Wilderness Project at www.ndakinna.com.

The Wiklatmu'jk
Parsons, Elsie Clews. "Micmac Folklore." In *Journal of
    American Folklore,* Vol. 38, Jan.–Mar. 1925.

"Swamp Woman"
Brown, Mrs. W. Wallace. "A Wabanaki Counting-Out Rhyme."
    In *Journal of American Folklore,* Vol. 3, 1890.

Jenu or Chenoo
Hager, Stansbury. "Micmac Magic and Medicine." In *Journal
    of American Folklore,* Vol. 9, No. 34, Jul.–Sep. 1896.

Leland, Charles. *The Algonquin Legends of New England.* Boston, New York: Houghton, Mifflin, 1884.

Rand, Silas Tertius. *Legends of the Micmacs.* New York, London: Longmans, Green, 1894.

"The Spreaders"

Bruchac, Joseph and James. *When the Chenoo Howls.* New York: Walker, 1998.

The Ndakinna Wilderness Project at www.ndakinna.com.

"The Thin Faces"

Chamberlain, A. F. "Some Items of Algonkian Folklore." In *Journal of American Folklore,* Vol. 13, Oct.–Dec. 1900.

Leland, Charles. *The Algonquin Legends of New England.* Boston, New York: Houghton, Mifflin and Company, 1884.

Speck, Frank G. "Montagnais and Naskapi Tales." In *Journal of American Folklore,* Vol. 38, No. 47, Jan.–Mar. 1925.

Jipijka'm

Whitehead, Ruth Holmes. *Stories from the Six Worlds.* Halifax, N.S.: Nimbus, 1988.

Kewasu'nukwej, the Invisible Tree-cutter

Alger, Abby L., and Mrs. Wallace Brown. *In Indian Tents.* Boston: Roberts Brothers, 1897. (See Al-wus-ki-ni-kess, the spirit of the woods.)

Rand, Silas Tertius. *Legends of the Micmacs.* New York,

London: Longmans, Green, 1894. (Here the tree-cutter is named Wegooaskunoogwejit.)

The Tioml or Totemic Helper

Rand, Silas Tertius. *Legends of the Micmacs.* New York, London: Longmans, Green, 1894.

Whitehead, Ruth Holmes. *Stories from the Six Worlds.* Halifax, N.S.: Nimbus, 1988.

Snakes Listening to Stories in Summertime

Bergen, Fanny D. "Some Customs and Beliefs of the Winnebago Indians." In *Journal of American Folklore*, Vol. 9, No. 32, Jan.–Mar. 1896.